S.W.A.K.

A novel of ultimate betrayal

S.W.A.K.

A novel of ultimate betrayal

Adriana Sifakis and George Sifakis

EVOLVE

S.W.A.K.: A Novel of Ultimate Betrayal

978-0-9916229-0-0 hardcover
978-0-9916229-1-7 ebook

Published by Evolve Publishing, Inc.
www.evolvepublishing.com

Printed in the United States of America

First edition May 2014
10 9 8 7 6 5 4 3 2 1

Dedications

Nonnie & Papa, my beloved Italian grandparents, thank you for instilling in me unconditional love, guidance, encouragement, and the pursuit to live out my dreams. These extraordinary gifts have carried me through my life, and have now been passed down to our three loving children, Alexa, George & Evangelia. ~ Adriana

YiaYia & Papouli, thank you for showing me the way. Your love, dedication, and work ethic helped shape who I am today and my promise to instill all of these values in our children. ~ George

Theo Despoti, who proved to us that miracles do happen. You are greatly missed but your love has left an everlasting light in our hearts and we feel your presence each and every day. ~ Adriana & George

Acknowledgements

To our incredibly supportive family who loves and cherishes us and our children unconditionally, we are forever grateful for you and love you back wholeheartedly.

We have had the tremendous pleasure of being surrounded by a countless number of exceptional friends, colleagues, and mentors. Individually, you have touched our lives in extraordinary ways. Your true and genuine friendship fills us with terrific feelings of joy, happiness, and an incredible sense of well-being—many of the greatest gifts that life has to offer.

We cherish the Greek Orthodox faith and community that has instilled in us a spiritual presence of hope, faith, and love. Metera, your love and support has been a shining light and constant source of inspiration; we love you.

A special thank-you to those who assisted with the process of getting this book to print. Lynn Schwartz, our incredibly talented writing coach who helped guide us through this monumental task, you are a wonderful woman and we are grateful for having the opportunity to work together. Like we always say, there's much more to come! We love you, Lynn!

We are thankful to Karen Kreiger with Evolve Publishing, a kind and compassionate woman who has shared her decades of experience and knowledge in the publishing industry and has been nothing short of a joy to work with.

Alexa, George, and Evangelia, you are the heart and soul of our world and we love you from the bottom of our hearts!

Prologue

Washington, D.C.

"May the Lord rebuke thee, Satan!

"May the Lord rebuke thee, Satan! May the Lord rebuke thee, Satan!" The second command was louder than the first, the priest's words precise and sharp. Backed by the power of the Almighty, he sang out over their heads as if the sanctuary were at capacity and then paused, waiting for the dictum to echo through the empty cathedral.

"Shudder, tremble, be afraid," Father Gabriel charged. "Depart, be utterly destroyed, be banished!" Father Gabriel's demeanor did not suggest the outrage that the meaning of the words carried, nor did his small, thin frame exude the physical force or aggression that might have been warranted on such an occasion. He moved through the prayer recitation in a deliberate and methodical manner. His objective clear, confident that when his task was complete, he would triumph.

She knew him as Father Gabriel. He was a familiar face at St. George's Greek Orthodox Cathedral, where her husband had taught her to worship. But today, she was not on familiar ground, did not know what to expect from Father Gabriel, nor what she would encounter in the cathedral. She knew only that she trusted him, a trust that was both innate and inexplicable.

She lowered her head forward, in part from fear and in part from shame, as Father Gabriel itemized each offense. "Thee who fell from heaven and together with thee all evil spirits: every evil spirit of lust, a day and nocturnal spirit, a noonday and evening spirit, a midnight spirit…"

She squeezed her husband's hand, his fingers interlocked with hers, and the moment he felt the pressure, he reciprocated, his grip so tight it caused their golden marriage bands to scrape against each other. Father Gabriel's words floated into the crevices of the cathedral, circling high into the dome, "Depart … Be gone … I adjure you … "

What was it that he suspected? What was it that Father Gabriel was certain had to be chased away? Out of her soul? Out of her heart? Driven away forever, so that she might become "whole and sound and free"?

Her eyes opened and she felt the courage to raise her head. Looking up, she saw them watching, the Byzantine icons that inhabited the cathedral, depicted in mosaic and acrylic, from the walls and ceiling. Did they know? Could they explain?

What was their judgment?

She tried to count them all. Were there 50? 60? 70? No, much, much more. Each holy portrait possessed a unique composition — the thickness and thinness of the lines, the color distribution. No two the same. They gazed down at her and she felt their embrace, as if in one quick whoosh, they were all transported to the ancient churches of Constantinople.

After months of worry, she and her husband had come to see Father Gabriel—to question, to unburden, to confess the bewildering, secret facts, to receive answers, but neither she nor her husband had expected Father Gabriel's response. "It is the devil's work," he said simply. "We will turn to the prayers of Saint John Chrysostom and Saint Basil for help."

She had not understood the implication of the prayers, but her husband had known. Father Gabriel, in his professional opinion, prescribed these prayers, as if he had been recommending a good dentist to pull out a painful, decaying tooth.

They were prayers of exorcism. And her husband believed that the prayers might protect her. Might protect them. When she heard the word "exorcism" her fingers turned icy, her breath short and shallow as if the infected tooth, which she had endured and ignored, now festered into the ultimate consequence, an incurable, terminal disease. She imagined the Hollywood version—a spinning head, screams of unspeakable profanity. Green bile spewing from her mouth. Would she shake? Convulse? Fall to the floor? And when the cross passed over her head, would her tongue slap and flap, forcing out rancid and unintelligible debris to anyone who would dare to bear witness?

"We should not delay," was all Father Gabriel said. Her husband knew he was right and deep down she must have known it too, because she let them lead her from Father Gabriel's office into the sanctuary.

Father Gabriel pushed on, "I adjure you, most wicked, impure, abominable, loathsome and alien spirit . . . ."

She was beginning to feel suspended, dizzy—mesmerized by the medallion of Christ, the surrounding windows fading into a circle of unbroken, natural light.

She felt the priest touch her head and then her heart with his cross, gilded and imposing.

The light pressure of the cross made her expect the worst and she opened her mouth so that she might release the inevitable, but nothing came out. Moments later she only felt immersed in relief, stripped of a thick and waxy burden.

Then she looked up and noticed Theotokos, Mother of God in the dome of the church ceiling. Theotokos, with arms extended, emerged in the light. Gathered around Her were nine medallions of Her heavenly attendants, the angelic hosts. All joined Father Gabriel with the business at hand.

"I adjure you," they seemed to chant. And she bowed her head again, this time not in shame and fear, but to join in the chorus of protective prayer, "I adjure you," she whispered. ". . . For He shall come without delay to judge all the earth, and shall assign you, and all the powers working with you, to the fire of hell, having delivered you to the outer darkness, where the worm constantly devours, and the fire is never extinguished."

PART ONE

*We must free ourselves of the hope that the sea will ever rest.
We must learn to sail in high winds.*

—Aristotle Onassis, twentieth-century shipping magnate

CHAPTER 1

Country Club Lane, Elizabeth, New Jersey

THE DROPLET HIT THE SNOW-WHITE COMFORTER. Lauren watched the crimson circle, no larger than a small garnet, hurry across the silk; it wiggled and widened, forming a splotch, flower-like with jagged petals. Lauren knew it was blood. Her blood. The color would soon lose its punch, but the damage would be permanent—the droplet joined the others, a field of flowers, which dotted the luxurious bedcover in faded, rusty brown.

Lauren touched the space between her nose and upper lip, the familiar fluid gooey and warm. Another nosebleed. Ma wouldn't be happy about the stain. "You need to be careful," Ma instructed Lauren. "In this house, we buy extra-nice belongings. We need to treat them right."

In the beginning, Ma had tried to remove the blood with tricks she read in *Hints from Heloise*—concoctions of baking soda, vinegar, peroxide, and meat tenderizer (which only works when unseasoned). But even the most touted household remedies didn't help. Lauren's nose bled often, an unpredictable steady stream. Not something Ma could scrub out.

"Hold your head back," said Ma, handing Lauren a wet washcloth and directing her to squeeze her nose between her thumb and forefinger, to close the nostrils tight.

"Ma, I can't breathe," Lauren resisted.

"You know what to do. Breathe through your mouth."

"Ma, what if it won't stop?"

"You know it will. It always does," Ma said, and then added the words Lauren dreaded, "It looks like you won't go to school today."

Although the cloth hid Lauren's eyes, Ma knew they would soon become pink and puffy. Crying unsettled Ma, and she was ready to divert any potential tear from running willy-nilly down her daughter's face. "We'll have fun today," Ma coaxed. "Maybe a little shopping, a McDonald's sundae. Maybe there's even a present for you."

Ma worked fast to assemble her words, trying to distract her daughter before the girl wandered off into a wilderness of disappointment. "No sulking allowed," Ma said. "Remember, every knock is a boost. And besides, you should feel grateful. There are plenty of kids much worse off than you. Imagine missing a leg? Or your fingers!"

Lauren knew she should count her blessings; she had heard about the legs and fingers before. She was sorry for those fingerless kids, but she wanted to go to school.

"Besides, what's happening in first grade?" Ma said. "I'll tell you. Not much. I can teach you anything that Mrs. Lee can."

Lauren held still, the bloody cloth clinging to her nose and forehead. She hated to miss again. It had taken Lauren some time to warm up to school. When Ma first dropped her off, she clung to Ma's leg and Mrs. Lee had to peel her away, separate mother and daughter, so that Ma could wriggle free and be on her way. Mrs. Lee had not given up, and over the course of several weeks she managed to draw Lauren apart from her mother without a fuss. Lauren liked school now, even looked forward to it.

At recess, Lauren always managed to snag a swing. She would nestle into the black rubber seat and pump, her legs moving back and forth with serious intent. Her fingers would grip the metal chains tight, and once she was sky high, where no one could hear, she'd squeal and shriek, her voice propelling into the air, traveling far beyond the Wanda O. Winfrey Elementary School playground.

Mrs. Lee (who knew a thing or two after thirty years of six-year-olds bounding through her classroom) had even told Lauren she had superior and advanced talents. Her penmanship was by far the best in class, since she never failed to make the capital "L" in "Lauren" straight and tall, perfectly aligned with the other five lowercase letters that obediently followed neat and proper, like well-behaved children.

Lauren's newfound affinity for school made it more difficult to keep her home and Ma knew she was still not in the clear. There was a good chance Lauren would choose to spend the day wrapped in a blanket of self-pity. So Ma brought out the big ammunition to fortify her fun-filled plans: "We'll even have Kraft Macaroni & Cheese for breakfast. What do you think?"

The smallest smile peeked out from under the sides of the bloody washcloth. Ma caught it and knew she was home free.

CHAPTER 2

THE NEIGHBORS ON COUNTRY CLUB LANE WERE TROUBLE. Ma
liked the name of the street and thought that living in a house tagged
with such an upscale identity could only bring good fortune. A little
over five years ago, Ma insisted that her husband Lou buy the three-
bedroom brick house with a finished basement and room to grow. Ma
had also liked the Elizabeth, New Jersey, location because it was far
enough away from Queens, New York and Lou's parents, Nonna and
Nonno. Ma had wanted out of Queens once and for all, away from her
mother-in-law—the buttinksy. Ma was sick and tired of Nonna's intru-
sions and child-rearing advice. When it came to raising Lauren, or any
of her kids, Ma didn't see any need for old-fashioned opinions.

"Country Club Lane," Ma told her mother-in-law, lingering over
"Country" and "Club" longer than necessary, as if the syllables were a
wedge of lemon she could rub into Nonna's wounded heart.

Even though the move introduced Lou to a heavy commute, forcing him to leave the house at six o'clock in the morning six days a week
to make his way to Queens and the Napolitano Brothers International
Garage, the family-owned auto repair shop where Lou was a sought-
after mechanic, he didn't mind. Lou liked to drive. Even more, he liked
to give Ma what she wanted. When Lou's parents questioned the prac-
ticality of the decision, which they knew had been instigated by Ma,

Lou blushed and offered a worn-out excuse. "You know what they say: happy wife, happy life."

The house did make Ma happy. At first.

The twins were three at the time of the move and quickly settled into dashing about the fenced-in suburban backyard with ease, never giving Queens a second thought. When Lauren was born, Ma would stroll down Country Club Lane, pushing the best stroller money could buy. Since Ma never paid top dollar for anything, she had scored the high-end Maclaren, the Cadillac of strollers, at a consignment shop. And so the tiny baby girl took her first rides in style, swaddled in pure white, with the twins skipping along behind.

The neighbors used to marvel at Ma—at how put together she always was. "She's so cute," Mrs. Cuomo would coo, staring at the itty-bitty girl. "Yes, I've already received my dose of double trouble," Ma would joke, referring to the twins in their matching cowboy outfits, "and now I've been blessed with yet another happy accident, my baby girl." And Alexandra Tosatto, who had three boys of her own, would laugh and nod with understanding. The neighbors would make a great fuss with "oohs" and "aahs," wondering how Ma could manage three children under the age of four with such composure. But over the years, as the twins grew into loud and stocky preteens and became Tony and Little Louie, the neighbors had started in on her one by one. And now, Ma was fed up with the whole thing.

Ma pretended to get along, keeping her anger in check with a strained politeness. She continued to greet Mrs. Cuomo, who lived next door with her widower son, Carmine. The other neighbors whispered that Carmine must belong to Hells Angels. His outfit, always the same, seemed to support that theory: leather pants and vest, heavy chains, and red-and-white insignia patches. Carmine, with his full mustache and straggly red beard, kept to himself. To the neighbors, that seemed to be the worst offense of all.

The Napolitano driveway was located next to the Cuomo front lawn, where Carmine washed and tinkered with his most cherished possession, his Harley-Davidson. Carmine buffed and revved up his motorcycle a few times per week, exposing fire-spouting dragon tattoos that crawled over his beefy biceps. Otherwise, Carmine stayed away from the Napolitano house and family. Ma was glad for that. She hadn't paid much attention to the rumors until Alexandra told Ma the Hells Angels' motto: "When we do right, nobody remembers. When we do wrong, nobody forgets."

Carmine's mother did not stay away. Mrs. Cuomo spent most of her time sitting on a low wooden stool in her yard-turned-heirloom-tomato-garden day and night. This prevented Ma from slipping into her Cadillac Eldorado, painted a custom pearl so it shimmered and dazzled (a birthday gift from Lou), without being trapped into conversation. Ma would listen to Mrs. Cuomo drone on about her grandson's latest computer accomplishments out in California. Ma wanted to shout at the old Sardinian. Who cared about his "accomplishments"? The kid was a friggin' bore. He definitely didn't take after his hoodlum father, who at least possessed some backbone. But Ma was good about it and kept her mouth clenched tight so that her true thoughts wouldn't escape and clobber the old cow.

Ma also tried her best to ignore Alexandra Tosatto's not-so-subtle remarks about Tony and Little Louie. "Our front door handle was greased in Vaseline again. I can't imagine who would want to cause such mischief," Alexandra would say snidely. "Can you?"

"Alexandra's got some nerve," Ma would say to Lou at home. "She's jealous. It's that simple. I'm good looking. I have nice things. That fatty is green-eyed with envy. They all are—the whole damn block."

As if the neighbors' harassment wasn't enough, Ma developed a new worry. It seemed rats were nesting among the roof rafters and traveling between the walls, settling in like part of the family, like they belonged. Ma had seen two or three dart along the darkened corners of the den— quick and subtle shadows. At first Ma questioned if they were real. She thought she must have imagined the whole thing. But lately, she heard a steady scratching behind the wood paneling at night.

"I want them out," she told Lou more than once, poking him until he rose from his slumber. So far, Lou hadn't been able to find the problem. But Ma knew the source. The rat invasion was Lori Molinari's fault. Even though Lori lived three doors down on the left, Ma knew she was a filthy pig who didn't pick up after herself. "She'll ruin the neighborhood," Ma warned. Lori's trash was everywhere, which Ma said was an open invitation to any rat within a three-mile radius.

CHAPTER 3

WHEN THE PHONE RANG, Ma was using a toothbrush to tease her hair into a pronounced pouf. The toothbrush was a beauty tip from a high-end stylist in Manhattan and even though Ma had not yet demonstrated any talent for hairstyling, the teasing was a ritual she honored. Ma's hair, thin and platinum blonde, was backcombed, letting the strands that greeted the world cover and hide their underlying support—a nest of hair, hardened by a generous spray of Aqua Net. It was a solid foundation, an attempt to make Ma's limp hair seem thick and pert. "It's important to keep up your appearance," Ma told Lauren. She had even given Lauren her own tortoiseshell comb, and mother and daughter practiced the art of the tease, side by side, at Ma's dressing table. When Lauren balked and said she was bored, Ma admonished her, "You have to invest the time if you're going to tease it right."

Ma ignored the call the first nine rings, but the caller was determined, and the pestering would not stop. That piqued Ma's curiosity, so she relented and picked up the white Princess phone receiver. The moment she heard her cousin Janet shout, "I've got terrible news," Ma knew she should not have answered.

It was another problem from her tedious family. The pack of them was a nuisance. But Janet was right. It was terrible news. News passed from Ma's estranged mother to an aunt, from the aunt to Janet, and now it was coming out of the white Princess receiver into her ear. The family spoke the language of distress. Ma could count on it.

According to Janet, it was Jack Anthony, Ma's older brother. This time, Jack Anthony was not busted for hot-wiring a car, mistreating women, selling cocaine, or scamming people to invest in his next "great business idea." This time was something different. Jack Anthony was in Bronx-Lebanon Hospital. He had shot himself in the head with a Hi-Point handgun. "It sounds bad," Janet told Ma.

When Ma put the receiver down, she finished the task at hand: her hair. She moved the toothbrush along her tired hair with deliberate, sharp, and rapid motions, determined to keep her hand steady. When she was satisfied that every stray bit of frizz had been reigned in and lacquered down, she was ready.

Despite it all—and although Ma had not forgiven Jack Anthony, would never forgive him for all he had done—they were family. Ma felt the pang of the situation. Maybe it was their common childhood. Maybe it was their shared blood, a kinship that coursed through the O'Donnell family whether they liked it or not.

Ma marched downstairs to the front door and opened it wide. The air was unseasonably warm, and the humidity that blasted into the foyer felt more like the dog days of a Jersey July rather than the September afternoon it was. Lauren, who scampered away from the dressing table when Ma answered the phone, was steering a black Schwinn bicycle, a hand-me-down from the twins, back and forth, up and down, round and round, on the blacktop driveway.

"Lauren!" Ma hollered. "Find your brothers. We're going to see Uncle Jack Anthony."

⌒∞⌒

Lou left the auto shop promising to meet Ma right away. Ma didn't drive on highways. Keeping tabs on every driver zipping along in multiple lanes, front and back, this way and that, made her feel out of sorts. And so Lou met Ma and their brood in the parking lot of the City

View Diner, which was conveniently located near an entrance to the expressway, a good meet-up spot for continuing on to the hospital in the Bronx. Lou pulled his truck into the parking spot adjacent to Ma's Caddy, on time to the minute, and hopped out to join his family.

It wasn't often that all five traveled together, a scenario that required both twins to ride in the backseat, Lauren placed between them with her feet on the raised hump. As usual, Tony had trouble keeping still. He didn't do well in confined spaces like the car, and chose to entertain himself by reaching over Lauren and pinching Little Louie's elbow, until Little Louie, fed up, closed page 98 of *The Call of the Wild*, stretched across Lauren from the other side, and socked his brother in the stomach.

"Settle down guys," Lou said out of habit, his voice lacking conviction or warning of punishment.

Tony had been nicknamed Live Wire in his early years due to his squirming, tapping, and humming ways, while Little Louie remained sedentary and quiet, most content when reading. Ma thought that the difference in behavior must be attributed to Tony taking more than his fair share of her energy in the womb. Despite their differences, the brothers got along—most of the time.

Ma had been punching buttons on the radio, skipping through the channels: Spanish salsa, 1010 Wins—"All News, All the Time," and heavy metal. None of them would do. But when Billy Joel, the raspy piano man (born in the Bronx like Ma), sounded his first few notes, Ma paused and waited for more. Billy's song came out years before. It seemed to settle her, a past memory calming her nerves. She sat back into the Caddy's leather seat, and as they made their way up the clogged expressway, Lou dodging in and out of rush-hour traffic, Billy Joel filled the car with song.

Ma knew the lyrics by heart. More than that, she knew their meaning. Billy crooned to her about seduction, about Catholic girls guarding their chastity for far too long. Ma knew the price Catholic girls paid. And for what? Billy was right—it was the good who died young.

Tony gestured a gag, groaning, "This song sucks. Can't we change the channel?" Lou was quick to respond. "Let your Ma listen to what she likes." And Ma, who usually would have been up to challenge Tony and push him back into place, didn't pay him any mind. At the moment, she was devoted to Billy.

The song's lyrics, and their irony considering the situation, seemed lost on everyone in the car except Little Louie. Did his mother not hear the words? Or maybe she did. What was she thinking? She couldn't possibly believe that Uncle Jack Anthony was good. Dying? Apparently. Young? Well, not exactly. Good? Not hardly.

None of the Napolitano children had been inside of a hospital, unless you counted their own birth, which only Ma remembered and therefore did not count (although Ma made sure each child was well aware of the excruciating, traumatic event when they had, one by one, forced their way out of her body and into the world). Three years older, the twins had no more idea than Lauren about what to expect from the hospital, let alone the ICU, as their medical knowledge was limited to information gleaned from repeat episodes of *Trapper John, M.D.* and *St. Elsewhere*. And so, when the doors to the Bronx-Lebanon Hospital Center parted, all three stepped through with a mixture of curiosity (to see a real hospital) and dread (to see Uncle Jack Anthony).

The ICU patient beds and nurses' station formed a horseshoe, a configuration that allowed the nurses, worn out from twelve-hour shifts, to keep watch over the patients. It was noisy—beeping, buzzing, ticking. A collection of screens, monitors, ventilators, drips, and tubes all worked together to breathe, pulse, pump, drain, and medicate. For the weak. For the infirm. For those who could no longer do for themselves.

Ma approached the nurses' station, her family trailing behind, and stood at the counter until a nurse broke away from her change-of-shift meeting pack and came to Ma's assistance. Ma handed over the pass she had received downstairs in the lobby and the nurse pointed to a patient bay surrounded by glass.

Ma looked through the glass at the bed. She did not see her brother and thought there must be some confusion, but the nurse pointed to the clear enclosure again and assured Ma that there was no mistake.

"That's Mr. O'Donnell," she said. "You may go over to see him." Ma was still not convinced. "He can't speak, but he might be able to hear you," the nurse added.

"Is he going to be okay?" Ma asked, regretting the question the moment the words jumped out of her mouth.

The nurse hesitated, attempting to select the appropriate response. Ma didn't wait for the answer. "Will he be all right?" Ma asked. She felt as if she were reaching back in time, asking their boozy mother if Jack Anthony would recover from a hangover or nasty black eye.

"This kind of head injury is difficult," was all the nurse offered. "I'm sorry."

She suggested that the children wait in the hall, but Ma would have none of it. Eventually the nurse gave in, adding caveats like, "under these circumstances," "they will need to be quiet," and "only two visitors near the patient at a time." Ma nodded and forced a small smile, but immediately ignored the directions and the five of them stood at the end of Jack Anthony's bed like a blockade to the outside, a family fence.

Jack Anthony was wired up like a science experiment spoof—unreal and extreme. Sticky pads on his chest monitored the electrical activity of his heart. A small sensor was attached to one ear, and a catheter threading out from his waist and down his right leg drained urine into a clear bag. A cuff wrapped around his arm connected to a large machine beeping a consistent rhythm. Small tubes ran into his neck and groin and a slightly larger one attached to a mass of bandages dressing his head. Another tube through his mouth connected to a breathing machine that hissed and clicked as it pumped oxygen. Numerous bandages held the intravenous lines and tubes in place.

"Will you look at all of this?" Ma asked her children. "Take a good, hard look at your uncle and cement it in your mind," she instructed.

Surprisingly, given the fact that he had shot himself through the temple, Jack Anthony's face was intact. Yet Ma, even though she had moved and was standing next to her brother, couldn't identify anything familial. Jack Anthony's face was puffy, swollen, and discolored. Purple-black puddles covered his face, arms, and legs. It was the sick, sallow yellow of his face that made Ma the most unsteady. The bed had been tilted up slightly and his hands and feet were raised on pillows. Ma thought he looked like a battered and discarded blow-up doll.

When Ma leaned in closer, his eyelids twitched open. "Jack Anthony," she whispered. "We've come." Ma didn't get a vocal answer back, but Jack Anthony's lips, crusty with a straw-colored fluid, closed slightly over the tube. Ma interpreted it as a sure sign of recognition. "We've all come," she said again.

Her family stood waiting for direction, but for once Ma was not sure what to do or say. How should she proceed? This time she had no control. Yes, Jack Anthony was tormented and troubled. Everyone knew that. Now his outside matched his inside. Ma could not help him. No one could.

"Well, I guess that's that," Ma finally announced, firm and matter-of-fact. "Kiss your uncle good-bye," she instructed, as if wrapping up some last-minute business.

Little Louie, Tony, and Lauren turned to their mother in unison, appearing like a much-practiced and choreographed slapstick move. All three were sure they had misunderstood Ma's words.

She said it again. "Kiss him good-bye."

No one made a move. Surely their father would correct her, change her course, or convince her that this request was unreasonable, impossible. The three turned to their father. Lou felt the pressure, but did not come to their aid—he would not cross Ma. He looked down and fixated his gaze on Jack Anthony's exposed right foot. The baby toenail was thick and hard, the color of parchment.

"Kiss your uncle good-bye."

Tony, realizing his father would not save him, spoke the first words of dissent. "I'll gag."

"Show some respect," Ma shot back, keeping her voice to a whisper.

"He smells," Tony complained. Ma frowned at her son. "This place creeps me out," Tony continued. "I'm gonna puke." He paled, as though the tubes and bandages covering his uncle's body had managed to entangle him, draining him of his lifeblood. He turned to Little Louie, hoping his twin would come to his rescue or at least share the burden.

On cue, Little Louie said, "I'll do it, Ma."

Little Louie moved toward the head of the bed. He hovered, trying to determine the best place for a kiss. Tears streaked the yellow skin and Little Louie worried that the pressure of his lips would cause his uncle pain. He found a spot above his uncle's right eyebrow where there wasn't a bruise, and—ever so lightly, barely making contact—set his lips on Uncle Jack Anthony.

Lauren followed Little Louie's lead. "Good-bye Uncle Jack Anthony," she said, and sent him a kiss, blown out over her small palm.

Tony held his ground and would not approach.

"Show some loyalty," Ma told Tony. "You, of all people." And then she told Tony something he had never heard before. "Jack Anthony is your namesake," she said. "You are named for him. You are bound to him."

Ma walked up to the bed and leaned down to her brother's ear. She whispered something she should have shouted years before, a whisper loud enough for Tony to overhear. "You're a son of a bitch, Jack Anthony." Ma straightened and walked away from the bed, past Tony, past the other ICU patients, past the nurses' station, and out of the Bronx-Lebanon Hospital Center.

It was dark when Lou drove them back to City View Diner to retrieve Lou's truck. They rode in silence. Lauren and Little Louie slept. Tony sat straight up, alert. He did not turn to watch the other cars rushing past either side of the Caddy. He stared forward, stiff and unmoving, as if any and all fidgeting had been knocked out of him for good, watching the pouf of his mother's hair lit by headlights, rocking back and forth.

CHAPTER 4

Lou woke with the urge to make his family Sunday dinner. He made most weekend meals, but felt like he would outdo himself this time. His family of five would gather together and break bread. They would move forward, beyond the trauma of the last week, clearing away the lingering details of Jack Anthony's death, which lay stagnant in the Napolitano home.

As usual Lou woke up at five o'clock and roused Wylie, his beloved Rottweiler. At their first meeting, Lou thought the black-and-mahogany pup appeared an exceptional canine, robust and alert even at ten weeks. Wylie had not lived up to Lou's first impression, nor the reputation of his powerful breed. Wylie, despite his massive build and 125 pounds, was rather shy and complacent; a listless, snoozing animal—an unrecognizable descendant of the hardworking ancient Roman guard dogs. Still, Lou and Wylie had become devoted companions with a shared understanding of each other's temperament.

Lou looked forward to his dinner plan. He tossed it around in his mind, trying to organize the multiple details and meticulous timing it would require. Lou liked to cook. It was one of his great pleasures. If he couldn't be at the garage or sitting in his truck with Wylie, smoking Winstons and listening to the radio, there was nothing he would rather do.

It had always been that way. As a young boy, he used to tuck himself under the kitchen table in Bayside, Queens, and watch his mother and grandmother, a recent Italian immigrant who spoke no English, create meals for their large extended family. Even though the kitchen was the domain of the women and men were usually shooed away, the two women were used to Lou being underfoot, and as he grew older, they let him stay. Lou loved the culinary cacophony of metal, cast iron, wood, and glass. The savory smells. And the end result—mingling flavors of joy and nourishment, which fed the hardworking, hungry diners.

Cooking wasn't for Ma. During the week when Lou worked long hours, she stuck to an easy-boil, prepackaged, or reheated routine. "I don't do mundane domestic chores," Ma informed the smitten Lou when he requested that she become his wife. "If you're looking for a dumpy Italian housewife, you'd better take another look."

Lou did take another look. He liked what he saw, a petite blonde with all the bells and whistles, appearing as fragile as a goldfinch. But inside she was mighty, with a mind of her own. Ma was nothing like the wide women in his family who, despite their sturdy frames, were unquestionably subservient. Lou was drawn to Ma's Irish spunk. Who cared if she didn't cook? Lou's mother cared. Nonna didn't like her daughter-in-law's attitude and thought a diet of frozen TV dinners was not how her eldest son and three grandbabies should be fed. But Nonna also knew it was her son's choice, and she would stand by him and not press too much.

In the early morning darkness, Lou's truck had a residue of dew across the windshield. Lou wiped it off with his shirtsleeve and Wylie jumped into passenger seat, and off they went to the 24-hour shopping market.

In the kitchen, Lou lined the inventory of ingredients across the turquoise Formica countertop like an army of goodwill—oregano, cracked pepper, garlic, onions, plum tomatoes, green olives, parsley, extra virgin olive oil, pasta, and Coca-Cola. He planned homemade gravy (just the way Nonna had taught him) with meatballs and sausages and ziti on the side. Maybe he would even add steak tips on the grill. And ricotta cheese pie. He couldn't forget the pie.

When Lauren came hopping downstairs into the kitchen around seven o'clock, Lou was delighted to see her. She was good company on weekend mornings, and he relished his time with her. The twins, now preteens, would sleep until noon for sure. Sunday was Ma's day of rest too. And since they had moved from Queens, Sunday mornings didn't include Mass with Nonna.

"Good morning, Princess," Lou greeted his daughter, noticing that the hives which had covered her neck and face earlier in the week were settling down, the redness fading. "You're just in time to be my extra-special assistant." Lou clasped his hands together and rubbed them up and down across his callous palms. "This is gonna be good—really, really good."

"Can I help?" Lauren asked, knowing that her father would not turn her down.

"I don't know," he teased. "I've got some big plans." Lou instinctively pressed his hand over Lauren's forehead, relieved to feel cool skin. No fever or nosebleeds today. Lauren was small for her age, petite like Ma, yet fragile on the inside too. While Lauren inherited Ma's appearance, she didn't seem to possess the underlying might. Lou worried that Lauren was weak and did not have the determination or strength to fight off the many ailments that dogged her.

"Can I help?" she repeated, pulling a chair up to the counter to stand on.

"Of course you can." Lou's speech was full-flavored Queens, an accent that had been dunked in hot oil and breaded Italian-style. "There is no way I could do this without you."

"Really?" Lauren was honored, but suspicious that this statement wasn't right.

"Now why would I say that if it wasn't true?" Lou pulled his white undershirt out and away from his olive skin like suspenders on an expensive suit.

"I don't know. But you might."

"Not on your life. You are my best helper and we are going to make the best meatballs and gravy anyone has ever tasted."

Lauren looked up at her father; she could see the little specks of green in his hazel eyes. She believed him. Ma said that Lauren was damn lucky that she looked like Ma and not her father, because Lou had one big Italian nose with no chin to balance it out. Lauren thought he looked handsome. Gentle and perfect.

"Let's get chopping," Lou directed. Lou pulled out the worn wooden cutting board and a paring knife and placed a yellow onion smack in the center. "We, my lady, are ready to chop. But we don't want any tears, so I am going to show you a magical trick."

"A trick to keep away tears?"

"That's right. Here's what we do."

Lou grabbed the onion and placed it under the faucet. "First, we drown the onion in the coldest water to dampen its stinging power. Then, just in case, we put a piece of white bread in our mouth. Nonna taught me that."

"Really?"

"Really!" Lou ripped off a piece of Wonder Bread, cushiony and white, and held it out to his daughter. Lauren put it in her mouth.

"Don't chew," he warned. "Or it will be too weak to combat the onion." Lauren followed his instruction, and resisted the temptation to chew and swallow. She lodged the bread between her tongue and the roof of her mouth and kept it still so that it became soggy with saliva.

"Finally, for even extra protection, we put on special onion glasses." Lou pulled a pair of swimming goggles out from a catchall drawer and placed them over his daughter's eyes. The rubber straps had long lost their elasticity and drooped loosely next to Lauren's neck.

"These aren't onion glasses," Lauren laughed at her father. He could be so silly.

"Cross my heart, they are special onion glasses," he told her. "They have extraordinary powers and keep all tears away."

"And now, we are ready," Lou said. "We need to cut, fast and quick. Place your hand on mine." Lauren rested her hand over her father's rough fingers. They danced as paired partners across the cutting board, the knife dicing the onion into the smallest chunks possible. Lauren eyed her father through her tinted goggles. His persistent chopping did not let up until the last strip of onion was sliced. She looked at the little mound of onions Lou pushed to the side of the board. They had done this together, as a team, and she had not felt any stinging or tears. She thought her dad was the best man in the world.

CHAPTER 5

THE NEIGHBORS WERE MAKING MA TENSE. She didn't want or need stress in her life. "Stress is the enemy," she told Lauren. Sometimes Ma would go out, but that was rare. More often, when Ma felt overwhelmed and needed to retire to her room with a cocktail of prescribed stress relief medication and a stiff drink, she would summon Christina.

Christina lived at the end of the lane, two doors past Lori Molinari. At fifteen, Christina was mature and serious about her future. She was her swim team's captain and an honor student who planned to major in economics when she got to college next year. Ma didn't think there was anything interesting about the girl—exactly the reason why she trusted Christina to watch her children.

The twins didn't like having a babysitter. Louie resented that Ma thought he needed to be looked after. He was too old for that. Tony might have agreed with his brother, or even mounted a protest, except for the fact that he lusted after Christina—her dark hair waved over her shoulders, reaching far down her back, wispy and fluttering over the top of her buttocks. Tony never missed an opportunity to marvel at Christina's ever-blossoming breasts.

Lauren adored Christina, and looked up to the ambitious teenage girl. Best of all Christina brought movies, a special treat since Ma monitored television and movie selections for the whole family, even Lou (especially Lou, so that he would not lust after the young starlets as they sashayed across the screen). Ma allowed a steady stream of news and crime shows. That was it.

This time, Christina brought *Sixteen Candles* and Jiffy Pop. The combination was momentous for Lauren. Even the twins settled in on the couch—Tony strategically scrunched next to Christina—and the four of them followed the fetching Molly Ringwald as she acted out the real stresses of being sixteen and misunderstood.

But Christina's babysitting relief only went so far. Despite Ma's attempts to keep the stress at bay, it was coming her way in bucket loads. The previous day, someone poured paint (the color of chili pepper) onto the Napolitano driveway during the night. Lou's truck was parked in the street, and he didn't notice the menacing puddle since it was still dark at his early departure hour. The boys, groggy and stumbling to the bus stop, had not noticed either. Like many mornings, Ma was running a good thirty minutes late and was in a rush to drop Lauren at school and get herself to an early French manicure. She opened the garage door and backed the Cadillac over the driveway. The white Eldorado, tires emblazoned with red-hot stripes, left a thin trail of fire on the pavement as Ma drove it down and away from Country Club Lane.

Unbeknownst to Ma, someone was watching her exit: Carmine Cuomo. He was busy polishing his bike and looked up in time to see Ma pull out. Carmine thought she was one hell of a woman.

Ma ordered Lou to do something. "Let's let it go," he countered. "Kids are just being kids." He hoped to bring Ma's flaming temper down to a low simmer. He knew how boys got into trouble and even noticed how his own boys, the twins, were beginning to separate into two individuals looking for entertainment beyond what Country Club Lane could provide. Ma went into a real spin. "You'd better find your balls and start acting like a man," she hollered, and Lou had answered in his soft, reassuring voice, "Sure. Sure."

That night, while Lauren and the twins were engrossed in popcorn and teen comedy, Alexandra Tosatto came stomping across the lawn in a screeching hissy fit. Ma emerged from her room and yelled to Christina that she would take care of it. Ma was worried that Alexandra's fist pounding would dent the front door and she opened it just a sliver. "Someone dropped *feces* into my mailbox," Alexandra wailed, managing to place special emphasis on the word feces. Alexandra didn't believe in profanity, even under times of great duress, but Ma called it like it was. "Alexandra, the neighborhood has turned to shit and somebody ought to do something about it." With that, Ma shut the door tight and pulled across the chain lock. She turned around and walked into the family room to see her three children. Tony didn't bother to look up from the movie, and Louie (who now insisted that the "Little" be dropped from his name) smirked between bites of popcorn. Lauren stood up, stunned, and waited for her mother to say everything was all right. And she did. "Forget about it," Ma said. "That Alexandra is one major nutcase. Go on back to your movie. I'll be upstairs."

Ma knew that what really bothered Alexandra was that Lou hadn't taken on the Tosattos' eldest as a mechanic apprentice at the Napolitano business. Alexandra's son had been in a bit of a rumble and probably wouldn't be allowed to finish his senior year of high school, which didn't surprise Ma one bit. Alexandra and her husband, John, had asked Lou if he would take him on and of course Lou, being Lou, was happy to agree. "Lou will sleep on it," Ma jumped in. She didn't want the neighbors getting too chummy. Ma had a rule about mixing friendship (or annoying neighbors) with business. The day after the Tosattos asked Lou about the job, Ma told Alexandra that Lou just wasn't up to it, and chubby Alexandra had been acting put upon ever since.

Alexandra was one thing; she could be handled, swatted down like an irritating mosquito. It was another neighbor—Lori Molinari, the friendly divorcée and dirty rat-lover—who really got under Ma's skin.

"She's got that high-and-mighty attitude like she's better than everybody," Ma would say. "The way she sashays around in her second-rate fox fur coat. She's not fooling anybody, least of all me!"

What irked Ma more than she would ever admit was the way Lori smiled at Lou. It was a blatant, come-and-get-me invitation. And when she smiled, Lou would blush like he was thirteen years old. "Never trust a woman like that," Ma told Lauren when they were alone. "She's been after John Tosatto and I can tell she wants to get her claws into your father too. Hell, she's probably after Carmine. She's nothing but a piece of stinkin' garbage."

CHAPTER 6

Ma was moving Lauren's bedroom to the basement. The twins needed their own rooms now, and Ma was feeling hemmed in. There was plenty of space for Lauren downstairs. "We shouldn't waste the space," Ma explained. "Every room needs to be used in order for it to breathe. It's important for the health of the whole house."

"Ma, it's too dark," Lauren protested, not wanting to be that far away from her mother at night. Tony had offered to take the room instead. He liked the idea of being off on his own, almost underground, but Ma turned him down flat. "It's time Lauren grows up a bit," Ma said, "and I need to keep watch on you boys." Tony rolled his eyes, but did not pursue the matter. He knew when his mother could not be budged.

In the end, Tony and Louie refused to be separated, preferring to remain in their shared room. Lauren was still relocated to the basement. Tony and Louie were corralled into carrying down Lauren's twin bed and nightstand, and were directed to center it against the wall so that the head of the bed faced the one half-window. Lauren loved her white wooden bed. A small pink flower was delicately carved into the headboard, and if you looked closely you would discover a small green bud as well. The matching nightstand held a pink ballerina lamp.

"I need a curtain on that window," Lauren said to Ma.

"We don't need to waste money on window cover-ups when it's so small," Ma answered. "It's a basement, almost underground. Who's going to see you?"

Lauren wasn't convinced, and so she climbed onto her mattress and stood on her tiptoes to peek out of the pint-sized pane of glass. Ma was right; there wasn't much to see, just the driveway and Ma's Caddy, which blocked any view of the Cuomos' nearby tomato garden.

The room felt sparse. Ma didn't approve of stuffed animals. She said they were sentimental and silly and provided children with an unnecessary crutch. Instead of the customary pile of cuddly creatures, Ma bought a special poster to brighten up Lauren's new room. Ma tacked the poster on the ceiling above the bed—a grey kitty and brown puppy snuggled together in a field of enormous daisies that towered over the baby animals. The message "Lean On Me" was written in white letters across the ultra-blue sky.

"Do you think this picture is real?" Lauren asked Ma.

"Of course it's real."

That night at bedtime, Ma left Lauren's new bedroom window open for fresh air. "It's not good to sleep in a stuffy room," Ma told her. Lauren couldn't sleep. No matter how tightly she squeezed her eyes, willing them to stay shut, she just couldn't sleep. Next door, Carmine was fiddling with his bike, revving it up, over and over. While he tinkered, he sang "Abracadabra" by Steve Miller Band. Lauren didn't know the words, but she recognized the melody from the radio. And now Carmine's voice, singing a cracked and broken lullaby, drifted through the little window. She thought she heard "reach out" and then maybe "grab ya." Was that right? "Abra-abra-cadabra" she was sure of. She strained to make sense of the words. And then, there it was again. *Grab ya. Grab ya. Grab ya*, pricking at her ears until they burned.

Lauren put her fingers in her ears and concentrated on the poster above her bed. She wondered if Ma might be wrong about the giant daisies in the field; they just didn't seem real.

Hours later, after Carmine had gone inside and she had succumbed to slumber, Lauren felt something near her. The presence made her eyes flash open. She stayed still and quiet, waiting. She knew something was there. Something in the room with her. Then she heard a scurrying noise like tiny nails across linoleum and she screamed into the night.

"Ma. Ma. Maaaaaaa!"

Lou appeared in an instant and snapped on the light, his abruptness causing the lamp to jerk back and forth, leaving the ballerina to dance in a very ungraceful fashion.

"Dad! There were rats!" Lauren told her father. "I saw them. Rats. Just like Ma said!" Lou crawled onto the floor as his young daughter looked on, waiting for him to do something, to protect her. Lou looked under the bed and examined the floor and corners of the room. He moved to the pecan-paneled hallway and up the staircase, the area dim even with the lights on. He cased every inch, looking for a trace of the furry culprit.

CHAPTER 7

THE MEN WERE GOING HUNTING. John Tosatto was turning forty, crossing the threshold into middle age. He wanted to commemorate the occasion with something momentous, something worthy of the passage. It was the perfect excuse to honor a life-long dream to go hunting for more than a turkey, grouse, or squirrel. John Tosatto was after the Holy Grail—moose hunting in the Western Maine Mountains. Lou and John's cousin, Sam, didn't need much encouragement to accompany him. The idea of tracking down these monarchs of the North appealed to them all.

It was John who found a remote lodge and an inexpensive, but experienced, guide who would lead them through marshes, river bottoms, and mountainous woods and teach them moose calls. John said the place guaranteed prospective bulls, and promised to get the hunters up close and personal. Lou couldn't wait. For weeks, they made lists, studied maps, and practiced mating calls. Proper preparation was key, and the men each collected the essentials: flashlight, cheesecloth, knife, first aid kit, thermos, compass, rope, and binoculars. And weapons. The brochure said a muzzle-loader, handgun, archery equipment, or modern rifle would put a trophy bull right in a hunter's lap.

This was a trip for men. Alexandra Tosatto supported the adventure. Ma didn't put up a fuss either and told Lou, "Knock yourself out."

As promised, there was a moose. It was massive in size, weighing almost one thousand pounds with an incredible horn spread of seventy inches. This king of kills had been snagged by Lou, not John, and Lou arranged to have the outfitters bring the animal out of the woods and back to the resort, where it was quartered and readied to take home to New Jersey.

Lou worried that Ma would balk, but returning from the hunt with the ultimate prize had tickled Ma's competitive streak and made her proud of Lou—so proud that she allowed the hulking animal, the oversized Bullwinkle, to hang over the mantel, its antlers extending far past the edges of the brick fireplace, diminishing everything else in the room.

Lauren couldn't believe it was real. Tony thought the moose was the most amazing thing he had ever seen and begged Lou to take him along next year. Louie thought the creature and his glassy black eyes watched over their family room with a permanent look of surprise, flabbergasted to find his final resting place in Elizabeth, New Jersey. Ma was so excited by Lou's accomplishment that she even felt compelled to open her home, and invited the neighbors of Country Club Lane to come by for beer and cocktails. And they came—to meet and admire the moose.

All was fine, even peaceful, for weeks, until Alexandra Tosatto waddled over one afternoon to present Ma with something else that the men caught on the trip. Something that John and Lou hadn't bothered to mention.

It was a clipping from the *Rangeley News*. On the front page was a photo of Lori Molinari clad in a fitted camouflage jacket and complementary orange hat, flanked by John Tosatto, his cousin Sam, and Lou. The three men shared the same goofy grin. Lori held a crossbow. Behind her, a recent conquest slumped on the woodsy ground, struck down by her fatal bow shot—one big, stupid moose.

CHAPTER 8

THE EXPLOSION ROCKED THE HOUSE AT 3:00 A.M., sending Lauren's ballerina lamp crashing to the floor, the ceramic dancer shattering to pieces. A second boom ignited flames. From her basement bed, Lauren could see an orange glow swoop over her window and then retreat. Just when she thought it was gone, it would reach out again, flashing back and forth like dragon's breath, providing the only light in the night and her darkened room. She tried to bolt up and out of the basement, but couldn't move. She was in shock, pinned down by fear.

Wylie started barking and Lauren heard her father yelling and pounding on the twins' door: "Get up! Get up! Get up!" Then she heard his feet, heavy on the stairs, coming to her.

Lou ran in and swept Lauren out of bed. She was still, frozen in Lou's arms as he maneuvered back up the rickety staircase and into the foyer. Lou heard the surge of an angry blaze beyond the front door, its smoky, biting fumes intruding underneath, twisting and snaking into the house.

"Go out the back!" Lou ordered the twins, who stood dazed, in a sleepy stupor at the bottom of the stairs. "Take your sister with you." Lou put Lauren down, her thin Cinderella nightgown sticking to her knees. Louie grabbed her hand and the three siblings fled outside into the night.

Ma was not a part of the frenzy. In her bedroom, she removed her satin nightgown and reached for a pair of black leggings and a white cotton blouse. She was aware of Wylie's whining out in the yard and her husband's shouts as he gathered up the kids. She aligned her blouse and did up each of the seven buttons.

Lou rushed back into the bedroom looking for Ma. "For God's sake, get out!"

"I'm coming," Ma answered.

"Now!" Lou's face tightened. "Now!"

"I'm coming," she repeated. This was one of the few times in their marriage (especially since the Lori Molinari moose-hunting fiasco—despite Lou's declaration of innocence and swearing on his mother's life that it was not his idea) when Ma did not question Lou. She obeyed his order and followed his lead, though first she slipped on a pair of black sandals and grabbed her purse and a sweater as if gathering the necessities for a mere trip to the grocery store.

The Napolitano family moved from the backyard, around the side of the house, and out into the center of Country Club Lane. Neighbors assembled in a wide range of sleepwear to take in the drama as the angry flames shot higher. Lauren saw Christina, the young babysitter, sitting on the curb next to Alexandra and ran into her arms. Ma chose to stay clear of Alexandra and stood off to the side on her own. She had not yet digested Alexandra's recent news. She hadn't decided if Alexandra was a confidant, the wife of a two-timing cheat, or the enemy.

Lori Molinari, that filthy rat-lover, was nowhere in sight.

From the street, the front of the Napolitano home was no longer visible. A black haze floated over from the driveway and settled like fog. The core of the blaze seemed to emanate from a vibrant orange center, like the eye of a storm in a Weather Channel illustration.

Mrs. Cuomo worried that the flames would leap into her yard and destroy her heirloom tomato garden in one fell swoop. Carmine, who was dressed (even at this hour) in full motorcycle regalia, seemed to have no concern for the tomatoes or for the Napolitanos. He sat staring into the flames, mesmerized by the fire's multitude of colors, his clunky silver chains hanging from leather chaps, glistening in the firelight. Only his mother could hear him humming "Abracadabra." Old Mrs. Cuomo did not find it odd that her son was serenading the fire tonight. Softly singing of heating up and cooling down. Of black panties and burning flames. She'd heard the song flow from her son's lips one hundred times before and never gave it a second thought.

John Tosatto was the one who called 9-1-1 after the first explosion, and as the sirens became louder, he busied himself with Lou in the middle of the action, blending into the scuffling, running, and shouting until the hoses were extended, sending a surge of water over the driveway. At first the flames seemed impossible to drown. They shot up wild and frenzied and did not weaken under the flow. But after a long forty-five minutes, they were defeated, left to whimper like a small, misbehaving child who didn't get his way after a tantrum.

When the smoke began to clear, Ma said it was a miracle that they were alive and that the house had been spared. In fact, the house had never been on fire, had not burned. Only streaks of black smudged the front facade, which John assured her could be restored with a fresh coat of paint. Ma's Cadillac was another story. It was in ruins. Still parked in the driveway where Ma left it that night, it sat, a metal skeleton, burned and charred with a few strips of once-white leather dangling and simmering off the frame.

"Nothing to be done now," Lou said to Ma. For the second time that night (and in so many weeks) Ma allowed Lou to speak without interruption—without shooting him down with bullets of raging profanity.

With the fire kaput, the firemen packed up the three trucks, the neighbors dispersed, and Lou spoke to the police about arson, insurance, and filing the necessary reports.

The firemen told Ma not to get too close to the crumbling car. So she moved up the edge of the driveway to study the damage and then made her way to the front door, which appeared sooty but unscathed, except for something brown and tattered that fluttered at just about eye level. Ma couldn't quite make it out. A scrap of paper? Debris from the car? Ma approached the entrance to her home and faced a handwritten note nailed to the door.

Burn in hell.

Ma would not stay another night in the house, not another moment on Country Club Lane. Just like that, the Napolitanos were gone.

CHAPTER 9

Belle Haven, Westfield, New Jersey

MA SAT IN THE KITCHEN OF HER NEW WESTFIELD, NEW JERSEY HOME. A young couple with two young children had snapped up the old house, and the Napolitanos were fortunate to have found desperate sellers in Westfield who were forced to accept Lou's lowball offer and an immediate closing date. "One man's misery is another's lucky day," Ma had quipped.

This house was larger, more appropriate for the family, especially since the auto shop prospered more than ever. Set back from the road, it sat on a hill with a long, curving drive. Inside were many modern and unexpected conveniences, like a master bedroom with a bathroom en suite, complete with a Jacuzzi tub. The kitchen had a large island, wine shelving, and an office cubby. The cubby desk had space for a typewriter and files, which Ma organized for bill paying and managing insurance claims (of which there were many—unfortunate events seemed to happen to the Napolitano family quite often). On the wall next to the cubby, Ma hung a bulletin board where she taped an enlarged glossy photograph of her Cadillac—burnt and ruined. From this cubby spot, Ma had a perfect vantage point for tracking and monitoring all activities in the adjoining family room.

Boxes from the recent and abrupt move were stacked throughout the house, towering in uneven rows, their contents waiting to be integrated into the split-level rancher. Lou would not find the moose head among these transported belongings. That item had been ceremoniously thrown out. For the moment, Ma ignored the boxy mess. She typed. It was a slow process, as Ma had not acquired great keyboard skills. For her purposes she worked out a slow and steady system. She would get the job done.

After several revisions, Ma was satisfied. It would do. She held the white paper in front of her and read the text one more time to admire her fictional prowess.

The letter read:

```
Dear Editor,

The following is the notice we would like to
include in tomorrow's paper:

Lori Molinari, a thirty-seven-year-old
divorcée, passed away in her home at 1329
Country Club Lane in Elizabeth, New Jersey,
according to the Union County Medical
Examiner's Office. Police were initially
called to the house on Tuesday after Molinari
was reported as missing and neighbors
complained of a foul odor coming from the
residence. Molinari's unfortunate demise was
a result of being trapped and buried alive
under mounds of debris that choked every room
of the home. A spokesperson for the health
department stated that it took firefighters
six hours to wade through the clogged
hallways to recover the body. The fire
department has cordoned off the residence for
decontamination and rodent removal.
```

Ma carefully folded the page in half and in half again so that it would fit inside an ivory greeting card, which said in a flowery font:

Today Is The First Day Of The Rest Of Your Life.

Be Happy.

She sealed the envelope, placed a LOVE stamp in the upper right corner, and addressed the letter to:

Obituary Editor
The Union News
Elizabeth, New Jersey

Across the back was Ma's final adornment in her slender, slanted script: S.W.A.K. Ma never forgot to embellish an envelope with the acronym —"Sealed With A Kiss"—a finishing touch when mailing out an important letter.

It *was* a happy day. In fact, it was the first day of the rest of Ma's life. Country Club Lane was behind her.

Ma may have put the old neighborhood behind her, but Tony had not. On Country Club Lane, Tony ruled. At thirteen, he reigned over a small band of sweaty neighborhood children ranging in age from six to twelve. Those under six were not welcome, as they more often than not had to take frequent potty breaks, or squealed to their mothers about the gang's secret activities. Outside of their small posse, Tony developed a reputation for bullying. He liked to whiz by on his bike, or even better, trail a lone child from behind, chanting accusations in a singsong falsetto.

"FATTY, FATTY, FAT ASS!"

"LITTLE BABY, BABY ASS!"

"DUMB, DUMBO, STUPID ASS!"

"DIAPER, PEE-PEE, SHITTY ASS!"

These were the selected favorites from his "ASS" repertoire. Sometimes he slapped the victim with the back of his hand for emphasis and this gesture almost always led to wailing, which Tony responded to with "PUSSY ASS!" before speeding off down Country Club Lane.

When anyone brought it up with Ma, she said, "Boys will be boys. It's in their blood."

On school days, Tony claimed the long black seat at the back of the bus and no one challenged him. He scavenged the chewing gum-infested floor for discarded pens and pencils, breaking them in half so that their edges became knife sharp and jagged. He propelled these missiles with a much-practiced expertise over crowded, three-kids-to-a-seat rows—aimed at the curly heads of studious girls who hovered up front, seated as far away from Tony as they could get, which only made Tony more determined to make a direct hit. Whenever Tony landed a bull's-eye, the girls shrieked and whined, "TONY, STOP IT!" or, "TONY, YOU ARE SUCH A JERK!" Tony would smirk and call back, "What's *your* problem, LITTLE TITTIE ASS?"

The worn-out bus driver, at the wheel for too long and using all of his concentration to remain in his own zone of private peace, would shout the expected and always ineffective, "Settle down," but did not turn around to address the outburst.

In the neighborhood, Tony shot his BB gun at random windows. He charged through Mrs. Cuomo's tomatoes, leaving her biggest and most beloved heirloom specimens smashed and oozing. His small troupe followed his lead without question, traipsing through the community after him as he called out graffiti instructions to those who were more than willing to please him. Although Tony was not tall, his shoulders were wide, telegraphing a manly strength when compared to the skinny, undeveloped bodies of his comrades. The kids even gossiped that Tony shaved with a razor and splashed his face with Aqua Velva. The petit bandit ensemble respected Tony, with his deepening voice, developing bicep muscles, and steel bravery. Tony had a "So what?" "Whatever" "Let-'em-try-to-make-me" attitude. Tony was irreverent. Tony was bad.

Tony was cool.

The gang would argue over which of Tony's feats were the "baddest," and it seemed there was a tie for first place. The summer before the Napolitanos moved away from Elizabeth, Tony had jimmied open the sliding glass door of the Smiths' house while they were vacationing in Cape May. The Smiths' living room became the gang's secret meeting hideaway for two weeks—a haven for drinking the Smiths' Schlitz (a beer most of the boys thought tasted gross) and endless cans of Pepsi. They raided a stash of grape Popsicles from the basement freezer, a stash that left purple dribbles across the beige wall-to-wall carpet. This prank was the ultimate for many. But several of the boys fondly recalled another moment from that same summer, a kind of summer grand finale—a humid, mid-August afternoon when Tony pried shy Mrs. Giglio's bathroom window open (while she lay in her darkened bedroom with a migraine), tossing a lit cherry bomb through the window and into the toilet.

Kerplunk! Pow!! BOOM!!!

The boys heard the explosion from behind a line of nearby laurel bushes with a mixture of disbelief, awe, and unwavering admiration for Tony, who ran from the window to join his loyal followers with cheetah-like speed.

At one time, Louie had been Tony's sidekick, but his older twin (older by four minutes) didn't have it in him for the long haul. Louie grew bored with Tony's antics and preferred to read passages from his multivolume encyclopedia set, a gift from Nonna. The present had annoyed Ma, since she thought the clunky books were nothing but a massive dust collector. During the daylight hours, the boys seemed to go their separate ways. At night, in their shared bedroom, neither could sleep unless the other was near, stacked into their bunk beds—Tony on top, Louie on the bottom—within close reach. And even though Tony felt his twin was a part of him in ways he could not express, embedded in his core, there were things that Tony did not want even Louie to know. Like the fact that the rumpled blanket, which Tony strategically draped over his face each night, was not to keep the light out as Tony said, but so that his thumb could rest over his lower lip, scraping against his bottom teeth. Undetected. Undiscovered.

Moving to a new neighborhood in Westfield and being enrolled in the eighth grade at Edison Intermediate School after school was already in full swing did not agree with Tony. No one knew him; no one feared him. He had been demoted, robbed of his powers.

When Mrs. Stokes, the no-nonsense guidance counselor, telephoned Ma for the fourth time in a week, she was not calling with good news. Tony had been enrolled for nine days and already Mrs. Stokes had concerns, which she began to enumerate with great gusto, the volume of her voice intensifying as she presented each crime to Ma.

1. Tony had been late to every class and found dawdling in the hallways.

2. Tony had not turned in any homework assignments.

3. Tony slept during all of the academic periods.

4. Tony disregarded the designated lanes of hallway passage when moving from class to class. These lanes were clearly marked by yellow tape on the floor. He refused to stay within the confines of the right-side lane, and wandered into the left-side lane, bumping and slamming into fellow students without apology.

5. Tony had pressed Kathy Philips up against her locker. (What Mrs. Stokes did not mention was that Kathy had not complained about the incident, nor the hard lump in Tony's pants that caused Kathy to turn a flushed rose. Kathy seemed to enjoy the attention, but Mr. Solomon, the pre-algebra teacher, had come across the episode, along with several other students. The students had formed a tight circle around the couple, all amazed that Tony was so adept with his tongue.)

6. Tony had been found in the basement of the building, reek-
    ing of marijuana.

7. And the final straw: Mrs. Stokes had taken it upon herself
    to inform Tony that his behavior "was not how a young man
    conducts himself at Edison Intermediate" and Tony had re-
    plied, "Blow me!"

Mrs. Stokes informed Ma that this behavior was unacceptable,
would not be tolerated, and required immediate disciplinary action.
Tony was suspended. No discussion. No second chances. Suspended
for a minimum of two weeks. "You will need to come and retrieve him
from the school this instant," Mrs. Stokes instructed Ma. "And before
we will even consider having him return to this educational institution,
we will need an apology, and we will need to see sincere remorse for his
outrageous and inappropriate infractions."

Ma had rallied, drummed up the strength to apologize to the tight-
ass witch, and told Mrs. Stokes that she couldn't imagine what had
gotten into her son. Moving is stressful, Ma pointed out, and perhaps
Tony was feeling overwhelmed, or perhaps he ate something; perhaps
the school lunches hadn't agreed with him. "He's usually such a good
boy," Ma said.

Ma did go to the school to retrieve her son, driving her rented yellow Ford Pinto. The used car was temporary transportation until she
could replace her torched Caddy, and leased to her at a rock-bottom,
bargain price. Practically free. No one wanted to drive the car since
word had come out that the Pinto had a design flaw—a propensity to
burst into flames when hit from behind. Ma wasn't bothered about the
car's dangerous reputation, but still, it just didn't suit her, didn't feel
right. She hated the hatchback style and detested the light ochre col-
or, a puke-like shade that reminded her of Jack Anthony's pallor right
before he died. Worst of all, she was getting mighty annoyed that the
insurance adjuster was taking his sweet time, literally weeks, to get the
Caddy's reimbursement claim processed.

"This school's a drag," Tony told Ma as he sauntered out of Mrs. Stokes's office after Ma signed the suspension papers and they headed to the parking lot. "It is the most B-O-R-I-N-G-ASS prison ever!" Lou would not be happy when he heard about this ruckus, but Ma understood. Tony had spunk, which he had inherited from her. He had no time for mundane, meaningless crap, or for idiots. He was growing up and he was no wimp. She could tell he would soon be a force to reckon with.

"You've got that right," Ma laughed and gave him a good knock on his right temple with her purse. Ma figured the best plan for now was to get the boy some lunch. And that settled that. Ma started up the Pinto and they headed to McDonald's. Two Big Macs, extra fries, two large chocolate milkshakes. Ma didn't eat, just poked at a french fry with the extra straw, until it had been smashed beyond recognition. But Tony was ravenous and ate it all—understanding that from now on, he would need to find ways to fortify himself, so that he could face down the Mrs. Stokes of the world. Face down his future.

Chapter 10

MA CHECKED THE CLOCK THE MOMENT SHE HEARD Lou pull his truck into the driveway. The clock read 7:02 p.m. Lou opened the front door and stepped into the large foyer of their new home. He was not yet used to the generous space, high ceilings, and grand staircase of their new surroundings, and stood on the white marble floor readjusting. He felt awkward, out of place. The Cararra tiles, silk wallpaper, and brass accents felt luxurious, grander than anywhere he had lived. Lou was not a fancy guy and not much for décor. He did not have many opinions about color, fabric, or furniture. That was Ma's domain, but the hard, glossy floor felt foreign to him. Stark and unforgiving. And though he could not feel the marble through his sturdy work boots, he suspected that if he brushed his bare toes across the floor, it would feel cold. It needed a thick rug with lively colors to warm it, cover up the harshness.

"You're over thirty minutes late," Ma shouted from the kitchen. Lou moved through the living room to the kitchen where Ma stood, placing four frozen chicken pot pies into the microwave.

"It's not so late," Lou answered.

"I will not tolerate it," Ma stated, closing the door to the microwave oven with a sharp clap.

"There was traffic," Lou said, nodding to the twins, who were slumped on the couch in the darkened family room. The twins, mesmerized by Don Johnson on a taped episode of *Miami Vice*, took no notice of their father's arrival home, nor did they acknowledge their mother's scolding.

"Traffic, my ass," Ma said.

"It was backed up. You know how it can get."

"Oh, I *know* all right." Ma rinsed her hands in the sink and reached for the white dish towel, wiping each finger separately, pulling the towel from the knuckle to the fingertip. "I *know* how backed up it can get—I *know* all about that, especially when there is a detour."

"There weren't any detours." Lou didn't wish to engage. He pushed his hair away from his forehead, which was dirty from spending the day under the hoods and chassis of troubled vehicles. "I need to clean up."

But Ma was starting to roll. She did not hear what her husband said, nor did she care to. "Detours to the old neighborhood?"

"Come on, don't be ridiculous. There were no detours," Lou repeated.

"Perhaps a detour to Country Club Lane?"

"Ah, come on, I'm telling you there were no detours. Not tonight and not any night." It occurred to Lou that marriage was like a used car. Once you'd driven 100,000 miles, the troubles began. You could make the car run, but it was high maintenance. Never an easy drive.

"I'm not an idiot." Ma would not accept lying, not from her children and certainly not from her husband. "You think I'm an idiot?"

"I don't. I never said that."

"Just one big idiot?" Ma was gaining steam, ready to blast.

"I do not think that," Lou said. "I think I need to clean up and I think you need to calm down. Get ahold of yourself."

"Of course, you do this to me now. Today of all days. The stress your son put me through this week. And now this." Tony, initially oblivious, sensed trouble and turned away from the TV to listen to his mother roar. Was this it for him? Would she turn him in? Right now?

"I need to clean up." Lou could feel his own anger gathering strength, rising up to meet Ma, up from his toes, a direct shot through his calves, knees, and into his stomach, where it sat, simmering.

"And tell me, how *is* Lori?" Ma had not forgiven Lou for the hunting trip. Lou had pleaded his case, his innocence, for weeks, sometimes even convincing himself that he had won her over, gotten her to believe him, but then the accusations would crawl back, growing to full force as ugly as before.

"How would I know how she is?" Lou said. "We've been through this before."

"I sit here, trapped, dealing with all this crap while you, while you're off visiting your whore in her filthy love nest."

"There is no love nest." The argument, its repetition, made Lou's head heavy. He felt like a caged mouse running on a spinning wheel. Round and round and round.

"What would you call it?" Ma said as if she had caught him red-handed.

"This is nuts. I'm taking a shower." Lou trudged upstairs to the bathroom. He held the ornate brass banister for support, his black boots dragging.

"Sure, go ahead," Ma shouted up the stairs, her voice chasing after him. "Run off and drown yourself in the shower."

The twins had heard these tangos between their parents before, and even more since the hunting trip, but they also knew that after the bomb, there would be quiet, a respite, and they could all begin again. During the shouting, their reaction was to turn up the volume on the television, Tony cupping his ears so that he could catch everything coming out of Don Johnson's mouth. He did not want to miss a second of the handsome actor aiming his Bren Ten, a stainless-steel handgun, at various unsympathetic criminals.

Lou positioned himself under the showerhead so that the water poured over the back of his neck and sore shoulders. He turned up the pressure and let it beat down on him.

Ma could hear the water running upstairs. "Go ahead. Wash off the evidence of that slut," Ma muttered to no one in particular. She wasn't finished and Lou had once again scooted away like a coward. The yelling got her heart pumping. She felt prickly and alert. This would not fly.

"Lauren," Ma called upstairs. "Get down here." Lauren did not need for her mother to call twice, and she appeared at the top of the stairs. She had a new room now; the Westfield house had placed her upstairs again, up and out of the basement, directly next to her parents.

"I want you to go out to your father's truck," Ma told her daughter. "and open the ashtray. I want you to pull out any butts and bring them to me." Lauren looked confused, her tiny face red and blotchy from the outbreak of hives that had kept her home from school that day. Ma steadied herself and explained once more to her daughter, "Go out to your father's truck. Open up the ashtray. Pull out any and all butts. Got it?" Her steel gaze made the required errand clear. Lauren nodded her head.

"You can put them in this." Ma handed Lauren a plastic Cap'n Crunch cereal bowl with a picture of the jolly cartoon pirate mouthing "Argh."

"Don't leave any behind," Ma said, reinforcing her request. "Get them all."

Lauren had never been alone in her father's truck before. She knew it was an important place for him. He often sat with Wylie in the truck and listened to the radio. "It's my thinking spot," he told her. She hopped up onto the running board. Stenciled white letters covered most of the ebony door: "Napolitano Brothers' International Garage: For All Your Automotive Needs."

As always, the door was unlocked and Lauren tugged against its weight. Lauren felt uneasy. To her, the truck door was like a secret vault, which, once opened, would thrust her into a space where she did not belong, or like the rabbit hole in *Alice in Wonderland*, where she might fall and fall and fall. It took three tries before she was able to pull it open. What did her mother want butts for?

Once Lauren opened the truck door and slid inside, settling into the passenger's seat, she worried less. The cab felt familiar and comforting—full of her father's smells: musty like dried leaves, with hints of oil and grease. The truck was never spotless like Ma's Caddy had been.

Instead it was filled with her father's tools of the trade, tools that made her proud. "I'm a doctor for cars," he had explained to her. "Cars need check-ups too. You have blood and a car has oil. If you don't keep it healthy, take care of it, the car can't do what it needs to do."

There was a worn and soft brown leather jacket on the seat, a wrinkled polo shirt with dark stains, and several small grimy rags. Metal boxes were strewn on the floor, full of screwdrivers, pliers, and bolts in assorted sizes, their twisty, curvy indentations making them appear like exquisite, handmade toys. A welding torch lay across a blue towel on the floor—all accoutrements from his mechanic toiling.

And there was music. Lou did not own many cassettes, but those tapes he did have he savored and played over and over again. Though Ma did not approve, Lou played David Lee Roth's "California Girls" so often that the plastic cassette cover had cracked on both sides and the shiny tape had come undone and wiggled out and across the floor.

The ashtray was shut. Lauren pulled the cover toward her, its hinges extended out, like little arms offering up a gift—grey and black ash, half-smoked cigarettes, chewing gum that had long lost its flavor and been placed back inside the striped wrapper, two pennies, and small white lumps of paper, which contained tiny bits of a green-black charred substance—what Ma called butts.

Lauren counted the individual stubs as she placed them into the plastic bowl, just as Ma said. One, two, three . . . The butts were small and she had to dig her fingers down into the soft ash to retrieve the buried pieces, pulling them out one by one. . . . Four, five, six . . . Her fingers felt dry and chalky. Seven, eight, nine . . . When she was sure she had collected them all, Lauren carried the bowl inside, careful not to spill.

Lauren presented the bowl to her mother; she licked her fingers to remove the ash. The taste was smoky and bitter, like dirt, and she spit it back into her hands.

"Look at this," Ma said, examining the debris in the bowl.

"Twenty-three butts," Lauren told her mother. "I counted them."

"It figures," Ma said. "He's higher than a kite." Lauren had no idea what her mother meant.

Ma placed the bowl on the counter and told her three children to come and eat their chicken pot pies. The tops of the pies were puffed and light brown and once a fork pierced through the crust, one could find bits of white chicken meat, peas, and chunks of carrot, all bathed in a creamy sauce. The children each placed a small pie on a plate and carried them back to the couch for eating. Ma never made one for herself. She did not like the way the thick sauce coated her throat. She poured a vodka and orange juice, which she could swallow with pleasure.

When Lou returned to the kitchen, he sat down at the table where Ma had plopped the last pie. The pie was cold; its crust deflated, sagging in the middle, sad, and tired looking; all the air that had once puffed it up into something edible had been released. Lou didn't care. He was washed clean. Ready to start over. He smiled at Ma.

The moment was right, and Ma smacked the cereal bowl down next to the pie. "Twenty-three butts," she said. "Lauren counted every last one."

"Lauren?" Lou asked.

"You heard me, you pothead. Your daughter dug them out of your ashtray and brought them to me," Ma said. "You must be stoned out of your mind. Cigarettes. Joints. More joints."

"Lauren brought them to you?" Lou asked again, not sure if he was ashamed because his daughter had found the evidence or because she had turned him in. Betrayed him. Lou looked at his daughter, who sat between her brothers on the couch.

"What's pot?" Lauren whispered to Louie. "Wasn't it in the chicken pie?" And Louie elbowed his sister hard. The message was clear: shut up.

"What do you expect?" Ma asked.

"What was Lauren doing in the ashtray?" Lou asked Ma again, wondering why his daughter had been digging into his indulgences.

"Don't try to change the subject. What a great example you are for your children."

"Enough," Lou said. He had to get Ma to stop. It was enough for one night. "That's enough."

"What do you think?" Ma charged forward, plunging into battle without a second thought. "Thanks to you, *Mr. Pothead*, Tony is in trouble at school. Where do you think he gets it from? I'll tell you where. From you! That's where. From you!" With that Ma poured the contents of the bowl over Lou's pie. Cap'n Crunch's jolly face turned upside down. The ash topped the crust like frosting; the decorative butts caught and held in the deeper crevices of the fallen pie.

Lou slammed his fists against the table, first the right, followed by the left, as if the first pound had not had the impact he intended to communicate. The pie popped up, rising from the plate, suspended for a brief moment, forcing the butts to roll across the table and floor. "It's enough!"

Ma, indignant and put-upon, made off to their bedroom upstairs and locked the door. She would not tolerate it. Would not. Would not. Would not.

Tony feared it was his turn. His father would now focus on his crimes, blame him for the disruption. Tony would be forced to give an explanation, to itemize Mrs. Stokes's long list of charges. His father would lecture and holler and punish. His father would tell him he was headed down the same path as Uncle Jack Anthony, his namesake.

But Lou did not ask Tony about any of it. Nothing. Instead, Lou walked to the edge of the bulky leather couch. "Lauren," he said, "what were you doing in the ashtray?" Lauren poked her head up: in the dark room, her father strained to see her face; only one side was lit by the television glow. The shadow made her face look odd and unfamiliar to him. The recent breakout of hives made her face bulbous and discolored. He thought she looked years older.

Lauren did not know how to answer her father's question. She did know not to mention Ma. "I was digging for butts," she told her father.

Lou said nothing. He walked out through the living room, across the marble floor foyer, and returned to his truck, where he sat for the rest of the night.

Chapter 11

Nonna and Nonno were coming to dinner on Sunday afternoon. It was their first visit to the new house—a pioneering trek from Queens to Belle Haven in Westfield, New Jersey.

Belle Haven. Ma loved the sound of it. This time she would not make the mistake of getting to know her neighbors.

Lauren was thrilled to see her favorite grandparents. The twins wondered what presents they might receive, as Nonna and Nonno never came empty-handed. Lou fretted over what to serve. Should he make the usual traditional Italian meal? Something new? He wanted it to be special, to make his parents welcome. He knew that the house, with its jumbo rooms and builder upgrades, would appear too ornate and showy for their simple tastes; however, it would also be a measure of their son's success. For that, they would feel proud. Ma felt only dread.

There were still dozens of boxes to unpack, and since the house was three times as large as the house in Elizabeth, the furniture looked insignificant, the rooms barren and incomplete. Across the back wall of the family room were French doors that opened onto an ample raised deck lifted high by long steel posts. During the day, the divided-light panes provided southern light, and a view beyond the steep, sloping yard to vacant wooded land. With fall in full swing, the deck was covered with decaying maple leaves. There were neighbors, but the houses had spacious grounds and were far apart (some even had acreage). Other than a friendly wave here and there, Ma had not yet met the residents of Belle Haven. She intended to keep it that way.

The house had two unique features. The first was that it was built on rock. The 4,000-square-foot dwelling hid most of the solid foundation, but the grey and craggy underpinning was exposed off to one side, jutting out like the ledge of a cliff. Here, the previous owners had perched a long wooden picnic table, which had weathered into splintery, pale silver.

The second distinction of the house was that it used two large propane tanks for heating. The metal vessels were at oddly placed steps from the front door, rather than disguised and hidden at the back. Ma thought it was a good thing that there was a long, curvy driveway, an intimidating barrier between the road and the house, because anyone spying the tanks could easily "blow the Napolitano home to smithereens."

Saturday, the day before Nonna and Nonno were to arrive, Ma was feeling a tight pressure in her chest. The twins were instructed to turn off the TV and sweep the deck; place the unpacked boxes into closets, under beds, and in the garage (any hidden corner); and polish all of the brass appointments (door knobs and stops, light fixtures, the banister) that had been left unattended and were now tarnished and green. Lou was to do the shopping and cooking, but he had gone into the auto shop early that morning and had not made it home by noon as promised.

Lou returned at two o'clock without groceries and with a long-winded excuse that it had been a busy Saturday morning at the shop. Carburetor, exhaust, electrical troubles—Ma would have none of it. She hissed and howled. She demanded to know where Lou was hiding his two-bit whore. She threatened up and down to tell Nonna and Nonno about Lou's druggie ways. After she exerted herself beyond the brink, squeezed out and used up every morsel of energy, Ma moved onto the newly swept deck with the comfort of her latest drink of choice, a Tom Collins. She needed space, less stress. She plucked a piece of ice from her glass and set it on her tongue, sucking hard, before she crunched the cube in two.

Then, looking out over the rock ledge and onto the picnic table, she saw them. It took her a moment to register what she saw, for the shapes to come into clear view. They darted, this way and that.

Hurry. Scurry. Furry.

Rats on the picnic table!

Rats in Belle Haven.

They roamed the top of the table searching for lost and forgotten crumbs. They scrambled up and down the table's legs, their claws anchored in the soft pine. There were two big ones with long tails that switched back and forth and three others, smaller, half the size, almost babies. It's a family, Ma thought. A goddamn family of rats.

Had they followed her to Belle Haven?

The realization came in a lightning flash, a bolt of knowledge that electrified her. It slammed her hard, and the knowing threatened to crush her to the core. In one miniscule instant she knew the problem, the source, the hideous truth. Lori's rats had wriggled into the moving boxes, made their home in the packing paper, and were carried out of Country Club Lane to Belle Haven with the rest of their belongings.

Lori, that filthy, no-good whore.

⚬⚭⚬

The rats were a private family matter. "Not to be mentioned to anyone." The mere idea of a new neighbor accusing Ma of bringing rats to Belle Haven made her head bob, little shaky tremors she could not still. Ma shouted upstairs to Tony, to bring his BB gun and shoot the invaders. "Aim for the skull," she howled, but by the time Tony had found his gun and joined Ma on the deck, the picnic table was bare and the rodents had gone, scampering away at the first notes of Ma's screeching.

Ma sent Lou to the hardware store and when he returned with two small glue traps, she continued carrying on. "Is there anything you can do right?" Ma hammered, and didn't settle down until Lou left and returned again with a bagful of assorted snap traps, cage traps, powders, and poisons, promising, over and over, that he would take care of the problem.

By the time Nonna and Nonno drove in from Queens to West-field the following day, Ma had pulled herself together. "Not a word to Nonna or Nonno," she warned her children. She knew her mother-in-law had never liked her, and if Nonna discovered the business about the rats, Ma would be pressed, and pushed, and picked at for sure.

Lauren perched herself on the front steps forty-five minutes before Nonna and Nonno's scheduled arrival. She didn't want to miss the first glimpse of her grandparents. After an hour, when she saw the small black car turn the corner into the driveway, she had to stare a moment longer to make sure it was not her imagination. "They're here! They're here! They're finally here!" Lauren hopped and clapped as Nonno maneuvered the winding driveway.

Lou, Louie, and even Tony gathered around the front door to greet them.

Ma hung back in the kitchen. "What a bunch of commotion for a couple of old geezers," she muttered to Wylie, who also seemed uninterested in racing toward the front door and preferred to snooze on the kitchen floor. "You'd think the Pope had arrived."

Nonno brought the car to a stop, got out, and walked around to open the door for Nonna. There they were. The pair wore matching knee-length khaki shorts and white T-shirts that exclaimed, "I'd Rather Be Golfing" under identical beige windbreakers. They were the same height (not too tall and not too short) and olive colored—browned from a recent trip to Florida, where they stayed in the small condo they kept for getaways and little escapes from Queens and the demands of the auto garage. As much as the couple matched on the outside, they were similar on the inside too. Not only as a result of spending forty years together as man and wife, but also because they had similar sensibilities—a gentleness, a loyalty to their own. Lauren thought they were glorious.

Before Nonna was through the door, Lauren spied the big tangerine bag stuffed with polka-dot tissue paper. "It's for you," Nonna said, handing Lauren the bag. Lauren poked through the thin paper and saw the doll. She never had a doll before. Ma thought they were silly. Lauren stared into the bag, savoring a secret wish come true.

"It's a Cabbage Patch Kid," Nonna said. "Everybody tells me this doll is what every girl wants. I hope that's true."

"Nonna, she's beautiful." Lauren embraced the doll, crushing its pillow-soft body against her tiny frame. She ran to show Ma. In the kitchen, Lauren held the doll out so that Ma could admire her.

The doll had bulging cheeks that protruded over most of the face, almost obscuring two tiny black eyes and a thin, smiling mouth. The hair was made of yellow yarn and wound into tight curls. The arms and legs flopped. The doll's puffy cheeks reminded Ma of Jack Anthony. "That is the ugliest thing I've ever seen," she said.

"She has a birth certificate," said Lauren, "and adoption papers."

"I'd send her back," said Ma. Lauren squeezed the doll close and darted off to savor her new treasure in the family room.

Nonno sized up the twins in the hallway. "Si dispone di una scintilla nei tuoi occhi," he said to Tony, who looked away, embarrassed by Nonno's overt display of affection. Nonno winked and slipped both Louie and Tony a crisp $50 bill, and they ran upstairs to their room, relishing their good fortune.

"How about a tour?" Lou asked his parents. As the three inspected every inch of the house, Ma could hear Nonna comment to her son as they entered each room, "It's so big, Lou." "Do you need a tub so big, Lou?" "I've never seen such a big closet." "Lou, the laundry room is the size of a house."

Nonno chided his wife, "Let the boy be. Sure, it's big. He's a big shot now. He's worked hard for it." Nonno laughed and gave Lou, a younger version of himself, a knock on the head.

When Lou, Nonna, and Nonno entered the kitchen, Ma pretended to be busy, wiping the counter clean with a sponge. "You've seen the house now," Ma stated.

"Yes, it's fit for a queen." Nonna gave Ma a quick embrace, while Ma stood stiff. She did not like Nonna's arms circled around her, their flesh touching, and held her breath until she was set free. Nonno kissed his daughter-in-law, one kiss for each cheek, and Ma squashed the impulse to take the sponge and scrub her face clean.

"This is for you," Nonna said, and handed Ma a rectangle-shaped present, neatly enveloped in blue wrapping paper.

"Thanks," Ma said, and pushed the gift to the side of the counter.

"Open it," said Lou. "Let's see what you got."

All eyes were on Ma as she undid the blue ribbon knot. She flipped the gift over and sliced the clear tape with her sharp nail so that the shiny cobalt paper parted to reveal a book, *The Classic Italian – Recipes Mama Made*. And a subtitle: *Easy, Step-by-Step Instructions for the Beginner.*

"Well, look at that," said Lou.

"Yes, look at that," said Ma.

"This ought to come in handy," said Lou to his mother.

"I hope it will," Nonna said, smiling at her daughter-in-law. Ma thought she might punch her.

Lou put dinner on the table and called for the kids. There was plenty of eggplant, meatballs, and linguine, but it was not the extravagant meal he had hoped to prepare. Since the rat fiasco the previous day, there had been no time for cooking, and this Sunday afternoon meal was takeout from Milano's Italian Family Restaurant.

At the table, Nonno made sure all the family members sat up straight and placed their napkins in their lap. The twins were told to remove their baseball caps, and elbows were forbidden to rest on the table's butcher block surface. "Let's respect the food placed before us," Nonno told Lauren and the boys. Ma thought he had a lot of nerve directing her kids in her home.

The meal went by without incident. There was shoptalk between Lou and his father, and Nonna chimed in about the warm Florida weather. Ma did not eat, but sipped from a coffee mug filled with vodka and orange juice.

"You boys are growing up," said Nonno, finishing his last bite of tiramisu. "You're young men now, almost fourteen. What are your plans?"

The boys stayed silent. No one ever asked them that and they were both unsure of the correct answer.

"Tony?" Nonno asked again. "What are your plans?"

"I don't have any." Tony hoped his grandfather wouldn't ask for the $50 back.

"I suppose one of these days you will," Nonno said. "When I was your age, I was already working. And how about you, Luigi?" It took Louie a moment to register that his grandfather was addressing him. Like his grandfather and father, he was Luigi too.

"Would you like to fix cars like the other Luigis?" Tony tightened when he heard Nonno address his twin as a kindred spirit, as if he was excluded from a special family pact, an inheritance passed on from generation to generation. He was stuck with his own namesake, Uncle Jack Anthony.

"I don't think so, Nonno," Louie said. "I'd like to study. I'd like to go to college."

"That would make us proud," said Nonna.

"Me too," said Lauren. "I'd like to go to college too."

"Well, that's not happening," said Ma.

"Why not?" Lauren asked.

"Let's just say, you're not exactly the sharpest knife in the drawer," Ma said.

"Don't be silly," said Nonna, who tapped her thighs and motioned for Lauren to come and settle into her lap. Lauren, like a young pup, jumped at the offer, crawling into the warmth of her grandmother.

"Lauren, you're not a baby—leave Nonna alone," Ma said. "Get out of her lap."

"She's fine," said Nonna, stroking her granddaughter's thin hair. "She can go to college. She can do anything she puts her mind to."

"I just don't believe in getting her hopes up for something that is not going to happen," said Ma. What Ma really thought was that the buttinksy was starting in again.

"She needs to eat more," said Nonno, as if announcing an important plan. "She's too thin and pale."

Ma gave Lou a look and he jumped into action to steer the conversation away from trouble. "Nothing to worry about with Lauren. She's been to plenty of doctors. They can't find a thing wrong."

"Maybe you haven't been to the right doctor," said Nonno. "She's frail."

"P-s-y-c-h-o-s-o-m-a-t-i-c," Ma spelled out.

"Nah, she's sensitive, that's all," Lou corrected Ma.

"My other son was sensitive too," said Nonna.

Here we go, Ma thought. And Nonna proceeded to retell the tired story of Nick, Lou's younger brother. Nick, who had been asthmatic as a boy. Nick, who had trouble making his way in the world. Nick, Nick, Nick. Ma disliked him from the start. Nonna coddled him. Gave him money for nothing. Lou was the one who worked hard at the family business, building it up, making it successful. Unlike Lou, Nick was too sickly to get his hands dirty and went to college instead, majoring in Renaissance art, which Ma thought made him a fancy pansy.

Ma's dislike for Nick turned to deep disdain when Nick named his firstborn, Luigi, after his father and brother. Ma viewed taking her husband's name as theft. And when Ma gave birth to the twins one year later, she named the older one Luigi, and called him Louie. Nonna objected at the time, saying one grandson named Luigi was enough, but Ma ignored Nonna's wishes. It was Ma's right to name her son after her husband, to name her son what she wanted.

Nonna blabbed, and blabbed, and blabbed about her golden boy, Nick, and Ma nursed her cocktail and kept her mouth zipped. After what seemed like ages to Ma, Nonna and Nonno departed. There were hugs all around, and Nonna took the opportunity to whisper in Ma's ear, "Use the book I gave you. Cook for your family. Everybody looks so skinny."

Lou went outside with Lauren to wave good-bye and when he returned to the kitchen, he felt a satisfied relief. "That went well," he said to Ma. "I think that went just fine."

And Ma said, "I can't wait to see that woman in a jar of formaldehyde."

Chapter 12

The Chapel-at-the-Mall was a church Ma liked to visit now and then. Lauren was on day two home from school due to a slight fever and a spidery rash that covered the back of her arms and legs. Ma thought an outing would do them both good—some fresh air, new surroundings. A little prayer couldn't hurt, and a little shopping was always good for the soul.

She also liked reasons to go out and about and to get behind the wheel of her new prized possession. The insurance claim from the fire finally came through, and Ma wasted no time ordering a spanking-new Cadillac Eldorado with all the bells and whistles. She haggled the price down by visiting the car dealership every day until the salesman finally caved and gave her the price she wanted. Then she brought the new car directly to the Napolitano auto shop for a custom paint job in the most beautiful shade of violet—the color of amethyst, her favorite gemstone. This beauty was a present to herself, and it checked all the boxes.

When Ma and Lauren hit the road, feeling the clean new tires rolling over the streets, Ma felt reborn into nobility, carried about in luxury. The color resonated with her, not the calmness of blue nor the fire of red, but a combination, the best of both, a hue that held mystery, magic, and power.

The Chapel-at-the-Mall was set up by the Carmelites. It was plain and small with the exception of two stained glass windows depicting figures of Mary. Between the windows was a plain wooden statue of Jesus on the cross. Next to the chapel was a gift shop, which sold trinkets and greeting cards.

The chapel catered to shoppers, mall employees, old folks looking to break up the day, and sleep-deprived young mothers looking for a respite from pushing strollers up and down the long indoor promenade. The no-fuss chapel suited Ma. There were no neighbors to wish well, no personal inquiries from the two priests who kept the place running. You were in and you were out.

Lauren and Ma took the elevator down to the chapel on the lower level. The noon Communal Mass was coming to an end, and Ma and Lauren slipped into a pew in the back. Ma closed her eyes and listened to the priest. He began a prayer to Our Lady of Mt. Carmel.

"O God, come to my assistance," he prayed.

The few worshipers sprinkled throughout the chapel answered, "O Lord, make haste to help me."

"Glory be to the Father and to the Son and to the Holy Spirit," the priest continued.

And the worshipers called back, "As it was in the beginning, is now and ever shall be. Amen."

Ma did not join in prayer, but moved her body back and forth ever so slightly, rocking to the rhythm of the familiar prayer. Lauren looked at her mother and followed her lead. She shut her eyes tight and let the words fill her head.

"All gracious God, may the prayers of the Blessed Virgin Mary, Mother of Carmel, protect us and bring us to your Holy Mountain, Christ our Lord. Under her protection you call us not only to be your servants, but also your children. We ask you to gain for us, from your Son, the grace to live as children in joy, peace, and love."

Before the prayer was complete, Ma tugged Lauren's hand, and they snuck out the door of the chapel. As they were leaving, Lauren could hear the last bits of the prayer, the words fading, disappearing.

"We turn to you for protection, Holy Mother of God. Listen to our prayers and help us in our needs. Save us from every danger, glorious and Blessed Virgin."

The gift shop was bright with fluorescent lights and contained rows of religious books, statues, jewelry, and greeting cards, which Ma took great pleasure in reviewing. The cards were ornately illustrated in gold and shades of blue and red. There was a card for every need: birthdays, weddings, Christmas, Easter, first Communion, Ordination, and anniversaries. The largest selection was devoted to sympathy and encouragement, comfort for those who suffered. Ma picked a dozen to buy. She didn't have anyone in mind to give the cards to, but liked to have them around.

Ma made her purchase from the woman at the register, an older, orderly woman wearing a sweater with two embroidered white ducks. The woman rang up each card with great care, checking the price, reading and commenting on each sentiment, and then tucking each card carefully under its corresponding envelope flap. Ma thought she looked and moved like a turtle.

Finally, with cards in hand, Ma called to Lauren, "Let's go."

Lauren was busy admiring a Mass card and didn't respond. The painting on the card depicted an idyllic, tranquil valley with verdant hills and a pebbled path that circled a blue pond. Lush trees bent over the path as if to gently guide and protect all who walked on it, and the light pink and yellow flowers that sprang up along the path made it seem like a happy place. Below the painting were the words:

A Healing Prayer
May your body be blessed with strength, your mind with rest, and your spirit with peace.

Ma called to Lauren again, "Let's go." Lauren pulled the card from the rack and ran over to her mother.

"Can I get this?" she asked Ma. Ma was about to say sure, until she noticed that the old woman, the slowest cashier in the world and the only cashier in the shop, had stepped away from the register. "I'm not waiting for her again. If you want the card, take it."

"But we have to pay," Lauren reminded her mother.

"I've already bought a dozen cards and I'm not waiting around for that slowpoke." Lauren looked unsure, not understanding, so Ma added, "Look, if they wanted you to pay, then they would have a competent person at the register, ready and waiting. Do you see anyone around?"

"No," said Lauren.

"Well, neither do I. So if you want the card, put it under your sweater and let's go."

Lauren looked at her mother and then again at the register. There was no cashier.

"Make up your mind," Ma said.

Lauren tucked the treasured card under her sweater and grabbed her mother's hand.

Ma smiled at her daughter. "Glad you came to your senses. You'll learn that it's best to follow my lead in life. Monkey see, monkey do." And they walked out of the Chapel-at-the-Mall gift shop and into the noisy promenade for a little more shopping.

CHAPTER 13

THE NEW YORK YANKEES WERE WINDING UP THE SEASON. There were only a few games left to play and Lou, for the first time since he could remember, had still not made the trip to the stadium in the Bronx. For Lou, it was an annual ritual, a tradition started by his father, who would take Nick and Lou several times every summer. An outing for Napolitano men. The memory made Lou teary-eyed.

This year, with the strain at home, Lou gave up on the idea of going until he got into some baseball talk with one of his customers, a young bond trader with Ferrari troubles. The trader pulled tickets from his wallet and presented them to Lou. The seats were nothing special, nor were they hard to come by. They were seats that Lou could have bought himself. The trader even apologized that they weren't better, explaining that he received one hundred tickets and these were his last two. Lou accepted the gift with grace; he had never been given Yankees tickets before. Lou interpreted the fact that the tickets had found their way to him as a sign, the arm of fate reaching out, insisting that he make the pilgrimage to Yankee Stadium like every year before. Lou was even more convinced that something larger was at play when Ma, who did not approve of Lou going out and about without her, consented with, "Sure, join the world of the cretins and make an idiot of yourself."

Since there were two tickets and Lou did not want to choose

between Tony and Louie, he asked Lauren to join him. Ma went along with that choice too. "If you aren't embarrassed to be seen in public with a clown like your father, then by all means, be my guest," she said to Lauren.

Lou had been distant from Lauren ever since she went through his truck's ashtray for butts. He felt embarrassed. He felt ashamed. And he could not deny that he felt betrayed. But he also knew that baseball was like salve on a burn; it could take the sting out. Baseball could cheer anybody. The Yankees playing the Boston Red Sox might be the remedy, a chance to restore their father-daughter camaraderie.

The day of the game, the pair climbed into Lou's truck, happy for the adventure, and set out for the Bronx. Lauren knew nothing about baseball, and Lou felt compelled to reveal the spirit of the game.

"Baseball is not just about brawn," he explained to Lauren. "It's a kind of collaboration between players. It's a place where big and little, lumbering and nimble, smart and not-so-smart come together. Everybody has a chance to shine."

The season had been less than stellar for the Yankees, but that did not stop dedicated fans from coming out, filling the stadium with enthusiastic cheers, hoping for a win. On this late September day, the season at an end, a crush of loyal hopefuls made their way to the stands. Lauren held her father's wrist so that he would not lose her. Lou knew the stadium well and they weaved in and out of the mob, climbing to their seats in rapid order. Even before sitting down, Lou motioned to a middle-aged man who was barking out the names of snack selections. A large box of goodies hung over the man's sweaty, ample belly, supported by thick shoulder straps. With Lauren's encouragement, Lou went all out—two hot dogs, two sodas, cotton candy, Cracker Jacks, and popcorn.

The field. The players. The crowd. Lauren took it all in. Pitch, hit, run—sometimes a slow amble and sometimes an all-out race to the next base. Regardless of the pace, the fans around them were happy to hoot, "He's out!" Or, "He's safe!" Lou smiled and smiled. Lauren thought he looked nothing like a clown.

The crowd, an assemblage of Yankee brotherhood, was up and then down, inhibitions left at the stadium gate, straining voices into one harmonious roar. Lauren didn't follow the game, but was delighted to toss handfuls of popcorn into the air every time the fans jumped up to holler, watching the kernel confetti float and land on the heads of spectators in front of them.

When #23, Don Mattingly, the team darling, was up at bat, the devotees were on their feet in a gesture of honor, waiting to see what they had paid for—that little bit of magic. Mattingly positioned and repositioned himself, moving from side to side. He reminded Lauren of Wylie, circling round and round until he found a comfortable spot to settle.

The pitcher threw the ball, only to have #23 step back. The pitcher tried again. The ball shot out for a second time from his practiced hand. Mattingly's bat struck, and the white circle knocked into the air with a hard force, which sent it sailing into the stands over hundreds of tilted heads. A wave of fingers reached up to pluck the ball from the air, but it seemed to be propelled by its own single intention and zoomed past, unattainable to those trying to capture it. When the ball reached its destination, it fell—WOMP—right into Lauren's lap and bounced against her thigh with a harsh slap.

"It's yours," Lou yelled, dancing about. "My daughter caught the ball!"

There was more hoopla as Mattingly rounded the bases and completed the home run. "Whoo! Whoo! Whoo!" The entire section where Lauren and her father sat shouted in unison, moving fists in vigorous circles. "Whoo! Whoo! Whoo!"

Lauren claimed the ball, its mark still red and stinging on her thigh. Lou lifted her up and onto his shoulders. "I knew it was an omen," he said. "I knew this would be a lucky day." Grabbing her father with one arm, she extended the other frail arm high, like a victor presenting the white leather treasure to all. In response, #23 moved away from home plate and turned toward the stands, toward Lauren Napolitano. Mattingly, the Yankees star, waved his hand back and forth to her in a gesture of solidarity.

From her perch on her father's shoulders, Lauren waved back, the ball snug in her other hand. She was on top of the world.

Chapter 14

Ma believed in looking good. It gave her a feeling of power, confidence, of having the upper hand. She made sure her platinum blonde hairdo kept the ever-invading chestnut roots hidden and covered. She wore clothes well, carrying them on her back like she sprang from a moneyed Scarsdale coterie and not a disheveled, scrappy Irish family in the Bronx (who Ma hated to admit were her true kin). Ma's hard-drinking mother wouldn't have known the difference between Kmart and Bergdorf Goodman, but Ma did. She had studied *Vogue* and *Elle*, even the sexier *Cosmopolitan*, and gleaned her fashion know-how from the glossy pages. Her petite frame was flattered by any design that highlighted darts and sharp pleats, or stretch fabrics that hugged her close and emphasized her lean contours. It was only the baggy styles, which had become popular of late, large and billowy, that didn't flatter Ma. They diminished her, made her look inconsequential, so she avoided those styles at all costs.

Ma's trim physique had more to do with a lack of appetite, a diet of stress and worry, and a vodka meal plan, than any vigorous workout. Unlike the other mothers with whom she was forced to interact, Ma was tight and flat. In those fleshy female areas where other women became lumpy, ample, and loose, she was almost concave. There was nothing soft or squishy about Ma.

The other mothers noticed. Ma would catch them grabbing a look. The clothes were all name brands, and Ma's skirts were invariably two inches too short. She favored sleeveless camisoles made of Lycra in all seasons, because Ma ran hot. Her tops were always purchased a size too small so that they stretched across her boyish chest, the spaghetti straps revealing defined and bony upper arms.

After three children, Ma could still pull it off. She knew the other mothers envied her and she played on it, made them drown in their jealousy stew. When Ma faced her New Jersey world, filled with harried women clad in stained sweatpants who, in their morning tizzy, had forgotten to take any care with their hair, she wrapped herself in Armani and Dolce & Gabbana and carried a Gucci handbag. Her tiny, size 5 feet slipped into Enzo Angiolini or Stuart Weitzman (on special occasions).

Still, Ma was never a spendthrift. She purchased these luxury items when she found them at bargain prices in upscale consignment shops, or as good knockoffs on Manhattan's Canal Street. Sometimes, when an insurance claim came through, Ma would splurge on a little gift for herself. After all, she earned it.

Everyone commented that Lauren looked just like her mother. If you examined them feature by feature it was true. It was their energy that didn't match up. Ma's high-intensity zoom and Lauren's sluggishness couldn't be more opposite. Lauren resembled an injured sparrow more than her fast-flying, zippy mother.

Lauren's stringy hair was baby fine, scraggly, and uneven, and her complexion was the color of watery milk. Most days, her stomach ached, which made her face look worn. Her arms and legs were sprinkled with mauve splotches—itchy rashes that she scratched until scabs formed. The scabs itched and she scratched through them. No matter how many times the doctors cauterized the vessels, blood dribbled from her nose.

The bevy of doctors who inspected Lauren, searching for a reason for her chronic discomfort, suspected that her troubles might be a result of food allergies, parasites in the stomach, or lactose intolerance.

But after several rounds of allergy tests, upper and lower gastrointestinal tests, barium x-rays, and antiparasite medications, they had yet to pinpoint the problem.

Ma was frustrated. Why couldn't this long string of doctors, some of the best in the state, pediatric experts who came highly recommended, come up with a satisfactory answer and help her daughter? A "fragile constitution" and "delicate immune system" were mentioned. Tests and more tests were ordered.

Ma thought that if Lauren looked better, she would feel better. After all, she was a girl, and an attractive appearance might give her the strength she needed. "You are never too young to learn the importance and power of good grooming," she told Lauren.

When Ma received a promotional coupon in the mailbox, she thought the angels had been paying close attention to her worries and sent a sign of support. The coupon was from Très Suave: House of Beauty, offering a complimentary Little Miss Beauty hairstyle for ages six to twelve.

Ma had never been to the salon. Très Suave was located on a main artery in a small Westfield strip mall next to Lucky Wong's Cantonese Delight and Howard H. Howard's Insurance, where Ma currently filed her insurance claims. The storefront was one big window, dressed with pink and gold draperies pulled to each side. Between the two satiny panels, a hot-pink glittery chandelier hung from the ceiling. The Très Suave sign was painted on the window in standout curvy letters that called out the French name in a majestic fuchsia.

Ma wasted no time in calling Très Suave and requesting their best stylist. The friendly receptionist suggested Daffnei as the perfect fit. Daffnei had recently graduated at the top of her beauty school class and had a gift for working with young girls, particularly those with straight hair. Customers said she was a true artist.

Ma and Lauren pulled up to the House of Beauty on a Friday in the early afternoon. Ma had yanked Lauren from school, telling the secretary that Lauren had another medical appointment. According to Ma, a beauty treatment was certainly therapeutic and would be more beneficial than any medical procedure so far.

Once inside Très Suave—an environment drenched in various shades of pink—Lauren and Ma were greeted with enthusiastic hellos. Lauren was promptly seated in a swivel chair upholstered in pink Naugahyde. The employees, all women, wore short black skirts or leggings, and a black company T-shirt with pink letters, touting the obviously thought-out slogan:

Très Suave Is Our Name
Beauty Is Our Game

There was no doubt that Daffnei was a happy hairdresser. Her cheerful smile did not shrink for a moment, and she made chirpy remarks in a breathy English accent. "Hello lovely ladies," Daffnei greeted Ma and Lauren, "aren't we lucky for this grand and gorgeous day?" Ma said nothing, and Daffnei chirped on, "Are you two loveys here for our complimentary haircut?" Ma squashed the desire to answer, No, of course not, we're here to go swimming.

Daffnei wasn't put off by Ma's lack of enthusiasm. She fluffed Lauren's limp hair, pulling it up and out and running her fingers over the scalp, examining the roots and split ends, assessing the situation, devising a strategic plan.

"It's a bit thin," was Daffnei's diagnosis, but not wanting to sound negative, she added, "But no worries, when life gives you lemons, you must absolutely make a lovely pitcher of lemonade."

Ma thought Daffnei must have been doused in powdered sugar in "Merrie Olde England" and didn't think she could take much more of Daffnei's grating, upbeat inflections. She stood silent, glaring.

"It's a bit thin," Daffnei said again. "I can give it a good, solid trim and even out the ends. A shorter style might give it body."

Lauren, for her part, was used to being poked and prodded. She sat obediently as the two women discussed her troubled hair.

"It needs bounce and volume," Ma said.

"We could try a perm," Daffnei suggested to Ma. "They are quite popular with young girls these days."

"Just a gentle wave," Ma agreed.

Daffnei pondered the situation a bit more. "I am just not entirely sure how her hair will respond to the chemicals. But we will give it our very best."

Ma was done with the conversation and Daffnei's irritating sweetness. Ma had decided. Now the English sugar pot needed to stop talking and get to work.

"It's decided." Ma gathered up her purse and keys.

"Ma, are you leaving?" Lauren said, startled to see her mother move toward the door.

"It seems like this will take some time," Ma explained, thinking that she would rather shoot herself than stay in Daffnei's bubbly presence for another second. "No reason for me to be here. I'll just be in the way," she said to Lauren. And then she added, "You're in good hands. Daffnei was the top of her class."

Lauren was not happy that Ma left. Nor was Daffnei. And Daffnei, sensing there could be tears, amped up the chipper chatter.

Daffnei started by explaining the perm process, the rods and chemical solution, the curly results she hoped they would get. She told Lauren about her hair history, how she had practiced in beauty school, first on mannequins and then fellow students, and how beauty school had prepared her for all the facets of the industry. While she was proficient in makeup, skin, and nails, hair was her passion, and she had known from an early age that she had an artistic flair for hair. As a child, she practiced on dolls, but quickly expanded to neighborhood girls and then to their mothers. She had come from Norwich, England to New Jersey to attend school. When she arrived, she didn't know a soul. Then she met fellow student Tommy Toffano and fell in love.

Daffnei's tales spouted out of her mouth like a geyser of perky words. For Lauren, the words had a magical effect. She not only forgot that Ma had made her escape; she was calm, entertained, and smiling.

She devoured a handful of hard candies before Daffnei took a breath.

Two hours later, Lauren held up a hand mirror as Daffnei spun her chair around so that she could view the front and back of her head from all angles. Lauren couldn't believe what she saw. Curls. Lots of them. They were wound tight like fiddleheads.

"You have such an adorable little face," Daffnei told Lauren. "The curls really highlight that. I think you are going to be very happy."

Lauren smiled, hardly believing she could ever have so much hair. On cue, Ma made her way through the front of Très Suave, past the Friday afternoon rush of Westfield ladies. From a distance, Ma got a first glimpse of Lauren in the large wall mirror. She stopped in her tracks, not quite grasping what she saw. Daffnei saw her and waved, beckoning her over to see the new hairdo, proud of her artistic prowess.

Ma stepped forward. Once she was standing over Lauren, she grabbed a fist of curly hair and tugged. When she released the hair, it sprang back into place. *Boing!* She tugged at another clump, stretching it as far as it would go from the scalp before releasing it. And another. *Boing! Boing! Boing!*

"What happened here?" Ma asked Daffnei.

Daffnei detected a note of unexpected trouble. "It's a perm. Doesn't she look adorable?"

"Adorable?" Ma turned to look directly at Daffnei. "She looks like a goddamned poodle."

Lauren recognized Ma's tone and interjected, "Ma, I like it."

"Look at this," Ma demanded. Daffnei peered into Lauren's hair for a closer look, examining her handiwork in case she missed something, but all she saw was artistic success.

Ma saw a frizzy, fried mess—Lauren's small head poking out from under a mass of curls, tight and kinky. Little flyaway hairs that had not been crimped into spirals stuck out this way and that. It was a halo of corkscrews curved around her daughter's face like a berserk bonnet.

"I asked for something gentle," said Ma, making each word precise, "A little oomph."

"Lots of girls get styled like this," Daffnei tried to explain, her enthusiasm waning.

"It makes her nose look gigantic." Ma held her breath. She did not scream or holler, pushing the desire down, forcing the rage to the back of her throat. Sensing something had gone wrong, the other women in the salon started to lean forward in their chairs and stare.

"I can't believe she did this to you," Ma said to Lauren.

"The perm might be just a bit tight," Daffnei conceded. "Maybe not your cup of tea, but it has been executed well."

"Executed? This is more like an execution. This is not a gentle wave. This is a disaster."

Daffnei realized that Ma would never be satisfied, would not recognize her expertise, and she did not have the manipulative powers to turn the situation around. "I think Lauren really likes it," she said in an attempt to send Ma in a brighter direction.

"I don't know what passes for competency in England, but in this country this is nothing but a mess."

"I think that might be a might harsh." Daffnei's smile and sunny demeanor had vanished.

"Are you kidding me? Were you asleep in that fancy beauty school? Your grade here is an F. Flunked out. Finis."

Daffnei was used to being praised, recognized for her skill and ability, and Ma's criticism of her artistry was too much negative energy for her positive outlook. She began to sob, first in little spurts and then in an all-out wail.

"Ma, it's really okay," said Lauren. "It's not too tight. I like it." Lauren's protests to her mother made no difference. Daffnei continued to sob, her shoulders shaking, her eyes red and glistening with tears.

"I'm the one who should be crying." Ma had lost her patience with the self-centered brat. Enough was enough. "You are an idiotic bitch, an English whore, and you've turned my daughter into a mess."

The manager, an overweight woman with a stern expression, stepped in. She swiftly removed Daffnei from the situation and sent her to the back of the salon where she was circled and comforted by a tribe of sympathetic beauty shop employees.

"I'll be seeing you in court," Ma said to the manager as she pushed Lauren up to the front of the salon, and out the door, past the shaking heads of loyal patrons.

Once in the car, Lauren tried again. "Ma, don't worry. It will grow out. It's okay."

But it was not okay with Ma. Her daughter looked ridiculous. "I'll fix her ass good," Ma promised Lauren. "Just wait and see what happens to her."

CHAPTER 15

MA SEPARATED THE TWINS. Now that they were fourteen and the new house had enough bedrooms, she thought they should no longer share. They were becoming different sorts and needed their individual space. Neither twin was happy about the separation, but knew it would sound babyish and unmanly to protest. Privately, they each felt unsettled and off balance, brutally ripped apart, a portion of their inner essence harmed. Of course, neither said a word.

Both boys tacked up "Private! Do Not Enter!" signs on their bedroom doors. Tony would not allow Lauren in his room. Ever. Despite the towels that he scrunched along the crack between the floor and bottom of the door, the entire family could smell the fumes that seeped out almost daily. Lauren didn't recognize the musty smell, but Louie did. So did Lou and Ma. Lou wanted to punish Tony, but Ma said, "Why bother? He gets his druggie ways from you." And Lou, worrying that it was true, kept quiet.

Louie welcomed Lauren into his room anytime. She would sit on the end of his bed after Ma retired to her room, while Louie, propped up on the floor with pillows, read book after book or scribbled in journal after journal. Ma thought this journaling business was a waste of time, peculiar for a boy, and couldn't figure out how she had ever given birth to a bookworm like Louie.

Louie kept a chess set next to his bed, a gift from Nonna and Nonno. Lauren didn't know how to play, but liked to slide the pieces around the board, the Queen chasing the King. She liked to hold the carved wooden miniatures in her hands. They were smooth and intricate. She thought they were beautiful.

Sometimes, if she pressed Louie, he would help her with schoolwork that she missed due to one of her many sick days. Cursive writing, minute math, the history of ancient Egypt. Eventually, Louie would lose interest and return to his own studies, books, and journals.

"What are you always writing in there?" Lauren asked night after night. Louie never read his words aloud, but told Lauren the truth. "Just thoughts. Ideas. Some things I might want to think about."

One night, for no particular reason or occasion, he presented his sister with a gift. It was a journal he made from one of his school composition books. Louie was not particularly artistic, but he covered the black-speckled cardboard with aluminum foil so that it was silver and shiny and cut a strip of red construction paper, securing it across the front with a large dab of glue. On the red strip he wrote, *Lauren's Private and Secret Thoughts.*

"But what can I put in this book?" Lauren asked her brother, honored that he thought she was smart enough to do the things he could do.

"You can write anything. Anything you want. You can even doodle. It doesn't matter," he told her, and she dashed back to her room to take pen to paper. She sat and stared at the journal for some time, worried that her first mark would ruin the book for good, and even worse, that Louie would be disappointed, would realize that she was not as smart as he thought, that she was just Lauren, a regular old dodo. Finally, she sucked in her breath, held her pen, and lightly touched the point to the paper. When she fell asleep the journal was at her side, its first page full.

Ma kept the house dark at night. She didn't believe in wasting electricity by leaving lights on. So it was dark when Lauren awoke some hours later. She tiptoed toward the bathroom. By now the dark hallway was familiar and she knew the trip by heart. To reach the bathroom, she passed by each brother's room. She passed Louie's first. His door, as usual, was closed. As she approached Tony's door, she heard a rustling of footsteps and was surprised to see his door wide open (a rare occurrence). His overhead light was on, which made the room seem as if it was under a spotlight.

She stood at the door for a few moments until Tony sensed her presence. Startled, he turned to her. He was dressed in an oversized black sweatshirt and black jeans. A black knit cap was pulled down over his forehead, stopping just short of his eyes. He held two open spray paint cans, one in each hand, the thick, black paint oozing down the sides of the metal. Tony looked at the shadow of his sister. They were two creatures sneaking about in the night. He held her wondering gaze, and then without explanation kicked the door hard with his black work boot, which Lauren instantly recognized as belonging to her father. The door shut and she could hear the cans rattle from the sudden movement.

Lauren forgot about her need to visit the bathroom and scurried back to her room. She slipped under her satiny bedsheet and closed her eyes, willing them to stay shut. Her new journal lay next to her, opened to her first entry. She had written slowly in cursive, forming each letter as perfect as she could. It was a simple entry: "Rats, rats, rats."

Chapter 16

After the perm fiasco, Ma allowed two months to pass. Sixty-one days. She did not forget. She waited. During that time, she learned Daffnei's schedule. On day sixty-two, Ma executed her plan. Sometime between 4:00 p.m. and 8:00 p.m., starting on Tuesday and continuing through Saturday, Ma poured herself a drink, sat down before her white Princess phone, and called Très Suave: House of Beauty. In her best English accent, which wasn't good, she politely asked to speak to Daffnei. Once Daffnei came to the phone, Ma waited two beats and then shrieked: "Fuckin' whore. Fuckin' bitch. Fuckin' toad."

After a few days of the same assault, Daffnei stopped coming to the phone. Ma proceeded to call the salon and slam the phone against the kitchen counter, greeting anyone who answered the Très Suave line with a series of loud knocks. When the recipient hung up the phone, Ma repeated the procedure. Over and over. Calling. Slamming. Calling. Slamming. On the ninetieth day, Ma dialed at an off-hour, and in her best Bronx Italian accent, which was better than her English imitation, asked if she might make an appointment with Daffnei. "Daffnei," the employee said, "moved back to England."

On the hundredth day, Ma drove by Très Suave in the early morning, before the salon opened, to view the curvy letters of the shop's sign. The letters, once a jubilant fuchsia, were blackened with spray paint.

The word *beauty* (from House of Beauty) was marked with a big black X. In its place a correction had been made. The word *ugly* now appeared scrawled in large, shaky black letters. Très Suave: House of Ugly. Underneath the revised name, written across the front wall, directly below the large window with the pink and gold drapes, was another message, a new slogan in the same scrawling hand:

Très Suave Is Our Name
Beauty Killing Is Our Game

Ma slowed the car to take it all in. The skill and artistry would be apparent to anyone.

PART TWO

How hard it is to escape from places. However carefully one goes they hold you. . . you leave little bits of yourself fluttering on the fences. . . little rags and shreds of your very life. . .

—Katherine Mansfield to Ida Baker, 1922

CHAPTER 17

Napolitano Brothers' International Garage, Queens, New York

WHEN NONNO HEARD THE CRASH, he was eating prosciutto on rye in the office, the Dijon lingering on his tongue as he reviewed the improved receivables with Helen, his longtime bookkeeper. In that suspended instant, he could not reconcile the Lamborghini Diablo—which he knew had been lifted five feet in the air by the mechanical hoist for a simple tire rotation—with the shattering sound that rocked the garage. In thirty years, the Napolitano Brothers' International Garage, a business renowned and trusted for its import repairs, for quality work and care, had never improperly secured a car, allowing it to fall to the concrete floor. Not once.

The magnitude of the echoing crash that reverberated throughout the garage let Nonno know that what he would find would be catastrophic. He dropped the sandwich on the wax paper and forced himself to stand, to move his feet, one step and then another, faster and faster, until he was running into the garage to the second service bay, where the car had been raised.

His instinct wasn't wrong. The black Diablo had slipped from the lift and now rested off-kilter on the oil-stained floor, its sleek, shiny hood and right side badly banged and dented.

Nonno called for help from the other workers, most of whom were not yet back from lunch. Only Helen came, her puffy red ankles and thick calves straining to make the distance from the office to the service area. Nonno was screaming, his words a hoarse, muddled mess. It was a noise he had never made before—an unearthly howl. Nonno couldn't see Lou, but he knew what was true. Lou, his beloved son and name-sake, was under the Lamborghini Diablo. Pinned. Crushed.

∽

Lou drifted back and forth, on the verge of life one moment and death the next. He hung in between, in a woozy limbo, unsure which way he would be taken. The doctors at Mount Sinai Hospital of Queens offered no hope and attempted, without complete success, to keep him pain free. Still, Lou was breathing. Just barely. That fact was a miracle.

Nonna sat at the edge of Lou's hospital bed and Nonno stayed in the nubby brown chair against the wall. Nonna was stiff and upright. Nonno slumped. In six days, Nonna had not budged. Despite the nurs-es' urging, she would not go home to rest, would not leave her broken son. Nonno had gone home to bathe and catch a nap now and again. He returned with bags of fast food, which he placed to Nonna's lips. Ma took the children back to New Jersey and put them back in school after the vigil's third day. She even stooped to call an old neighbor, Christina, their Country Club Lane babysitter, who agreed to leave school to come to Westfield, sleep in the house, and watch over her brood.

Not Nonna. She stayed on, determined to will her son well.

Hour after hour, light after dark, Nonna calibrated her short, tense breath with Lou's irregular gasps. In and out. In and out. She prayed to Mary. She summoned the angels who had protected her in the past: Mi-chael, Gabriel, and Raphael. She recited every prayer she ever commit-ted to memory. Most of all, she guarded her son from any disturbance, like a watchdog sensing danger, full of fury, ready to assail anyone who came too close to the hospital bed. Including Ma.

Despite traditional marriage behavior or even legal rights, Nonna took charge. She wouldn't allow Ma near the bed for any long peri-od of time. Nonna wanted to keep her son calm and stable. She was determined, at all costs, to keep him breathing.

Nonna allowed Ma in the room for brief visits and to sit in the hall chair placed next to the hospital room door. Ma accepted the demotion, the stripping of her wifely rights. She did not fight her mother-in-law, but the insult burned and lingered. Ma consoled herself with one thought: she would wait until the time was right and then return the favor.

In the meantime, Ma brought her camera and snapped photos of her husband. Lou had broken or fractured most of his bones—forearms, hands, ankles, clavicle, pelvis, and spine. There was internal bleeding. And his face had been injured—cheekbones, chin, and nose. Wires crisscrossed his purple face, keeping the bones from collapsing. Ma photographed it all, from a distance, close up, from the side, and straight on. *Click. Click. Click.*

"Are you crazy?" Nonna scolded after the first click, astonished that Ma would want to record the horrific event. "Let my son have his dignity."

But Ma wanted exactly that, a record, something to bear witness. Evidence. And when Nonna would nod off, her head dropping forward, her eyelids falling against her will, Ma was ready. When she heard Nonna's little sputtering snores, Ma took action. *Click. Click. Click.*

On the seventh day, Nonno appeared with the priest, a crucifix, candles, and holy oils pressed from olives. Ma, the twins, Lauren, and Lou's brother Nick waited in the doorway with baited breath as Nonno and the priest entered the room.

Nonna knew what it meant when she saw the priest in his black shirt and pants, and his gentle expression moving into the room toward the bed. She fought back. She hit Nonno, the man she had loved for over forty years. She pushed on his chest, pounded and slapped, and chased both the priest and Nonno out of the small room.

"I will not give him up," Nonna told them. "He will not be given last rites."

Nonno had understood and accepted each blow without protest.

The priest also understood, familiar with this type of behavior during deathbed situations.

"It is Anointing of the Sick," the priest whispered to Nonna, his hand resting on her back. "It is to bring spiritual and even physical strength to him."

Nonna repeated her warning, which sounded more like a plea: "I will not give him up." The priest nodded and stayed in the hall without a word. They would wait.

After an hour, Nonna stood from the bed. "He needs God's strength," she said. "I am only human." Nonna made space for the priest to get close to Lou. She then allowed Nick, Ma, the twins, and Lauren to crowd the small room. The priest sprinkled them all with holy water and then stood over Lou.

"Through this holy anointing may the Lord in his love and mercy help you with the grace of the Holy Spirit." The priest placed his fingers over Lou's hands and whispered, "May the Lord who frees you from sin save you and raise you up."

Once the priest began the ritual of the final blessing, Ma inched out the door. Leaning against the tiled wall, she welcomed the chill of the ceramic squares against her bare arms. She had already been witness to her brother, Jack Anthony, inviting death from a hospital bed. Now her husband. Both of them could have prevented it.

Ma's three children watched the priest wave his hands over their father. Louie reached for Lauren's hand. It was a gesture that meant as much for him as for his little sister. When the priest left, Lauren went into the hall and hugged her mother tight. She circled her arms around Ma's waist and pressed her head against her stomach. Ma let Lauren stay. They were not a family big on hugging or comforting, but Ma tapped Lauren's back, quick little tip-taps, as if typing on a keyboard.

"Is he going to die?" Lauren asked Ma. Tony and Louie, who had joined them in the hall, waited for the answer too.

"That's what it looks like," Ma answered. Lauren cried. And Louie cried. Even Tony's eyes felt itchy and sore.

But Ma didn't weep. Not one tear. Not at the hospital and not at home in the privacy of her New Jersey bedroom. There was nothing moist to squeeze out of her. She felt flat and dry like cardboard. She knew the truth of it. She was not a crier and Lou, her husband, the man her family had thought she was lucky to have landed, had betrayed her. Repeatedly. She knew he must have misjudged the balance and positioning of the Lamborghini on the lift. One tiny moment of carelessness. She also knew that his carelessness was most likely due to the fact that he was high—a fact that Nonna and Nonno wanted to know nothing about. She had tried to tell them months ago, to ask for their help, and they had ignored the problem. Ignored her. "Stop trying to stir the pot," Nonno told her.

Yes, Lou had betrayed her. With Lori Molinari. With his parents. And now with his financial obligations. He was weak and couldn't go the distance with her or for her. At least she wouldn't starve, wouldn't be out on the street like a filthy rat. The hefty life insurance policy that she insisted Lou carry had been mandatory in their marriage from day one. She had seen to that. If Lou decided to leave her now, to depart this world, so be it; she certainly wouldn't starve. Far from it. That fact gave her great comfort—enough to sleep without worry or tears all through the night.

CHAPTER 18

Belle Haven, Westfield, New Jersey

THERE NEVER WAS A LIFE INSURANCE CLAIM. After six weeks in the hospital, Nonna's steadfast prayers had brought her son back. Much to the doctors' surprise, Lou had rallied and come out of the worst. He would have a long and difficult recovery ahead of him, but he was stronger; he was on his way.

Nonna fought to bring him to Queens, to his childhood home, where he would be cared for, nurtured with motherly love, and properly fed. Ma would have none of it. She was done letting Nonna run the show. Ma was his wife, the legal decision maker, and she claimed both her husband and her rights. It was recommended that Lou be moved to a convalescent home, but Ma was weary from weeks of not managing her own life and the people in it. Against all advice, she returned Lou back to his New Jersey home, where he would stay with his wife and their three children.

A Short List of Lou's "Cannots"

- Cannot walk
- Cannot talk
- Cannot make it up the fancy staircase to the bedroom
- Cannot use the bathroom on his own
- Cannot dress himself

- Cannot feed himself
- Cannot work
- Cannot make money to support his family
- Cannot apologize to his wife
- Cannot have his mother by his side

The list of "Cannots" seemed endless. For the first time in her adult life, Ma turned to her own family, the O'Donnells, for help. That Bronx Irish clan was nothing but trouble for Ma. She married Lou at nineteen and stayed away from the O'Donnells as best she could. Her four brothers (Jack Anthony, Pat, Bill, and Liam) all left home at an early age, fleeing Bessie—their hard-drinking, hard-punching, widowed mother—and their dilapidated Bronx neighborhood, in that order. Of the brothers, only Bill was around to help. Jack Anthony, Ma's favorite brother, was long gone with a shot to the head. Pat was institutionalized at sixteen and still receiving shock treatments. Liam, the youngest brother, had gone missing. There was also a younger sister, Nora. She was considered "slow," stayed behind with Bessie, and never found the means to get out and move on.

The news of Lou's precarious health had wound its way through the O'Donnell family, undercover like a snake, which led to phone calls from relatives who had been silent for years. There was one thing about the O'Donnells—they surfaced when death was in the air.

As luck would have it, Bill had a twenty-four-year-old son. (Recently released from a three-year prison sentence for armed robbery.) The crime was unimaginative and desperate—holding a gun to a young mother's head as she packed her Kmart shopping bags into the trunk of a used, ten-year-old Honda. He forced the young mother to remove her two toddlers from their sticky car seats and hand over the keys to the rusting vehicle as well as her purse and diaper bag, which carried all of $1.50 in loose change.

Bill told Ma there was a bright side. First, his son conquered his heroin habit (was forced to by the circumstance). And second, he received top-notch culinary training as part of his incarceration. Now Bill's son was looking for a new start, a new town, and a place to live. Ma was looking for brawn, someone to lift and carry, someone to watch over Lou, someone to make dinner.

That is how Jimmy O'Donnell, Ma's jailbird nephew, ended up in the Napolitano home in Westfield, New Jersey.

The twins were excited to have a felon in the house. It was as if one of their crime TV shows had jumped off the screen and moved into the house in Belle Haven. They quizzed Jimmy late into the night about prison, the guards, the inmates and their crimes, solitary confinement, and the food. Jimmy, who wasn't much for talking, relished the attention from his eager young cousins and embellished tales of action-packed robbery, nasty rapes, and grisly murders to keep the twins alert, begging for more.

"Is this shit for real?" Tony asked Jimmy, hoping the answer was yes, but sensing his cousin's real crime was lying.

"What else would it be?" Jimmy answered. "I've seen it all. Some very crazy shit."

Jimmy hadn't looked like much of a criminal to Tony. He was squat and short, a smaller member of the O'Donnell clan, who weren't known for their height, and he chewed his fingernails—a habit that Tony associated with nervous middle school girls. Louie could tell Jimmy was the real deal. He may have been stubby, but there was a coldness about him. He was mean. He lacked remorse.

The dining area off the grand foyer was set up for a patient, complete with a hospital bed placed in the center of the room. Ma purchased a used black leather La-Z-Boy recliner for Jimmy as a place for dozing while on watch. The twins popped in and out to see their bedridden, mute father. They were happy to see him alive, but without words they were at a loss for what to do and did not stay long. Lauren came more often and stood next to the bed.

"Are you just going to stay there staring at him?" Jimmy would ask Lauren.

"Yes," Lauren would answer.

"You're probably giving him the creeps. Would you want someone staring at you all day?"

"It depends on who was doing the staring," she told her cousin. Lauren would touch the ends of Lou's fingertips, and if Lou was awake, he wiggled his fingers back. It was their code. For now, it was enough.

Lou was not yet able to open his swollen eyes more than a sliver and he could not smile, but his children felt his presence, even when he was napping, which was most of the time. Ma would swoop in and circle the bed every few hours to make sure her systems were in place and that Jimmy was not slacking off on the job.

After a week or so, Ma thought Jimmy was working out well. He did not exude warmth, nor did he talk to Lou. He didn't think there was a point. Jimmy performed his duties: feeding broth from a small spoon, placing an ice cube on Lou's tongue, emptying his catheter. And he took over dinner responsibilities, making the family something new each night. Jimmy liked the rigid structure of Ma's hourly schedule and followed it precisely. There was only one thing that hindered his success: Lou's dog, Wylie.

Wylie had been out of sorts and grouchy during the weeks that Lou was hospitalized. Now he constantly hid under Lou's bed in the dining room-turned-recovery ward. Before the accident, Wylie was docile and pleasant, lounging around the various rooms of the house, a familiar fixture who stayed out of the way, under Ma's radar. Since Lou's return the old Rottweiler would not budge, would not come out from under the bed, and had to be dragged outside for walks. Wylie only made quick trips to the kitchen to gobble down the dry food poured into his bowl—food that was no longer garnished with extra gravy or scraps, treats that Lou never forgot. The dog's stubborn attitude reminded Ma of Nonna's behavior at the hospital, and Ma was never putting up with that nonsense again. Not from Nonna and definitely not from any dog.

Wylie did not welcome Jimmy. He barked at the intruder for over an hour when Jimmy first stepped through the door. When Jimmy entered the dining room to adjust Lou's bed, change the bedpan, or refill Lou's spill-proof cup with water, Wylie would begin a low growl. If Jimmy tried to bend down and reach under the bed to drag Wylie out by the collar, the dog would snap and snarl. Only Lauren could coax the animal out, put on the leash, and trot him into the yard. Once outside, there was always a seemingly endless amount of urine released over the grass, a golden spray that Wylie had held in for far too long.

"The dog doesn't like me," Jimmy whined to Ma.

And Ma knew it was only a matter of time before Wylie would sink his teeth into any one of them. "I'm sure you'll figure something out," Ma said.

Ma had lots to figure out herself. She sat at her desk sorting through the health insurance claims, papers large and small, which covered the cubby desk. Invoices, both hospital and household, arrived daily. Bill collectors phoned. Ma was alone with it all. Nonna and Nonno were not invited into Ma's New Jersey home. When they pressed, Ma put them off.

One morning, while the twins and Lauren were at school, Nonna and Nonno pulled into the driveway and knocked on the door. Neither Ma nor Jimmy answered.

"I know you're in there," Nonna cried. "Answer the door." Jimmy stood next to Ma in the foyer, silent, only a few feet from where Nonna wept on the front steps. In the dining room Lou could hear his mother's call. He waited for her to burst through the door.

"I have a right to see my son," she moaned. "You can't keep him away from me."

But Ma could and she would do just that.

In the end, Ma and Jimmy heard Nonno urging Nonna back into the car. "It's okay," he said soothingly as he pulled her away from the propane tank she leaned on for support. "Next time. We'll see him next time."

Ma smiled at Jimmy. He knew to stay quiet. He was an O'Donnell and he stood by her without instruction. To Ma, that was everything. For generations, the O'Donnell reputation was soiled, littered with heinous crimes, suicide, and addiction. That was their legacy. And most of the time they were loyal to their own—particularly when it came to being destructive or damaging to others.

Nonno was loyal too. Despite the fruitless drive to Westfield to see his son, he would not give up. Ever. For the sake of his son and for his three grandchildren, Nonno telephoned Ma and offered to help with expenses. Of course, Ma knew there were strings attached—strings that would wrap around her neck and choke the life out of her.

CHAPTER 19

ON THE KITCHEN WINDOWSILL, LINED UP BY HEIGHT, were Ma's prescription drugs. Eight bottles, which contained brown, green, blue, and pink pills of varying sizes, a rainbow of colors, all prescribed to keep Ma's nerves in line. To keep stress, and the havoc it caused on her stomach and bowels, numb and silent.

Taped to the window ledge and below the pill bottles, Ma displayed the most gruesome photographs of Lou in the hospital—his injured face, inhuman and aubergine colored; his damaged body, weak and unforgiving; his broken spirit. The pictures, highlighted by the morning sun, were a loud reminder to Ma, a reminder to them all.

Since she was a child in the Bronx, growing up unsupervised with five siblings, Ma prided herself in beating down and outsmarting whatever life slammed in her direction. There was nothing a little vodka cocktail couldn't handle. But since Lou's accident, she felt she was losing her grip, her hard-won control slipping away. Ma was not one to give in. She would focus harder, raise herself up, even if she had to claw her way back.

Wylie continued to cause trouble. Like Ma, the stress seemed to make him ill. He started throwing up blood. Still, he refused to come out from under Lou's bed.

"Poor doggie," Lauren said, trying to persuade him. "Come out for a little treat." Lauren's voice used to work on Wylie. This time he snapped at her little fingers as she waved the salty cracker.

"What a fuckin' nuisance," Jimmy said. "He smells up the whole damn place."

Jimmy took the end of a broom and poked him, but the dog would not move. Jimmy released the tight bed brakes and rolled Lou's bed to the other side of the room. Doing so let him clean up the stinking mess, but Wylie, once exposed, slunk across the floor under the bed yet again, even as Jimmy hollered and struck him with the broom.

"Won't you come out, Wylie," Lauren sang. She said his name again, drawing out the vowels: "Wylie, please come out and we can help you. Buddy. Buddy."

"He'll come out when he's hungry," Jimmy predicted. "And when he does, I'll be waiting." Jimmy struck the end of the broom handle against the floor.

But Wylie would not leave his hideaway. Each time Jimmy moved the bed, depriving the sick dog of shelter, he found a fresh pile of pink vomit to clean up. What really irked Jimmy was that with each round of this tiresome competition, Wylie mustered up enough fight to prevent his capture by baring his sore teeth and dragging his hind legs across the floor, out of reach and under the bed. Under Lou.

This went on for some time until one afternoon when Tony arrived home early, having left school without permission, to find Ma in her room and Jimmy settled into the La-Z-Boy. Wylie was out from under the bed and lay slumped against the recliner. The lights were off, the drapes drawn. All three (patient, Nurse Jimmy, and dog) were napping. The smell hit Tony hard and fast. That undeniable odor, grassy and musty, he would have recognized anywhere.

"Shit. Holy shit," Tony yelled at his cousin and raced upstairs to his room to find that his recent purchase, a plentiful stash, had been raided. It was gone, every last bit. It was clear who robbed him of his only pleasure. Tony ran back downstairs to confront his older cousin, ex-criminal or not. Ma, wondering about the noise, followed Tony into the dining room.

"Jimmy's been into my room," Tony challenged.

"Why would you think that?" Ma asked.

"Because stuff's missing," he told his mother.

"What kind of stuff?" Ma asked the question even though she could smell the answer. And Tony knew Ma's question was complicated. If he answered with the truth, she would punish him.

"What stuff is missing?" Ma asked again.

"Nothing," said Tony, defeated. "Nothing."

Ma turned, flipped on the switch for the dining room chandelier, and pulled back the heavy drapes.

"Better let some light in now," Ma said. "Tony, take Wylie outside." Tony, not wanting to be anywhere near Jimmy, called Wylie.

"Hey boy, let's go." The dog didn't move.

"Take him out before he makes another mess," Ma said.

Tony moved toward the recliner. Wylie did not wake. Tony bent down and pushed the heavy dog with his foot. Wylie's head lay in an odd position, limp and unnaturally bent to the side.

"Wylie," Tony called, but the dog still did not move.

Ma came closer, looking down at the Rottweiler, Lou's best friend. "I guess you two came to an understanding," she said to Jimmy.

Jimmy stretched his limbs and climbed out of the recliner to join Ma next to Wylie. "We did," he answered.

That evening, Tony, Louie, Lauren, and Ma followed Jimmy out onto the deck and down the stairs to the rock ledge and picnic table. Jimmy carried Wylie, the dog wrapped in a white linen sheet donated by Ma. The dog was heavy, and despite Jimmy's brawn, the weight was a struggle for him. Wylie's head flopped to the side with each step. Jimmy set Wylie down across the picnic table, in the exact spot where Ma had seen the rats.

Several feet away from the table and off the rock ledge, Jimmy dug a shallow hole in the hard ground. The Napolitano family buried their dog and said their good-byes while Lou lay awake and alert in the late afternoon light of the dining room.

At dinner, when Jimmy served up his newest creation, a flavorful concoction similar to chicken cacciatore, Tony, Louie, and Lauren refused to touch the meal.

"Did you hurt Wylie?" Lauren asked Jimmy, breaking the silence.

Ma answered for her nephew (out of loyalty, in O'Donnell style, without instruction). "Of course not," Ma said to her daughter. "The dog was old. You know how impossible he'd become. I guess God decided he'd worn out his welcome."

Lauren poked at her chicken, dragging it around the thick red sauce. Tony pushed his plate away, and Louie stood up from the table. "I've got a lot of homework," he said, and excused himself.

"Suit yourself," Ma said. "I for one think Jimmy has outdone himself tonight." Ma picked up her fork and began to eat. Most nights, Ma did not have much of an appetite. Tonight she was ravenous.

CHAPTER 20

THE MONTHS WENT SLOWLY. Winter passed into spring. Tony and Louie stayed holed up in their rooms, appearing now and then for Jimmy's meals. Lou was better. Physically. He could sit up for a few hours at a time, feed himself the meals Jimmy brought him, walk a few steps, and talk (although his voice was light and shaky). Other than "please" and "thank you," Lou didn't have much to say to anyone. His spirit had not yet mended. Louie thought it was most likely broken beyond repair. It was one thing to be bedridden and at the mercy of others, but Wylie's demise sent Lou wandering into depths. Even Lauren could not cheer him.

With Lou out of work, money was tight. Ma continued to refuse help from Nonno and Nonna and kept them away. Instead, Ma filed for the usual worker's compensation, disability, and food stamps. She fought with Blue Cross for hospital health insurance reimbursements, which required endless forms and ongoing battles. She never forgot to check the box that all payments should be sent directly to her and not the hospital or doctor. When she received the checks, money meant to pay the medical bills, she cashed them fast. The doctors and hospital could fight their own battles.

She had other ways of making money too. She juggled property and casualty insurance claims and initiated lawsuits, all in an attempt for ready cash.

Ma's To-Do List of Insurance Claims and Filed Lawsuits

+ **Claim:** fallen hickory tree on back deck

+ **Claim:** flooded basement due to faulty water heater

+ **Claim:** three-carat diamond anniversary ring gone missing from bedroom after workers fixed plumbing

+ **Claim:** Lou's stolen truck, found stripped of all parts, including tires and tools

+ **Filed:** $2 million dollar lawsuit against Lori Molinari for harassment and hiding rodents in the Napolitano moving boxes

+ **Filed:** $10 million dollar lawsuit against Napolitano Brothers' International Garage for safety violations and gross negligence

The kitchen desk cubby was Ma's headquarters. She organized a growing and mountainous pile, each claim in a separate color, with meticulous notes in neat and careful longhand. With the mounting claims, Ma had come to know Mr. Howard H. Howard, an insurance agent, whose offices were coincidentally located next door to Très Suave: House of Beauty. Howard generously worked above and beyond the call of duty when it came to helping Ma with her processing efforts.

"You sure have had your share of bad luck," Mr. Howard H. Howard said one afternoon when Ma stopped by with the paperwork summarizing her latest mishap. He tripped over an uneven and crumbling curb outside of Theo's Diner in the same plaza as the insurance office and salon. Howard pressed his fingers, the skin scabbed and peeling, over Ma's small hand.

Ma let Howard's hand stay, courting him like an actor in a Tennessee Williams play. "I rely on your kindness," she told him, emphasizing *kindness*.

Howard blushed. "This nasty little black storm cloud will move along soon," he offered, hoping his words would encourage Ma to allow his hand to linger a moment more.

"Mr. Howard, you can count on that," Ma said, sneaking her hand out from under his palm.

Ma also acquired a job at Lauren's school. She was what they called "a floater," which meant she was a teacher's assistant who moved between various classrooms, an extra pair of hands helping the harried teachers wherever and whenever they needed her. Ma made Xerox copies of worksheets, organized art supplies, arranged for projectors and TV sets, and acted as a general resource for any number of miscellaneous tasks. Ma didn't dislike the work. The teachers were grateful for her help and fawned over her, complimenting every bit of assistance she provided. Most important, Ma was her own agent, working alone, floating from classroom to classroom without any specific accountability.

Ma's position at the school made it more difficult for Lauren to stay home. Lauren made it to the classroom more often (despite the chronic ailments that continued to plague her) and her dismal grades began to climb.

Ma was fighting the finance war on all fronts, but stress was waging its battle too, taking its own toll. Since the accident, she spent more and more time locked in her room with medicine bottles and cocktails while Jimmy cooked the meals, did the laundry, swept the front porch, and kept the house in order. Jimmy O'Donnell stood by Ma and picked up the slack.

Jimmy contributed to the family income when he could. Ma didn't ask questions and Jimmy didn't supply explanations. There was no spoken agreement between them, but Ma could count on fifty or a hundred from Jimmy every so often. Even $300 now and again, here and there. She also noticed that while Tony did not openly speak to Jimmy since the day Wylie died, they both disappeared at the same odd hours.

Jimmy reminded Ma of Jack Anthony. It needled her. She could see her brother in Jimmy, as if Jack Anthony was calling her from the grave. There he was with his square face, thick neck, and muscular forearms with bulging veins. Ma would never admit it, not in a million years, but she missed Jack Anthony. Sometimes the feeling threw her off. She studied Jimmy, trying to determine what it was that made her pine for Jack Anthony—her impossible brother who was stolen from her.

Was it Jimmy's eyes that brought Jack Anthony back? His thin upper lip? The way he chomped on his tongue like a stale piece of gum, squeezing out the last dab of flavor? What was it about her nephew that was all Jack Anthony? She couldn't decide on any one thing, but she knew Jack Anthony was there. She felt Jack Anthony's presence whenever Jimmy stood before her.

Lately, Jimmy's physical familiarity—the recognizable expressions; his sharp, quick laugh that was like a machine gun spewing bullets—got her to thinking. Remembering. Dredging up the past, memories filled with torment and anguish that she had pushed away, thrown out into the garbage years ago. The memories resurfaced and stomped around her head.

She could not deny that Jack Anthony had stood by her. Always. Whenever Mother Bessie raised a stick or a hammer, or if the neighbor boys taunted her, and the time when her oldest brother (Bill) brandished a knife, it was Jack Anthony who stepped in. Protected her. It was Jack Anthony who brought her food when Bessie lay in a drunken slump on the living room floor and their father was hauled off in a paddy wagon with all the neighbors gawking. But it was also Jack Anthony who left and moved away with a giggling girl. Left Ma alone. Alone to fend for her nine-year-old self. For that, she despised him.

When she thought of Jack Anthony now, dead and gone, having left her again, she plucked at her hair. At first, it was an unconscious reaction. A quick pluck here. A tough tug there. Pulling the thin strands out, one by one, with a yank. The sharp pinch moved her mind away from the memories, brought her back into the current world. Since Ma didn't have much hair to spare and the habit had become something more than she could control, the scalp directly above her left ear developed a definite bald patch—a clearing, like a once thick-forested land stripped and marred from overlogging. The bare scalp was red and sore, tender to the touch. To cover the spot, Ma made a new part on the right and swooped over the hair to the damaged area, a bit of borrowing to hide the barren spot. It was the same technique aging men often try, except Ma was not losing her hair to age or maternal genetics; she was ripping each hair out from the root.

Chapter 21

One afternoon, returning home from her floating duties, Ma walked into the dining room, where Lou sat in the recliner, staring at the wall.

"It's enough now," Ma said. "It's time to get on your feet." Lou dropped his head so that his chin touched his chest.

"Just because you won't look at me, doesn't mean that you are going to sit here like a blubbering blob for the rest of your life. It's time to get at it. You didn't die and it doesn't look like you are going to anytime soon. So stand up. Be a man."

Lou did not raise his head.

Ma had already informed him that he would not, under any circumstances, be returning to work at the Napolitano Brothers' International Garage. The accident was, after all, Nonno's fault. As far as Ma was concerned it was a clear case of criminal negligence. The hoists should have been checked more regularly. The straps securing the Lamborghini were old. And who had been looking after, watching over Lou? Ma never mentioned the drugs, but she blamed Nonna and Nonno for that too. They had been warned.

Lou was familiar with Ma's opinion on the matter. In those days while he lay in the hospital bed, drifting between life and death, Ma made it clear. She reminded him by day. She reminded him by night.

"Look at what they've done to you," she said. "Somebody is going to have to pay." Even after Lou could speak, he said nothing. His get-up-and-go was gone; he didn't have it in him to fight her, or his mother, or his father, or even that new resident in their home, Jimmy O'Donnell.

Like Wylie, Lou was not budging. He was not getting up. He was not moving on. He sat in the recliner and wept. "I'm sorry," he sputtered. "I'm sorry, but I can't."

Ma needed a strategy and it was Lauren who came up with an idea. "Dad needs a puppy," she said. "A happy puppy."

"Just shoot me," Ma replied, but the idea began to take root over the next week, until it sprouted into a prospect that seemed to make good sense. Ma had never seen her husband dragging before. Lou had always been energized, raring to go, and now he had crashed to a dead stop. She didn't know what to do. Maybe Lauren was right. A new dog might do the trick.

Ma took Lauren across the four-lane road from Howard H. Howard's Insurance and Très Suave: House of Beauty to an identical strip mall of one-story, beige concrete structures. This side included the store Puppy Love. Ma walked through the door with a clear purpose: finding a puppy that would bring Lou out of his funk.

The store was larger than it appeared from the street. There were the obligatory shelves of pet food, dog beds, kitty climbers, squeaky toys, tanks of tropical fish, and small white mice that circled round and round. And the main event—puppies.

Lauren inched up close to a glass wall that ran along one side of the store. Behind the glass were three rows of small metal cages with a puppy in each. Yorkies, terriers, poodles, a basset hound, and even a boxer, his long gangly legs making him look like he had been folded up, collapsed, and forced into a cage far too small.

Lauren pressed her face against the glass. There was a Chihuahua, which had become a popular choice, and was attracting quite a bit of attention from both those customers intending to buy and those who behaved like they were at the zoo. Ma took one look at the tiny, hairless creature. "Not on your life is that thing getting into my house. It looks like a giant rat."

Lauren spied a cream-and-apricot puppy with floppy ears at the end of the row.

"Ma, that one. That's the one!" She moved her hands along the glass, leaving a trail of smudged fingerprints, so that she could look directly at the animal. The tag attached to the cage said: "Cockapoo. $800. Male. 8 weeks old." Lauren tapped on the glass and waved at the puppy, but the puppy did not stand, did not even look out with his black, glassy eyes.

"He looks sad," Lauren said to Ma. It was true; the cockapoo did not meet and greet Lauren's attentions. He was subdued, unlike his caged neighbors, who forced their snouts through the cage wire, scratched their paws against the metal bottom, and yelped. *Yip. Yip. Yap.* One particular poodle in a cage next to the cockapoo cried and scrambled, trying to get Lauren's attention, but Lauren was only interested in the morose puppy.

"That's all we need, another killjoy around the house," said Ma. "Let's find another."

"He's the one," Lauren protested. "I know it."

It was then that Matt, the pale and freckled young salesman, appeared, ready to do his job. "Would you like to play with him?" he asked Lauren.

"Yes, please," she answered.

"The cockapoo is a good choice for you," Matt told Lauren.

"What a bunch of baloney," Ma answered. "Let's have a look at that boxer."

Lauren thought Matt must understand these matters. Matt had auburn hair, the same color and wavy texture as the cockapoo. His neck and wrists were decorated with an ornate tattoo, a black snake, and he had multiple piercings—his nose and lip pierced once, the left ear three times, and the right ear five times. Each hole carried a small gold ring. Lauren was not impressed by Matt's tattoos or piercings, but she did take notice of his white doctor-like jacket. Matt wore the uniform over his black T-shirt and jeans. The loose jacket was embroidered over the pocket; sewn in red thread was, "Matt. Your Puppy Placement Expert."

Matt ignored Ma's direction and went to get the cockapoo. He brought the puppy out of his cage and around the glass wall and put him into Lauren's arms. The puppy lay still, except for his tail, which switched back and forth.

"What else do you have?" Ma said to Matt. "We need a dog with some spunk. Not this little mopey, droopy thing."

"He's got spunk," Matt told Ma. "He's just not ready to reveal it."

"This is the one," Lauren told her mother. "I know it. I think I'll call him Simba, just like the Lion King."

"We are not calling him anything," Ma said. "In fact, the only thing we are saying to this dog is good-bye."

Matt took the cockapoo back from Lauren and handed Ma his business card. "In case you change your mind," he said.

Ma had no patience for gushy sentiment and they left the store without the dog. Lauren cried all the way home. "He's the dog that's meant for us," she moaned. "I can feel it in my bones. I know it."

Lauren rarely objected to Ma's decisions, didn't go against her wishes, and Ma was taken aback by her daughter's emotional outburst and aggressive campaign on the car ride home. Lauren, between wails and shrieks, used unsettling phrases like, "The angels have sent him to us," "It was meant to be," "I know it in my heart," "God sent him to us as a sign," "He is meant to be ours," and "He doesn't belong with anyone else." It was too much.

At first, Ma was irritated. She needed this tantrum like a whack to the back of her head. These were obviously the words of a silly young girl, and yet, the rapid flow of reasons and the confrontational way in which Lauren delivered the message made her feel like Lauren had become unrecognizable. To Ma, it felt like Lauren was speaking in some strange, possessed way. As if the messages were flowing through the child from a larger, unknown plane.

When they reached home, Lauren ran to her room and threw herself across the bed.

Ma pulled the Puppy Love card out of her purse.

Call Matt

Puppy Love

Which Puppy Is Meant To Be In Your Life?

Ma hadn't noticed the tagline on the card before. She dialed the number to Puppy Love and asked to speak to Matt. The young woman who picked up the phone gave Ma the bad news in a tiny voice.

Matt had left for the day and would not be back for two days. And the cream-and-apricot cockapoo could not be put on reserve as Ma requested because the puppy had been placed with another family, the Millers, and was being picked up at the end of the week when they paid their balance.

"There must be some mistake," Ma told the tiny voice.

"I'm sorry. The puppy is no longer available."

"We were just there," Ma said. "The puppy liked us."

"I'm sorry. Someone else has already put down a deposit."

"Matt said we could have that dog," Ma countered.

"Ma'am, you can't have the puppy. It belongs to someone else now."

Ma knew she would get nowhere with the measly girl. "Yes, I understand," Ma said. "Thank you. Thank you so much." Despite her words, Ma never intended to offer any true gratitude to the bitch.

That droopy, mopey puppy was rightfully Ma's. No one was going to tell her that she couldn't have it. She could and she would. When Lauren emerged from her room later that evening after refusing to eat any dinner, Ma called her over to the kitchen cubby.

"I've decided we'll get the puppy," she announced to Lauren. And Lauren squeezed her mother with all her might until Ma managed to worm away from her daughter's ferocious grip.

"There is one slight problem," Ma mentioned. "Someone else is trying to steal the dog from us. But don't you worry. The dog should be ours. Just like you said."

Lauren looked up at her mother. Any doubt she might have felt was diminished by Ma's confidence. After all, Lauren knew that when Ma wanted something, she always got it.

Ma was on it. The next morning, knowing Matt was off and could not create complications, Ma dialed Puppy Love.

"Good morning," Ma said in her most chipper voice. "I hope you can help me. I purchased that cute little cockapoo yesterday and I just can't recall if I used my name or my husband's."

"Are you Mrs. Miller?" the clerk asked, and Ma was relieved that it wasn't Tiny Voice from the afternoon before. Things were going to go her way.

"Yes, that's me. Mrs. Miller," Ma said. "I can't find my receipt at the moment and I want to confirm the balance. I know we agreed to come in later this week to get the little fella, but I want to surprise my husband with a present. Between you and me, my husband's been ill and I want to cheer him up. I don't want to wait. This will mean the world to him."

"Of course," the clerk said. "The balance is $435."

The moment Lauren and Ma left the school that afternoon they drove straight to Puppy Love. Ma walked directly to the sales counter.

"Good afternoon, I'm Mrs. Miller and I'm here to pick up our cockapoo." Ma counted out the $435 in cash. As far as Ma could tell, Matt and Tiny Voice were not around. The clerk went to get the puppy and handed him to Lauren. There was a complimentary blue leash and collar attached to the dog.

After Ma and Lauren walked out of Puppy Love with the cockapoo scampering along behind them, Lauren asked, "How come you said you were Mrs. Miller?"

"Because fair is fair," Ma said. She would explain the rules of the road to her daughter. "We saw him first. This puppy was ours. You said so yourself. Never hesitate to take what is meant to be yours. Besides, I've been screwed plenty in my life, so it doesn't matter if I give a little screwing right back."

Lauren picked up the baby cockapoo and held him tight. Her mother was right.

When they arrived home, Ma called the boys to join them in the dining room and meet the puppy. The twins and Jimmy came into the room where Lou sat in the recliner.

"Are you fucking kidding me?" Jimmy asked with a groan.

Lauren walked up to her father and held out the puppy. "This is for you," she told him. She placed the puppy on Lou's thighs and the little cockapoo seemed to understand, staying put in Lou's lap, his little pink tongue licking Lou's hand, over and over.

"He'll need a name," said Louie.

"Rambo," Tony suggested. "How about Rambo?"

"The dog already has a name," Ma announced. "His name is Jack Anthony."

CHAPTER 22

Whether it was puppy Jack Anthony's homecoming, Ma's restless nights and lack of sleep, the combination of pills and cocktails, or the memories that pestered her, she could never say. That night, Jack the puppy scratched at the bedroom door until Ma unlocked it and the puppy scampered down the stairs. Ma followed puppy Jack, weaving her way to Jimmy's room. Now that Lou was more mobile and able to take care of himself, Jimmy slept in the guest room downstairs. Ma heard giggling and the puppy scratched on Jimmy's door. It was unlocked and Ma opened it wide, allowing the puppy to run in and begin hopping up and down at the side of the bed. There in Ma's guest room bed, right under her nose, was Jimmy, naked and sweating with some tittering girl.

"What's all this?" Ma asked, struggling to take it in. "What's going on here?"

"That seems obvious," Jimmy said to Ma in a snotty tone, showing off for the girl. "So if you don't mind, you and your little dog need to be on your way."

"What's obvious is that you have a stranger in my home in the middle of the night."

"She's not a stranger," Jimmy corrected. "I think we now know each other quite well." The shadowed girl burst into drunken snorts, which evolved into loud, broken hiccups.

Puppy Jack began to yap after each hiccup was expelled.

"What's your problem?" Jimmy asked, sensing that Ma was as shit-faced as he was.

"My problem is that you have brought a whore into my home."

"Get the whore out of my house," Ma ordered, leaning over the bed.

Jimmy raised his hand to Ma. His palm clapped her cheek. The smack pushed Ma back and she gazed at her nephew with disbelief. Why was Jimmy angry with her and not the girl? It was the whore he should smack, not her. Jimmy had it all backward.

"That's not a nice way to talk about my friend," Jimmy said to Ma.

"I want her out of here now," Ma said, looking like she was about to scream.

But it was clear to both Ma and Jimmy that the girl was not going anywhere. Even though Ma was ready to rage, the combination of in-ebriation and exhaustion kept her from mustering up the fight. Instead, she quietly sat on the edge of the bed.

"What are you doing now?" Jimmy demanded.

"I can't sleep," Ma said, her mood switching to that of a fretful child. "I'm so tired. I can't sleep one wink."

"You're drunk."

With puppy Jack cradled in her arms, Ma stumbled toward her kitchen cubby and sat down in the dark. She could discern the familiar mound of colored files and the photo of her burnt-up Caddy. She had been wrong. Dead wrong. Jimmy was not like Jack Anthony O'Donnell. Not at all. Jimmy had to leave. She wanted to make sure to remember it in the morning. Ma added it to her "To-Do List."

CHAPTER 23

Dear Journal,

Louie gave me a poem today. It is called "Hope" by a lady named Emily Dickinson. She is dead. I think Louie knows about everything and everybody even if they are dead.

I don't know who Emily Dickinson is. Louie says she is famous and I should learn her poems.

I DID NOT want to tell Louie that I don't exactly understand Emily's poem. But I DO like how it sounds when I read it out loud quietly in my bedroom and I know it has something to do with hope. And I really, really, REALLY LOVE that Louie gave me this special gift. So this is what I decided to do. ARE YOU READY???

I am going to COPY part of this poem into the pages of my secret journal (a gift from Louie that I LOVE!).

THIS IS MY PLAN!!!! I think I might copy these words over and over until the hope of the poem gets inside my brain and then I can tell Louie that I know what this poem means. I think that would make him VERY HAPPY!!!!!

"Hope"

By, Emily Dickinson

Hope is the thing with feathers

That perches in the soul,

And sings the tune without the words,

And never stops at all,

And sweetest in the gale is heard;

And sore must be the storm

That could abash the little bird

That kept so many warm.

I've heard it in the chilliest land,

And on the strangest sea;

Yet, never, in extremity,

It asked a crumb of me.

Copied by Lauren Napolitano

Belle Haven, Westfield, New Jersey

CHAPTER 24

Ma honored her "To-Do List" and crossed off the tasks one by one. She was patient with the growing agenda and tended to each item like a child, nurturing and nudging its progress. Once an assignment was placed on the list, written in Ma's slender and slanted script, it was permanent. Some items took months, even years, to complete, but Ma was loyal and patient with each entry. Once on the list, it could not be disregarded or forgotten.

In the past three years, Ma had filed over two dozen insurance claims, which Mr. Howard H. Howard helped her shepherd. All returned with a reimbursement. Lou's stolen truck and tools, the missing three-carat diamond anniversary ring, the flooded basement, and the fallen hickory tree over the back deck had all been good to her. Ma removed each claim from her list with a thick red marker in a grand flourish and filed the paperwork away. A small amount of worker's compensation ran for two years after Lou's accident, and the less reliable health insurance reimbursements arrived in small spurts. The two lawsuits had not gone as well.

The $10 million gross negligence lawsuit against Napolitano Brothers' International Garage came up for trial eighteen months after the accident. In the end, a $200,000 settlement was reached, which satisfied Ma for the moment. Ma decided not to hold out for additional funds, calculating that Lou's eventual inheritance from the business would be worth far more.

The day the check arrived, Ma disassembled the dining room's make-shift convalescent station. The hospital bed frame and recliner were discarded to a neighborhood charity and the mattress was thrown in the trash. Lou now made his way upstairs to their bedroom, but to ensure that all would not be forgotten, the photographs of Lou's hospital days remained taped to the kitchen window. Jack, the new puppy, had not been part of Lou's recovery as expected. The dog preferred Ma. And Ma's bed. Jack wasn't very welcoming when Lou arrived back in the bedroom.

Nonna and Nonno paid the settlement without complaint. They wanted to help their son and if this was how they could get him back on track, then pay up they would. They wanted Lou not only mended, but well. They wanted him in their life. Not a word was uttered against Ma. It was a tiny price to pay.

The other lawsuit, the case alleging that Ms. Lori Molinari hid rodents in the Napolitano moving boxes as a form of harassment, was thrown out by the judge for lack of evidence. While the judge may have thrown the suit out and moved on to the next case (perhaps with a snicker behind the scenes), Ma had not moved on. She kept the item on the "To-Do List" and added a large star.

Lou made astonishing physical strides. He recovered, with a few exceptions: a limp in his left leg, joints that ached in extreme weather, and a face that looked off-kilter and smashed. He resembled a battered boxer with a crooked nose, his left temple and cheek sunken like a water-worn gulley. Lou's demeanor was affected as well. He was quiet now. He had few words for his family and he never squabbled with Ma. On some Sundays he would drive to Queens to visit Nonna and Nonno. Most of the time he went by himself; sometimes he brought Lauren and the twins, but he almost always went without Ma. Nonno pressed for Lou to return to the garage, but Ma would not have it.

After several months of searching, Lou found a job teaching car mechanics at a vocational school in Newark, New Jersey, a distance of only fourteen miles from Westfield. The school was close enough for Lou to handle the drive and far enough that he felt like he was out in the world again. The school offered students a wide range of basic training for automotive, diesel, and motorcycle technology. There were classes in diagnostic techniques, fuel and emission systems, electrical systems, and transmission and drivelines.

Lou found his niche in collision repair. He taught students auto body repair and construction, the ins and outs of bodywork, surface preparation, welding, cutting, and dent repair. He connected with the challenge of bringing a wrecked car back to life, making it road ready again, and his soft and patient demeanor, coupled with an abundance of knowledge, made Lou a favorite with students, particularly with those who struggled and needed extra encouragement.

The pay was low, but the work was without pressure, and since Ma had found ingenious ways for an ongoing stream of supplemental cash, they had managed to keep the house in Belle Haven and prevent fore-closure. At home, Lou had, bit by bit, placed himself back in the kitchen to resume preparing meals for the family. Nothing fancy, but good enough. Jimmy found more and more reasons to be out and about and didn't defend his culinary territory. He often missed dinner.

So far, Jimmy was proving difficult to remove from Ma's "To-Do List." While she wanted Jimmy out of her house immediately after that unpleasant night, she didn't want to incur any trouble from Bill, or any of the O'Donnell clan, nor did she want Jimmy blabbing about her in-discretions. Many months passed before the opportunity presented it-self and, in a bizarre alignment of the stars, she finally got her way.

It started with a sparring between Ma and one of the teachers she assisted. The fussy Miss Cole complained that Ma had Xeroxed an exercise worksheet for her sixth grade math class on a slant, so that the column of twenty-five fraction-to-decimal equations tilted like the leaning tower of Pisa.

"This work is sloppy and unacceptable," Miss Cole said to Ma, and then added, "It will make the kids cross-eyed." Ma replied, "Looking at your fat ass for an entire year is what will make these kids cross-eyed."

Miss Cole complained to the principal, and the principal suggested that Ma might like to transfer to the newly open position of school crossing guard. Ma went down to the Westfield Traffic Safety Bureau, the supervisors of the Crossing Guard Program, and joined the ranks of fifty-two other guards whose posts ranged from one-and-a-half to three hours daily. It was perfect. Ma was on her own, outside, away from the Miss Coles of the world. She felt a special surge of power when she blew her whistle and waved her arms for direction, commanding children from the sidewalk into the road and across to safety on the other side. In the crosswalk, Ma had the final say. She was in charge.

Ma was surprised and pleased to learn that crossing guards collected their paychecks every other week at the local police station. Ma had followed true crime stories and television detective/crime/mystery series for years. She could discuss in great detail the gruesome killings perpetrated by Jeffrey Dahmer and David Berkowitz, more commonly known as "Son of Sam," and the fantasy crimes played out on *CHiPs*, *Charlie's Angels*, *Columbo*, *Miami Vice*, and *Magnum, P.I.*, which she watched regularly with the twins. And certainly she was privy to a slew of O'Donnell stories, featuring relations who landed in jail and prison. Despite her familiarity, she had never spent time in a police station and didn't know what to expect. She entered to retrieve her first paycheck with equal parts titillation, admiration, and dread.

Steve, a lumbering veteran detective who worked at a desk covered in years of reports and documentation, took a liking to Ma. He would come up to the counter each time Ma came in, making a point of inquiring how she was adjusting to her new duties. Ma was flattered by the attention, and asked Steve for his advice about traffic flow and safety. He was happy to consult, and invited her to sit with him at his desk so he could give her a thorough understanding of the topic. After some weeks, Ma asked him about his most interesting cases from previous years. Steve shared stories of arrest after arrest, crime after crime, cold cases, and dangerous encounters. Detail after detail. After a couple of months, Ma let it out that she was having trouble at home.

"I'm doing my best to help someone who has problems," she confided to Steve, "but I'm afraid my no-good, jailbird nephew has gone off track again."

Steve was concerned more by what Ma didn't say than what she offered, and listened with his full attention for the subtext.

"I'm so worried that he's a terrible influence on my twins. My husband, who's been ailing for years, is not up to the aggravation," she said.

"Let me know what I can do," he told Ma. "Anytime."

"You're so sweet, Steve. We'll manage. We just have to."

On future visits, each time Steve asked, Ma would say, "God only gives us what we can handle."

"Don't try to handle it all on your own," Steve told her.

"I wouldn't even bring it up," Ma stumbled, "except there have been some incidents. Steve, I'm afraid for my safety." Ma lowered her head. Steve looked down, too, when he heard Ma's words. It was as though both were bent in prayer, embarrassed and awkward. He wanted to help her, this little wisp of a woman who possessed boundless strength, but he also knew that she was too proud to give him any specific details that might allow him to do so.

It was true Jimmy spent more time with Tony, and Ma was seeing less and less cash, which Jimmy used to provide on a regular basis. On her way home from the police station that day, Ma thought about her family. Tony was flunking three out of five high school classes while Louie was ranked third in the class, but rarely came out of his room. Lauren, now a teenager, chatted on the phone with girlfriends, winding the spiral cord around her arms like it was a decorative bracelet.

Her three children were drifting, each in his or her own way, each in different directions. Ma felt like a wave had crashed into her life and swept her children away from her side. Despite her efforts to cling, to hold each of them tight, they had let go of her hand, released her without warning. It was in this mood that Ma saw the posters around Westfield for a Billy Joel concert at Madison Square Garden. Billy had been born in the Bronx, and although he had shot to the top, had courted and wed the beautiful model Christie Brinkley, Billy knew about hard knocks and survival. He knew about the rough patches of life; he knew about family.

Ma purchased five tickets. She did not buy a ticket for Jimmy. She hired a limo complete with driver and wet bar to take them to Madison Square Garden in Manhattan. It was a splurge, but one she was willing to make.

The afternoon of the concert, Ma ironed a shirt and pants for Lou, Louie, and Tony and a flowery dress for Lauren. She did not have to iron her own rose pantsuit, which she purchased for the occasion. Ma, usually not one for domestic chores, felt fully satisfied to guide the hot silver appliance across the board. She liked to witness the steam and heat pressing into the fabric, leaving a rigid and distinct crease down the front of the pants, the side of the shirtsleeves, and the pleats of the dress.

As they waited for the limousine, the family gathered in the kitchen. Lou came downstairs last and stood in his appointed outfit. Black pants, a blue striped shirt, and polished shoes. He looked at Ma.

"Am I okay?" he asked her.

"It's hard to see past that wreck of a nose," she told him, but she gave him a smile and that was enough for both. Ma looked from Tony to Louie to Lauren and felt proud of her crisp and pressed family. They all felt her approval as they stepped into the white limo and made the drive to New York City. To Madison Square Garden. To Billy Joel. It was as if this excursion was an announcement to Westfield, to Manhattan, to Billy, to the world: Look at us; we are a perfect family.

The concert was sold-out and short, but tough Billy was on fire. He pounded the keys and sang "Uptown Girl," "Piano Man," and "My Life." He bounced up and down. He hopped. He bopped. He stomped. The crowd could not, would not, stay seated, and they danced in the aisles to their favorites. Even Ma stood and let the folding seat snap back behind her. She swayed to the music, letting go of her usual worries.

The lights went dark and the crowd waited. Waited longer in silence. Slowly one spotlight emerged center stage, highlighting the scrappy Billy, who had come out from behind the piano and stood alone before the crowd in his black pants and red dinner jacket. He began to sing "An Innocent Man" in his beloved, raspy voice. He sang about those who had been fools, those who had been burned, about those who now feared being vulnerable, the melody trailing behind his raw energy. Ma nodded in agreement, an affirmation of Billy's message. "That's right, Billy Joel," Ma called to the stage, to coax this Bronx-born boy to continue singing the truth. "That's right, Billy. I'm done listening. Nobody will ever tell me a lie again."

Gradually, three guitarists emerged in a faint glow behind him, Billy emphasizing the lyrics with harsh finger snaps into the microphone. And like Billy's words, Ma was thinking of somebody else too—somebody who had hurt her when she was just a little girl.

And when Billy screeched out the refrain, the same as the title of the song, he forced his lips against the round tip of the microphone as if in the middle of a prolonged, private, and passionate kiss.

If the stars are aligned, odd things can happen, and so it was the night of the Billy Joel concert. At that very same moment—just a sliver in time on a Saturday night in Westfield, New Jersey—two police officers stopped a young man named Jimmy O'Donnell as he walked out of Mike's Pub. They seized and searched his knapsack and found an assorted supply of pills and white powders. In the same instant that Billy sang of past hurts and damage, Jimmy was busted.

Jimmy resisted his arrest, spitting and kicking and punching. He shouted every profanity he could recall, spitting out bile as his only defense. In the darkness of Madison Square Garden, Ma sang along with Billy, mesmerized, enunciating each syllable. I am an innocent man. Oh, how she loved the song.

The two police officers had not anticipated trouble, and were annoyed by Jimmy's savage resistance. The older officer, bulky and lumbering, struggled to maintain control over the suspect. Jimmy stomped and pounded and flailed until he was finally maneuvered and placed in a headlock, his face pressed against the aging policeman's. In a last-ditch effort to be freed, Jimmy lunged forward and sank his teeth into the officer's ear with a hard chomp, like Wylie might have done to Jimmy if he had had the chance or the strength.

"Holy Shit," the policeman cried. "He bit me." And as much as the officer screamed and threatened, Jimmy would not let go, would not pull his teeth out of the tender ear.

The other policeman wrestled Jimmy away from his friend and partner. Jimmy may have been defeated, but he carried something that belonged to the officer. Clamped between Jimmy's bloody teeth was the upper half of the policeman's ear. Miles away, Ma stood, ears perked, listening to Billy Joel.

There was a pause before the Garden's full houselights went on. The brightness lit up every face in the crowd. Billy began to shriek, "It's still rock and roll to me," spraying spit, his teeth bared. "It's still rock and roll to me." Ma began to dance, to shake, to shimmy. Even Lou and his three children stood to clap, bringing their hands together with loud smacks. Billy grabbed the microphone stand, dragging it across the stage like a thin dance partner, and it seemed to Ma that Billy was dancing with her, frenzied and wild, without missing a step.

The ringing woke Ma early the next morning. After several rings, Ma picked up her Princess phone.

"I need your help," Jimmy pleaded.

Ma did not answer.

"I need your help," Jimmy repeated, explaining the situation.

"Why on earth would you ever think that I would do something like that?"

"I'll do whatever it is you want. I will. I promise."

"Jimmy, there is nothing I want from you. I don't know why you would say such a thing." Ma hung up the Princess phone and placed it back into the receiver. She turned to Lou, who lay on the other side of the bed, and said, "It seems that Jimmy has gotten himself into a heap of trouble. Violated his probation. We won't be seeing him again."

Ma rose and went down to her kitchen cubby and "To-Do List." She took out a red marker and crossed out two words: Jimmy O'Donnell.

No one in the family—not Lou, not Lauren, not Louie, and not Tony—ever mentioned Jimmy again. No one cared.

CHAPTER 25

Dear Journal,

It has been ten days since I found out that Vince Cohen likes me.
And here is the really AMAZING thing. Vinny (that's what I call
him) likes to hear what I think about things even though my grades
are not like his (whose could be???). But still, he talks to me like
I am as smart as he is. He asks me questions about life and when I
answer he even says stuff like, "I never thought about it that way," or
"Good point," or "I'll have to consider that." Whoa!!! Do you think I
could be in love???
Lauren, a 9ᵗʰ grade girl almost in love

❧

Dear Journal,
Vinny held my hand in the hall at school today in front of every-
body. History in the making!!!
Lauren, a girl definitely in love

❧

Dear Journal,

I am increasing my vocabulary for Vinny.

SOME SYNONYMS FOR LOVE

Admire, adulate, be attached to, be captivated by, be enamored of, be enchanted by, be fascinated with, cherish, delight in, exalt, hold dear, idolize, long for, lose one's heart to, put on a pedestal, think the world of, thrive with, treasure, venerate, wild for, worship . . .

SOUNDS RIGHT TO ME!!!

Lauren

∽

Dear Journal,

Ma let me go to Vinny's house for dinner. His family is so nice. Mrs. Cohen (Vinny's mom, her name is Joanna) told me I was really cute. Ha! Mrs. Cohen made an AMAZING dinner. Roast brisket (something Mr. Cohen loves) and yams. I have never eaten yams before. They are an orange, rusty color and so good. Who knew? Mr. Cohen looks like Vinny and doesn't say much but has a nice smile (just like my Dad) and Vinny's little sister was happy to see me and she gave me lots of hugs.

But here is the BIG NEWS!!! Tonight at dinner, Vinny's mom asked me what I wanted to do after I finish high school (even though I'm only a freshman). I know that Vinny might be a psychologist (like his father), or a lawyer (like his uncle), or a doctor (his mother is a nurse). Vinny is not sure yet (he can do anything). I told Mrs. Cohen that I didn't know what I should do. Mrs. Cohen said that she thinks I am an EXPLORER at heart. Then she said that the EXPLOR-ER spirit could manifest (she uses big words like that and I had to look it up) in lots of great ways. How does she know???

The whole family is brilliant. Vinny held my hand under the table almost the WHOLE TIME (except of course when we had to use both a knife and fork!!!). The best part was chocolate mousse cake (HOME-MADE) for dessert.

Lauren, a happy EXPLORER in love

~

Dear Journal,

We're still going strong! I think this is some kind of record. Six weeks! I don't think Ma likes me spending so much time at the Cohen house. She said, "He's no ball of fire and those Cohens are stuffy and snooty." But still, she drove me over for dinner (again!!!). This time I got one of my bloody noses. Wouldn't you know? The blood just had to drib-ble out of my nose and over my blouse onto the white cloth napkin. UGH!!! Mrs. Cohen is a nurse so she knew what to do. She had me put my head back to stop the blood and she put some club soda on my blouse for the stain. Nobody made me feel embarrassed. When Ma picked me up, Mrs. Cohen walked out to the car with Vinny and me to tell Ma all about what happened. She recommended that Ma take me to the doctor. That's when Ma told her about my problems. Ma told her about taking me to a ton of doctors and no one could really help me. Ma even got a little tear in her eye when she was telling Mrs. Cohen that she was beside herself about what to do.

Ma told Mrs. Cohen that she thought I probably am just very sensitive to the weather and probably allergic to just about everything. Mrs. Cohen held Ma's hand to comfort her and told her, "As parents, we all have our challenges." She also told Ma that she could give her some good doctor recommendations and Ma said she would be forever grateful for that. I told Mrs. Cohen I was sorry about staining her napkin and she gave me a big hug and told me not to give it a second thought. It was kind of emotional and then Vinny KISSED me on the lips. In front of everybody!!! I guess he still likes me in spite of the dribbling blood at dinner and hearing about my health problems. I think my world has just changed!

Lauren, a "new person"

CHAPTER 26

MA AND LAUREN WERE HEADED TO HAPPILY EVER AFTER, which sold bridal, bridesmaids, and prom dresses. Ma wanted Lauren to look pretty; she was in the ninth grade, and this was her first high school formal. Ma wasn't invited to her own high school dances and was eager to have Lauren attend. Lauren surprised Ma with her effortless transition into high school. Lauren made all kinds of friends, who called her on the telephone, invited her to parties, and seemed to genuinely like her.

Despite her constant illness and ongoing aches and pains, Lauren was full of silly girl giggles and high school enthusiasm. She was even thinking of trying out to be a cheerleader. She seemed confident about venturing into a world without Ma, sure of herself in new ways, her ideas getting a bit too big for Ma's liking. Ma hoped that Lauren would at least have the good sense to dump Vinny, who had hung on for far too long. Vinny and his nosy mother. Ma wished for a senior on the football team. Even a junior. Somebody who was a man.

Happily Ever After was located across the road from Puppy Love, where Jack, the family dog (a.k.a. Ma's dog) had been purchased, and on the opposite end of the plaza that housed Très Suave: House of Beauty and Howard H. Howard Insurance. It was a busy and popular area of Westfield, and there was a long line at the intersection, with cars trying to make it across the wide avenue before the light turned red. Ma was in the left lane waiting her turn. Just as she pressed her foot on the gas to move the Caddy forward, a speedy blue Mustang in the adjacent lane scooted out in front, cutting her off. Ma slammed on the brakes and stopped at the long red light.

"What the hell was that?" Ma hollered. "Did you see that?"

Lauren had seen the Mustang cut them off. She had also seen who was in the driver's seat. "It's Lori Molinari," Lauren said.

"It can't be," Ma said.

But it was. And they watched the Mustang zoom across the avenue into the Très Suave: House of Beauty parking lot. Lauren could still make out the car well enough to see it pull up and stop.

"Did she see you?" Ma asked Lauren. "Did she see me?"

"I don't think so."

"What the hell is she doing in our neighborhood?"

Although Elizabeth and Country Club Lane were less than twelve miles away from Westfield, Ma had never crossed paths with Lori before and didn't intend to start now. Lori had no business driving a car on the same road as Ma, visiting the businesses Ma frequented. When the light turned green, Ma followed Lori's route and slowed in front of the Howard H. Howard's Insurance building. There it was, the little blue Mustang.

"This will not stand," Ma said.

The passenger was just getting out, dropping her keys and lipstick into a large leather bag. And indeed, Lauren had not made a mistake. It was Lori.

Ma didn't recognize the car, but she sure recognized Lori in tight raspberry pants and a clingy yellow sweater.

"Some married loser must have given her that car," Ma muttered.

"Are you going to say something to her?" Lauren asked. Ma wanted to screech; she wanted to sock Lori in the face, but she didn't. She waited for Lori to enter the House of Beauty and watched the receptionist escort her to the back of the salon.

"This is our neighborhood," Ma said. "She shouldn't be here."

Ma stepped out of the Caddy and walked over to the side of the blue Mustang, her key in her hand, erect and ready. She circled the Mustang once and then twice for good measure. A thin, deep scratch wrapped the car like ribbon. Lori would not know who vandalized her car, but she would no doubt interpret it as a warning. She would know not to come to the area again.

Ma joined Lauren in the car. Her anger was gone, washed away. "Are you ready to buy your dress?" she said to Lauren. "I want you to look beautiful."

Ma kept her word. Inside Happily Ever After, mother and daughter sorted through racks of dresses—dresses with feathers, sequins, and lace; some strapless and some off the shoulder, some with sweetheart necklines and some that plunged, some with pouf sleeves, and some with clingy bodices. There was a dress for everyone. There was a dress for Lauren. It was love at first sight. The dress was hanging on a rack off to the side when they spied it. It shimmered in the spectacular, iridescent hues of a peacock's plumes—aqua, teal, cobalt, and jade—an explosion of jewel-like colors that sparkled under the light, with delicate fine lines of gold etched into the blue, like veins in rare marble.

Lauren held her breath as she tried it on, hoping it would look as good on her small body as it had in the showroom. Hoping she would dazzle Vinny. When she walked out of the dressing room and did a twirl, even Ma took an extra breath. How her daughter was growing up, moving from a little girl to a delicate, exquisite woman.

"Well?" Lauren asked.

"It's nice," Ma said. Seeing her daughter glittered up like a fresh-faced starlet caught her off guard. It was more proof that Lauren was slipping away, faster than she could control. Ma was impressed by Lauren's intoxicating first blush of beauty, and even more delighted that they resembled one another, but it was impossible to feel a steady joy when there was also a relentless, nagging grief that ate away at her heart.

"Please? Can we get it?" Lauren asked.

How could Ma say no? How could she say yes or any answer in

between? So Ma didn't hesitate. Didn't try to argue. Didn't bargain down the staff. She simply wrote the check.

CHAPTER 27

THE MORNING OF THE FORMAL, before Lauren opened her eyes, she felt a familiar twinge. Her skin tingled and throbbed. She held her breath and went to confront her bedroom mirror. Standing before the glass, she absorbed the image reflected back at her—a sleepy, swollen girl. A puffy mess. It was nothing new, but confirmed her suspicions. Hives. Lots of them. Rosy red blotches with wide centers and spidery tentacles, reaching out, claiming her chest, upper arms, and legs. Worst of all they covered her face. More were on their way, waiting to erupt like rapid fire. First one, then another. *Pop. Pop. Pop.*

She dove back into bed, hiding her head inside a cavern formed by two pillows. She knew the routine all too well. Ma would give her the steroids that the doctors prescribed for these outbreaks, but the antidote wouldn't fight the red invasion fast enough, wouldn't erase the damage in time for the evening's event. She was crushed. Why of all the days in her life? Why did this have to happen to her now? It ruined everything.

Lauren rolled onto her side to take one more look at the spectacular dress, which hung over the back of the door, a pair of satin shoes custom dyed in a complementary blue resting on the floor below the gown. She had imagined dancing in the shoes for weeks. Tapping, hopping, and sliding to the sounds of Paula Abdul, R.E.M., Madonna, and LL Cool

J, a star-studded tape the music committee meticulously complied—a committee that Vinny, the only freshman member, was proud to be a part of.

There would be no dancing now. The tears started out as an erratic sputter, but once she gave in, they came full force, accented by breathy gulps and stuttering shrieks—a rush of grief splashing out onto her white satin pillowcase.

Ma heard the racket and peeked through the door. "What's all the drama?"

Lauren turned her head to face her mother. "Have a look for yourself," she cried. She raised one arm, the other, and both legs, offering up the evidence of her worst nightmare.

"What happened to you?" Ma asked, but it was not a question she expected Lauren to answer. She could tell what happened.

"What do you think?" Lauren fired at her mother, and Ma felt the sting of her daughter's nasty tone. She bristled briefly, but chose to let her daughter's anger bounce off her.

"What always happens to me?" Lauren wailed, thumping her fist against the pillow. "Every time! Every time! Every time!"

"We are not going to let this get the best of us," Ma coaxed, her voice soft with empathy. "Let's see what we can do."

"There's nothing to do. I can't go looking like this."

"Of course you can go," Ma encouraged. "So you won't look your best."

"Look my best? Did you see me? I'm hideous!" Lauren began to wail again, having admitted to the reality of her situation.

"You need to get a hold of yourself," Ma said. "This is a small thing that doesn't matter. You can still have a good time. Vinny will expect it. It wouldn't be nice to disappointment him, would it?"

Lauren considered her mother's question before she shouted back, "Vinny won't want to be seen with me. I look like a repulsive freak!"

"Just a few bumps." Ma knew she needed to corral her daughter's outburst into submission. "Look at me," Ma directed. "Look me in the eyes so I know you understand."

The instruction and firm voice caught Lauren's attention and she turned to face her mother, hoping that Ma could provide some magical solution.

"Every knock is a boost and God only gives us what we can handle," Ma told her. "You can handle this one. It's a piece of cake. Things could be much worse." Now that Ma warmed up, she was ready to roll. "What if you had to go through life with a cleft palate? Or a missing nose? What if your face and arms were burned beyond recognition, fried to the bone? What if a firecracker blew your eyes out? What if a shark gnawed your leg off? These things can happen. They happen every day and I think you ought to consider yourself lucky. I think you should count your lucky stars that all you have to complain about are a few little bumps."

The horrific images of Ma's everyday traumas quieted Lauren. She didn't want burned flesh or missing noses occupying space in her brain. "My friends will think I look ridiculous," she said, but her words were drained of their conviction; they were just the last bits of the tantrum as it petered out one little driblet at a time. "No one will want to talk to me."

Ma took this opportunity to make another point. "If you ask me, you have too many so-called friends. They can't all be true. Besides, if they're real friends and not just users, like I suspect most of them are, they won't let a few little hives get in the way of liking you."

"I wanted to look pretty," Lauren whispered.

"It's a dance; the lights will be low," Ma encouraged, and then Ma came up with the perfect solution. "I know what can fix this." She now had Lauren's full attention. "A little distraction is what we need—a bit of glitz." Ma left the room to retrieve the glitz, and Lauren shifted to her back and stared at the ceiling, wondering why her body always betrayed her.

Ma returned with a necklace and gently settled it on Lauren's bed— a diamond pendant in triple succession. Three circles of exceptional stones that captured the morning light, brilliant and glittering like a burst of fire. "This can make anyone dazzle."

"You'll let me wear this?" Lauren asked with caution, since Ma had never suggested anything like this before.

"Yes, I will. And there's one more thing." Ma slipped something out of a small velvet pouch. She unclasped her hand so that Lauren could see what matched the necklace in brilliance and beauty. There it was— Ma's diamond anniversary ring, the ring reported missing.

"Wasn't that stolen?" Lauren asked.

"That's right, but it mysteriously reappeared." Ma laughed. "From the looks of you this morning, it seems it has come back into our lives at just the right time."

"I can wear them? The ring and the necklace?" Lauren asked. The implications of the found ring were far beyond her. "Are you sure?"

"Yes," Ma said. "But you must be careful. I only bring these out for special occasions."

In early evening, when Vinny arrived in his rented baby blue tuxedo and jade cummerbund—an outfit coordinated to match Lauren's dress—he made his way to the Napolitano front door while his father, the evening's chauffeur, waited in the car. Lou welcomed Vinny into the foyer and stood with him until Ma and Lauren joined them. Vinny's first sight of Lauren, splotchy, red, and sparkling, was not what he expected. Unsure of what he was witnessing, he cocked his head to the side and asked, "Lauren, are you okay?"

Lauren knew she would have to give Vinny an out, let him off the hook. "If you don't want to take me to the dance I understand," she said, suspecting his verdict would send her back upstairs, weeping into her pillow.

Lou and Ma stayed silent too, all three waiting for Vinny's decision.

"I want to take you," Vinny told her without one trace of doubt. That was Vinny. Always true. Lauren knew that on this night she had at least one loyal friend.

"Take their picture," Ma said to Lou.

Lou remained where he was, standing on the sidelines. He want-ed to tell his daughter that she looked beautiful. He wanted to snap a photo of her in the gorgeous dress standing next to the fine young man. But she didn't look beautiful at all and he didn't want to record, to make permanent, how she looked this night—admitting that her discombob-ulated constitution was always messing things up, damaging her best memories. Lou put the camera down on the side table unused. "You'll have a good time," he said, hoping that what he told his daughter would be true. Ma said nothing.

Like any girl of fourteen covered in an uncomfortable rash, Lauren felt miserable, ugly, embarrassed, and insecure. Still, at her core, she also possessed her own treasure, which was as fiery and strong as her moth-er's diamonds. Its brightness radiated and always found the power to drown out any decaying depression—the vivacity that made her glow and beam and shimmer.

"Lauren, I'd like you to go to the dance with me," Vinny repeated to his best friend. Lauren took his hand and the two went out the door to the driveway, where Vinny's father waited in the car—ready to whisk them off to the formal, where they would dance right into their future.

CHAPTER 28

Tony worked nights as a waiter. When he had dropped out of high school the previous year, Lou surprised everyone and spoke up. He told Tony that a job, some kind of employment, was mandatory. Tony's hours at Famous Harry's were late. By the time he sent his last customer out the door, cleaned up his station, and stacked chairs, it was often close to two o'clock in the morning. With a wad of cash tips in his pocket, he was ready to frequent after-hours nightspots with other staff, outings organized by the head bartender, Sean, who possessed an endless supply of fake identification for those who found themselves in Tony's situation: underage.

Tony showed no interest in any vocation and slept most of each day, waking only to make it to his five o'clock shift at Famous Harry's. He was handsome, what Ma called "sharp," and attracted a bevy of female companions. Tony wasn't picky as long as the women (for his companions were not always girls of his age) presented as blonde. Tony placed no effort in courting these women, but they came around anyway. Many mornings, Ma would find a naked female or two streaking through the hall to the bathroom, or sprawled nude and cozy in Tony's childhood bed, snoring and hung over.

Louie tried to motivate his brother, but it only made Tony surly, angry with his more ambitious twin. Ma intervened and told Louie to stop pestering Tony and that maybe, just maybe, if Louie joined the rest of them in the real world, or managed to get laid now and then, he would start to get his own priorities straight.

Louie also stayed up late, but for different reasons. He was studying. At the end of high school, he gained admittance to three colleges—including Princeton, his first choice—but when he announced to Ma that he was vacillating between the study of Renaissance art, his longtime passion, and his new interest, medieval literature, Ma tried put a stop to such nonsense. "Why would you ever want to study a bunch of useless crap with a bunch of tight-assed highbrows?" Louie would not change his direction no matter how much Ma squawked. Even Lou did not understand his son's choices and offered no support. "For a kid who is supposed to be as smart as you are, you've grown up to be a numbskull," Ma scolded. Although Louie was not loud and kept to himself, he could be as stubborn and unwavering as Ma. He would not change course.

So that was that. Ma declared to the first valedictorian of the family that she was not paying for any college, would not spend one dime on "horseshit." Nonno and Nonna tried to intervene but only made matters worse by convincing Ma to stand her ground. To the shock of the high school administration, Louie Napolitano enrolled in the local community college and started a job working full-time at the library. He was knocking out his core classes one by one, saving his money with a relentless drive. He paid Ma her monthly rent, and then put the small amount that was left into his bank account, hidden safely away from his brother.

The night of Tony's car accident was the last straw, not for Ma or Lou, but for Louie. Tony had borrowed Ma's Caddy to take to work, something Louie was never allowed to do since Ma said he was the worst driver in the world. Instead, Louie used a bicycle for transport although he preferred to walk or ride the bus. The bicycle was a gift from Nonno that he received in middle school. He had long outgrown its small frame and was forced to lurch forward over the handlebars to make the pedals work. But Ma lent the Caddy out to Tony now and then, and on this night, after Famous Harry's closed, Tony proudly crammed some of the staff into Ma's car for barhopping. Around four o'clock in the morning, those who were left—Sean the bartender and two willing blondes—made their way back to the Caddy. They were two blocks from Famous Harry's when Sean suggested they return to the restaurant to carry on the party and pick up a few beers. Sean had a key. Tony, woozy and barely able to grasp the steering wheel, was able to maneuver the car back to Famous Harry's, but he was not able to find the brake or make the Caddy stop. It torpedoed through the front window and into the dining room, where it stalled directly in front of Sean's bar.

The burglar alarm sounded, blasted glass fractured, and the building's wood siding split and splintered. On impact, tables and chairs were pushed out of order, crumbled. Bar glassware tumbled off shelves, leaving messy mounds of wreckage. The police found the four passengers frozen in their seats, stunned. An ambulance came for the girls and Sean, who were bloodied and dazed; and Tony, who was unscathed and sassy, was escorted to the precinct where Ma and Lou, after several hours, managed to get him released and home.

Sunday morning, while Tony slept the incident off upstairs in his room, Ma was at her kitchen desk, trying to make the episode go away, trying to locate her contacts at the police department, including Detective Steve, who she found out was on indefinite disability after a lunatic hoodlum bit off the top of his ear.

"Well, now what?" Louie asked his mother. "Are you going to finagle this too?"

"What kind of snotty remark is that?" Ma barked. "We're lucky he's alive. Thank God your brother wasn't killed."

"Ma, isn't it even more important that he could have killed a lot of other people?" Louie answered, with a boldness that was unlike his usual quiet manner. "Don't you get it? Tony was drunk. He was the driver."

"Aren't you even glad he's alive?" Ma asked.

"That's not the point." Louie's frustration with his mother's logic could no longer lie dormant inside of him.

"Well, what's the point, Mr. Smarty Pants?" Ma shouted.

"He's out of control, Ma!" And there they were, his true thoughts unleashed. "That's the point. That's been the point for years."

"Have you done one damn thing to help him out of his slump? You're buried in your pompous studies and give him no attention. What have you done for him? Nothing, that's what. Nothing."

"What have I done for him? What have you done for him, Ma? I've been watching what you've done to him for years."

Ma would not tolerate Louie's contemptuousness. She didn't need his newfound impertinence. Not now. "Your brother has some problems, that's all, just like lots of boys do, just like your father did, something your frilly head doesn't understand. Did you ever, for even one second, lift your head out of your books to help him? Your own twin? Don't you dare put that guilt on me. You're selfish through and through. I have never been able to figure you out, Louie. I am ashamed to call you my son."

She finally said it to him, an unspoken truth he suspected for years. "That's no secret, Ma. No newsflash at all. I guess it's time to get my selfish ass out of this house."

"Don't threaten me, Louie. We've got bigger problems to deal with."

"It's no threat." Louie was done. The argument no longer fueled his buried fury. His path was clear. He knew he would not stay one more day in his mother's house.

"Good riddance," Ma said, but her son's behavior was so odd and unlike him, it threw her off, made her feel dizzy and weak. She misjudged him. Hadn't seen this coming, had never realized that he was the one to worry about.

Since he didn't own a suitcase, Louie grabbed a large black trash bag and went upstairs to his room to claim a few possessions. He placed his schoolbooks and journals in the bag, along with his glasses, one pair of jeans, three T-shirts, and his sneakers. Lauren stood in the doorway, wide-eyed, watching her brother shove his belongings into the bag.

"Louie," she begged. "Please."

He felt the deep tug from his little sister's request, but he couldn't honor it, could not stay. "I'm sorry," he told her. He slung the plastic bag over his shoulder and raced down the stairs, through the foyer, and out the front door. He did not say good-bye to his father, nor to his twin— who, despite everything, truly was and always would be an integral part of him. He walked past the houses of Belle Haven, out of the neighborhood. He didn't know where he would go, but he knew this much: he never belonged in Belle Haven and he would get as far away from Ma as possible.

CHAPTER 29

Dear Journal, Day of Doom.

Day of Dread.

Louie's gone!!!

What will I ever do without him?

My heart is a black hole.

Lauren

CHAPTER 30

As LAUREN'S HIGH SCHOOL DAYS CAME AND WENT, she busied herself with a growing gang of girlfriends and Vinny, who remained constant and as devoted as ever. Her grades weren't great, never approaching the level of Louie's, but they were steady. And although she still continued to accumulate a fair number of sick days, she pressed on, determined to do the best she could.

Since Louie's departure, Ma put up fewer protests, raised fewer obstacles to Lauren's social life. Ma did not feel well. Three days after Louie ran off, Ma fell to the floor, doubled over with unbearable pain, and spent three days in the hospital. Bleeding ulcers were the explanation. Since then, Ma took to retiring to her bedroom by half past seven each evening, and Lauren was left to chat on the phone hour after hour.

Tony had been out of work since the car accident last year. Famous Harry's had not pressed charges, but Ma promised to reimburse the restaurant for the substantial damages the insurance company did not cover. The payment was pending. Sean had fared better. He was able to keep his bartending job because the owner (the "Famous" Harry) could not deny the numbers, recognizing Sean's large and loyal following.

Sean stopped by the house to hang with Tony now and again. His visits became more frequent after he had a new view of Lauren, sixteen and beginning to appear less and less like a scrawny little girl.

It was Ma who noticed the way Sean took in Lauren, looked her up and down in unsubtle gulps. It was also Ma who invited Sean to dinner on Friday night, a night that almost always included Vinny. Vinny's weekly appearance was not an arrangement that Ma liked or encouraged. She just preferred to tolerate Vinny in her own house as opposed to letting Lauren traipse over to the Cohens yet again, spending even more time with those stuffy, interfering parents.

Vinny arrived late that Friday night. Sean, Tony, and Lou were already gathered around the table that was covered with Ma's customary Italian takeout. Ma was telling Sean about Jack's canine training class, when Vinny rang the bell and Lauren skipped off to let him in.

Jack, the cream-and-apricot puppy, never connected with Lou after their initial meeting. There was a solid, mutual distrust, and Ma took Jack, her brother's namesake, as her own. Despite the fact that Jack was a thirty-pound cockapoo, a docile breed, Ma decided the dog should learn guard dog basics and signed him up for a class that taught attack command training in Japanese. The instructor, a former Marine who schooled ferocious breeds like the Doberman, German shepherd, and Rottweiler, scoffed when Ma first presented the cockapoo. Jack surprised them all. He was small but tenacious and obedient, reacting to Ma's every command.

Sean didn't buy Ma's story. "Come on now," Sean teased Ma, "I can't believe that a little squirt like Jack could ever attack anything."

Perhaps it was the challenge Sean presented her, perhaps it was the fact that Ma felt obliged to defend Jack's dignity, or perhaps Ma noticed that Sean looked mighty fine in his tight jeans. Whatever it was, Ma turned to Sean and said, "I suggest you watch this."

As Vinny approached the table, Ma whispered a Japanese command into Jack's ear. Jack flew off Ma's lap and jumped onto Vinny. He growled and snarled at Vinny. He nipped and yipped, baring his teeth.

"Jack, stop," Lauren shouted at the dog. "What's gotten into you?" The dog would not stop. He fought his way above Vinny's tennis shoe and bit his ankle—one, two, three times.

Even Tony perked up and joined in. "The damn dog finally lost it!"

Ma was hooting like it was the most comical thing she ever witnessed. Lou tried to wave the dog off Vinny with his hand. The gesture made zero impact. Jack carried on. Realizing that the dog wasn't about to give up and was out to harm him, Vinny began to look pale and frightened. He tried to shake Jack off.

Sean stood from the table as if he had been waiting to make his entrance. He scooped up Jack, holding the wiggling and wild cockapoo by the back of the neck. "Why you little devil," he scolded the dog. "Leave this poor kid alone." Jack relaxed into complete submission while the family, amazed and awed, watched Sean calm the dog. Like magic.

"I hope you don't mind," Sean said to Ma.

"Not at all," she answered, her face and chest flushed with arousal.

"Are you okay, kid?" Sean asked Vinny, who could only give an affirmative nod.

Sean handed the dog over to Ma. "Good boy," Ma whispered to Jack. She offered him a liver snap treat and cooed in a singsong voice, "That's my baby, baby, baby."

"I am so sorry," Lauren said to Vinny. "I don't know why Jack would behave like that."

And Sean winked at Ma. "You are one spunky Mama."

There was something magnetic about Sean. He was slick and polished. Irresistibly smooth. Ma was a fan. Not just for his husky, broad-shouldered good looks, which were quite arresting, but for his aggressive, stand-up-and-take-charge energy. Sean wasn't taking a backseat to anyone. He looked at Ma, his high eyebrows dramatically arched over impish grey eyes. He was ready for any prank, anything she could dish out. Sean was familiar and comforting to her—he epitomized the Irish Bronx.

At the table, Sean placed himself between Lauren and Vinny. The comparison was hard to ignore once Vinny and the larger-than-life Sean sat side by side. Vinny became childlike, pimply, and insignificant. Sean ate with gusto; he was voracious and vocal—licking, slurping, sucking—unashamed of his substantial appetite and the raw, natural sounds he emitted while enjoying his meal. In the commotion, Vinny lost all appetite and was left to stare at his plate, humiliated and overwhelmed.

"Come on, kid. Eat up." Sean elbowed Vinny. "I think you need your strength." Everybody laughed, except Lauren, who worried for Vinny. She noticed for the first time how soft he was, nervous and filled with anxiety, how easily bowled over.

"So how old are you, Vinny?" Sean asked. "About twelve?"

Vinny hesitated, but answered, "I'm sixteen."

"Are you kidding me?" asked Sean. "No shit?"

"That's right, I'm sixteen," confirmed Vinny. "Just like Lauren."

"Relax, kid. Everything is A-OK." Sean chuckled and sent Ma another special wink.

Sean was first to finish. He dabbed red sauce off his broad chin with Vinny's untouched napkin and tossed it to the center of his own plate. "Well, that hit the spot. Thank you, Napolitano family. If you all don't mind, I'd like to take your lovely daughter out for some dessert."

Lauren balked, and halfway through an uneasy excuse Ma interrupted, "Lauren would love to go. How nice of you to ask."

"Vinny's still eating," Lauren said to Ma. "Let's not rush him. He's our guest."

Sean was used to getting what he wanted, when he wanted. Lauren's minor protests didn't bother him. "No problem. I'd say Mr. Sixteen is not too hungry tonight, so we'll drop him at home on our way out."

"It's okay," Vinny said to Lauren. "I'm pretty tired anyway."

"I guess so," Sean confirmed, giving Vinny a solid man-slap on the back. "I thought that little dog might make you pee your pants."

Unlike Ma, Vinny did not like Sean. He said nothing in the car and after Sean dropped him off, Vinny stood on his front porch, demeaned and defeated. It had been one rotten day. His ankle was sore and throbbing. Jack had no doubt left a dental imprint. He knew he should go inside the house and check out how much skin Jack had torn off, how deep the bite went, and apply an antibiotic, but he avoided it. Inside, his mother and father would want to know why he was home early and why he was so gloomy. He didn't know what to tell them. Vinny was sure that something momentous had transpired this night, but he couldn't begin to articulate it. So he slumped onto the porch chair and watched his girlfriend speed off with a handsome twenty-six-year-old in an orange Chevy Corvette.

Sean had barged into their lives unannounced and without warning, making Vinny Cohen invisible. For Vinny, life seemed horribly unfair. He understood this much: Lauren would venture away from him,. Maybe not tomorrow, or next week, or even next month, but she would be gone from his life. Poof! Just like that.

CHAPTER 31

LAUREN'S SENIOR YEAR IN HIGH SCHOOL provided a smorgasbord of emotions for Ma. Lauren's hive breakouts continued full force. Ma said it was the stale air that flowed throughout the large high school, a building that surely carried an assortment of airborne diseases and contaminants. Ma suspected that mold collected in the crevices and corners of the halls, potent and ready to attack her daughter's delicate immune system. And then there were the students. After all, the building was populated with the public, filled with all sorts of unclean teenagers and their dirty habits.

Lauren's formidable outbreaks, sore joints, and chronic stomach nuisances did not keep her from attracting a slew of friends. Ma did not appreciate the attention her daughter received and was aggravated by the giddy, giggling girls pulling Lauren this way and that, surrounding her with clouds of nonsense and noisy chatter. Ma knew female friendships weren't genuine—not something to trust or count on.

Lauren's popularity gave her a growing strength, and her all-consuming friendships with Katie and Layla made for an inseparable trio. Ma felt sure the girls egged Lauren on, were the reason her daughter was bold and mouthy, offering her opinion when Ma did not want it and then clinging to her point of view when Ma expected her to back down. Lauren buzzed with future plans now—all kinds of crazy-ass thoughts like college, pie-in-the-sky careers, and moving away—none of which were acceptable or realistic to Ma.

But Ma was also proud of Lauren and her pretty, feminine stature, her undeniable resemblance to Ma. With the exception of Lauren's nose, which had become more pronounced since puberty, Ma could recognize herself in her daughter. It was the nose she would have to watch. It was without question Lou's nose, which Ma felt might be waiting to burst forth and expand across her daughter's perfect face.

Lou's nose or not, Lauren snagged the charming Sean. Both Ma and her canine sidekick, Jack, were delighted with Sean's ongoing presence in Lauren's life and the Napolitano house. Sean made himself at home, and since he still lived with his own parents, sharing space with relatives never bothered him. Nothing was off-limits to Sean, not even Lauren's bedroom.

Deep down, Lauren was not committed to her older, handsome boyfriend and sometimes she missed Vinny and felt bad that he was so easily deleted from her life. Lauren came to accept Sean as a familiar part of her life and routine. So did Ma. Ma encouraged the alliance, Lou kept quiet and sided with Ma, and Tony glommed on to him with high hopes for connections in a world he only knew from the periphery. Lauren's girlfriends admired her grown-up relationship, and they frequently turned to her for expert advice about daily high school romance—dramas they could only play out with inexperienced and awkward high school boys. Katie and Layla made it a habit to come to the house just to stare. Sean was a sight to behold.

Lauren was no longer bothered by the way Sean smelled. At first the scent was overpowering; the long-lasting odor would cause her to inch away and turn her face from him. Like with Lou in earlier years, there was a constant aroma of marijuana, but Sean also liked fragrances and colognes which announced his presence before he entered a room. He collected a wide assortment and assembled the bottles across his bedroom dresser, where his mother made them part of her daily housework, respectfully wiping the glass clean, keeping them free of dust. As some people appreciated wine, Sean understood the subtleties of the scents, the blends and mixtures—intoxicating hints of jasmine, spice, sandalwood, musk, and cedar. He favored "Acqua di Gio Pour Homme" by Giorgio Armani, Calvin Klein's "Obsession for Men," and "Le Male" by Jean Paul Gaultier. The colognes were an expensive, necessary indulgence for Sean, an integral part of his virility.

In the beginning, Lauren was easily directed by Sean. A decade older, he seemed worldly and sure, and he loved to present her with one gift after another—a pink topaz ring, a diamond bracelet, a Gucci handbag, a cashmere sweater. But as she progressed through her senior year, that same sureness made Lauren start to feel as if Sean viewed her as a child. In fact, his pet name for her was "baby doll." While she knew little about his whereabouts, he was privy to her daily schedule. If he arrived while she was chatting on the phone to Katie or Layla, he would slip the telephone receiver out of her hands without any courtesies to the girlfriend on the line. "That's enough of that," he would say.

Nonno and Nonna seemed to be the only family members who were not enthusiastic about Sean. Nonno had an uneasy feeling about Sean and did not find him a suitable companion for his young granddaughter. "What is it that you do?" Nonno questioned Sean, but only received a short reply of, "A little of this, a little of that." It was true that Sean still worked at the bar, but there were also rumors of probation and weekly check-ins with, as Sean called them, "the Feds."

Nonno had taken to showing up at the house. He had not been well for some time. Since Lou's accident he seemed to suffer from apathy and a chronic depression. He no longer tended to the garage the way he had in the past and business was off. He was hospitalized in the spring with internal bleeding and received a blood transfusion. The doctors discussed the possibility of intestinal cancer, but Nonno chose not to pursue the matter.

Nonna did not join her husband on his jaunts to Westfield. She felt troubled in Ma's house and sent Nonno with tokens of food and greetings of love instead. When Nonno did appear, walking through the front door like he owned the place, Ma found an errand to run or locked herself in her bedroom complaining of headache or fever. Lou would chat with his father, but it was Lauren who Nonno came to see.

For months, Nonno stopped by the house with college catalogues and brochures that Lauren piled in her room. Combined, they were a travelogue of higher learning, representing all regions of the country, schools small and large, public and private. Lauren's grades were not good enough to let her consider the top tier, but her record was satisfactory enough to consider something with less prestige. "A solid state school," Nonno said.

Lauren read every page of every catalogue, not missing a word, memorizing school departments, admission requirements, and course offerings. She was most interested in broadcast journalism.

"Ma and Sean don't seem to like the idea of college," she told her grandfather. "Ma doesn't think I'll do well." Nonno grabbed her hands, harder than she expected. "Sure, everybody's got something to say, but I know you can do it. And because I know this, I will help you pay for it."

When Lauren revealed Nonno's generous offer to her parents, Ma only said, "That'll be the day. He's a tightwad through and through."

Let him pass on Lou's inheritance, Ma thought. The building was what was really worth money. Ma barely tolerated the fact that her father-in-law was coming around again. She didn't like him slinking through the house with information that pointed Lauren in the wrong direction, an opinion she often voiced to Sean. "What's good enough for us, Seanie, doesn't seem to suit your hoity-toity girlfriend. She thinks she's something, doesn't she? You must be spoiling her a bit too much." And Sean would slip his strong hand around Ma's little waist and tighten his grip. "Don't you worry, gorgeous," Sean reassured, "I've got plans for your little girl." Ma felt the flush, the pressure and warmth of Sean's fingers, and she would recall the moment long after he moved away from her.

Sean and Ma had become pals. He would often sit with her in the kitchen. Lauren, bored by their banter, found excuses to remove herself to her room for homework. Tony kept company with the TV, and if Lou stayed, he was quiet, barely there. Ma and Sean created a game they called "What's Worse Than This?" Both true crime aficionados, they could go round and round, topping the other with the details of horrific crimes. The game's only rule was that the crime must be true— Ma suspected that Sean sometimes cheated and made his stories up. Simple assault, murder, or clichéd crimes of passion were not good enough material for this game. They relished the freakish, outlandish examples of heinous behavior. They went back and forth, exchanging ghastly tales. Sean described to Ma, in slow and thorough terms, the plight of a woman who, when insulted about her weight by a cousin at a three-day family wedding, stabbed the relation to death. "That's not a good one, Seanie," Ma said, disappointed that Sean had come up with something so lame. "That's all you've got?"

"Hold on," Sean cautioned. "Hold on." His tone promised there was more to come. And Sean delivered. It seems the criminal in Sean's story was so offended that she not only stabbed her cousin repeatedly, but also dismembered, seasoned, and cooked him. She served the dead victim to unwitting relatives on the third day as her contribution to a grand, celebratory feast—giving whole new meaning to "family meal."

"Top that!" Sean challenged Ma. Ma was up for the competition, charging back with the details of a man who hacked his interior designer to death because she had the audacity to criticize his rather sparse décor. He used the designer's blood to paint abstract art over his bare, beige walls.

"Not bad," said Sean to Ma.

They both agreed that the hotelier who burned his wife in a bonfire because she would not give up smoking was a first-rate entry. The wife apparently signed a prenuptial agreement with an amendment limiting her to six cigarettes per week, and her death was a result of not honoring her agreement. Since both Ma and Sean knew the story, it was disqualified from the game.

Sean was good company, and Ma was not bothered by the fact that he was not employed in a traditional manner, a concern that was beginning to trouble Lauren. Sean had not disclosed the specific details of his past to Ma or Lauren, but Lauren had heard rumors of his being on probation for a heist involving money laundering and Las Vegas. Lauren suggested he find a job other than working at the bar and his other obligations that called him out in the night. She envisioned something more traditional, something where he didn't work all hours.

"Don't I treat you right, baby doll?" he would ask her. "Don't I lavish you with goodies?" She admitted that he did.

In the middle of the school year, Sean bought himself a present and picked Lauren up from school in a new Mercedes. "I thought now that you're almost a high school graduate, I'd better make sure you are riding in style."

Katie and Layla stood on the pavement in front of the school, marveling at Sean and his new wheels. They thought Lauren was the luckiest girl in the world. Lauren was less impressed with Sean's new purchase and responded with, "How can you afford this?" There had been little scraps of information and rumors—fraud, gambling, drug sales—doled out in bits and pieces, nothing Lauren could piece together as a whole, nothing that made sense. When she mentioned it to Ma, she was told, "I think we could all learn a thing or two about making ends meet from Seanie."

Ma began to wear Lauren's clothing: the faded jeans and cashmere sweaters. She borrowed jewelry that Sean bestowed upon her daughter. Sean didn't mind. "Just like sisters," he said. It didn't really bother Lauren either. She would do anything to please Ma and generally tolerated her antics. Lauren knew better than to speak out against Ma. If she did, she knew she would get in big trouble. What did get to Lauren were the jokes at her expense—she had become the inspiration for Sean and Ma's pranks. The yearbook incident was the last straw.

As the school year wound down, Lauren came home one afternoon to find her brand-new yearbook on her bed, opened to the page of her senior photograph. The photo was a good likeness, her blonde hair parted on one side, her eyes communicating irresistible warmth. She looked happy. Underneath her photo was the class tribute. Lauren Napolitano: "MOST POPULAR SENIOR." But the photo had been tampered with, altered with black marker over the glossy page. Little devil horns were drawn into her blonde hair so that they popped out just above her head. A thick, curvy mustache wiggled under her nose, and a pointed goatee was placed at her chin. She could not believe anyone would mar her yearbook, disfigure her face.

"Who did this?" Lauren flung the book onto the kitchen table where Ma and Sean sat drinking cocktails.

"What are you talking about?" Ma asked.

"This. This is what I'm talking about," Lauren hollered. "My yearbook is ruined with some stupid devil horns. It's all marked up." Lauren held the defaced yearbook up for them to see.

"Well, how would I know what happened?" Ma inquired.

Lauren would not back down. "I think you do know."

"Listen, Little Miss Popularity, I don't know who did it, but I guess if the shoe fits. . ." Ma teased.

That made Sean laugh. "I think what you mean to say is . . . if the horns fit. . ."

Lauren slammed the book closed between them and ran back upstairs to her room. She threw herself on her childhood bed while her mother and boyfriend poured another drink. Eventually, Ma went upstairs to retrieve Lauren, and found her daughter lying facedown on the bed clutching the old Cabbage Patch doll that Nonna gave her when they first moved to Belle Haven. The doll had frayed over the years. The thinning fabric barely covered its signature bulging cheeks, and the black eyes had lost their deep saturation and were now a dirty grey. It was Lauren's only cuddle toy, and Ma always resented Nonna for bringing it into her home, knowing full well that Ma objected to dolls and stuffed animals.

"I don't know what happened to your yearbook," she told Lauren, "but it's no big deal. Somebody's just being funny."

"Well, who is that somebody?" Lauren charged.

"Who cares? Come on downstairs for dinner. Sean's waiting and you don't make a man like that wait," Ma said without answering the question.

Lauren refused to look at her mother; only the doll stared at Ma—straight on, with that insipid grin. "Why worry about a little high school photo?" Ma asked. "You're almost eighteen, a woman, the girlfriend of a real man, and you'd rather cling to some lousy doll like a baby. It's time to throw that horrendous thing out."

"It's a present from Nonna and I think she's beautiful."

"Have you looked at that thing? It was ugly then and it's even uglier now."

Lauren embraced the doll, crushing its familiar pillow-like body against her own in an embrace the doll received countless times before.

"I have a feeling there's an engagement ring in your future if you play your cards right," Ma said. "So get rid of that thing."

Ma snatched the doll out of Lauren's arms and ran back down to the kitchen. Lauren, taken aback, had never seen her mother run before. She chased after her. "Give it back," Lauren whined.

Ma ran into the kitchen as if charging toward the end zone, ready to score a major touchdown. Sean looked up and Ma tossed the doll. "Catch," she told him.

As any good teammate would, Sean caught the doll, while Lauren, the clear opposition, leaped into the air to claim her back.

"Baby doll, baby doll," Ma sang out. "Oh, baby doll, oh baby doll. I'm wondering if there is anything but nonsense in your head."

And Ma, now in possession of the cherished object, held the doll by its legs, flagging it against the kitchen table with a hard rap. Once. Twice. Three times. The doll took it without resistance. *Whack. Whack.* Still, the smiling face remained—frozen, unharmed, and oddly out of place with the violence being unleashed upon it. The doll's resilience amazed them all, and Ma took to the challenge, slamming the doll's head harder and harder.

"Whoa! Baby, baby," said Sean, amused that Ma was going all out.

"What are you doing?" Lauren said. She stopped yelling and turned pale.

"I'm trying to see if there is anything but a load of nonsense in this head." The doll's head whacked against the table. Again. And again.

"Cut it out, Ma. It's not funny," Lauren said.

Ma thought it was funny and kept on. Lou, who said little during the shenanigans, moved out onto the deck for a cigarette. He hated commotion and when it started up he would slink away and become a shadow in the quieter parts of the house, making himself invisible. He also knew better than to go against Ma.

Ma began to toss the doll into the air, juggling it up and down. The little cloth bundle remained unfazed and accepted all treatment without injury.

In the end, Ma triumphed over the doll. She took a kitchen knife and sawed the small head off, leaving the severed section to plop to the floor, its stitched grin intact. Jack scooted over to inspect the head. He sniffed it and clamped on, claiming it as a new plaything. The pup shook his head and started to pull the white stuffing out. It was only then that the doll's face collapsed—its bulging cheeks sagged, sunken and flat. The smile was no more.

CHAPTER 32

Since the yearbook and doll incident, Lauren felt a growing irritability toward Sean. The mood lay festering and sore, and she was unable to shake it off. She wondered why Sean joined in when Ma teased her. Why didn't he stand up for her? As usual, the joke was at her expense. As usual, Sean responded to her concerns with, "Girl, you need to chill. It's all in fun."

Ma sensed Lauren's diminished interest in Sean and anger toward her, a pulling away from both mother and boyfriend. She was planning to see Lauren married soon, and tried to remedy the situation by buoying up her daughter's spirits with a new car for her eighteenth birthday: a silver Chevy Camaro. Lauren was thrilled with her mother's grand gesture and loved the car. Sean did not. "It's a girl car," he said. Sean preferred to do the driving and didn't want to ride in the Chevy as a passenger, or, even worse, be seen as the driver. Lauren's new gift stayed parked in the Napolitano driveway. Unused.

Sean liked to drive his Mercedes. He felt an undeniable rush when he sped down the road at racing speeds. Lauren liked it less and less. The aimless driving with no particular destination in mind, a favorite pastime for Sean, bored her now. She felt trapped on these excursions and longed to have somewhere to go. She pressed him more and more, reviewing familiar territory of the same tired, stale questions and concerns.

"It was a fuckin' doll," Sean responded for what felt like the ninety-ninth time. "Why are you hell-bent on busting my ass? How many girls your age ride around with a guy like me in a car like this?"

"How do you pay for these things?" Lauren asked. "I don't think you make that much at the bar."

"Here we go again," Sean said. "I can't work just anywhere. You know that. You know the circumstances. But you don't hear me whining. I've made my way. And you, baby doll, don't seem to complain about the benefits."

"I want to go to college." She let it out. Now she had to tell him what she had been hiding for over a week. "I've got three college acceptances. They came in the mail last week. I want to choose one."

"Oh yeah?" Sean asked, surprised at her success. "Where?"

"California, New Hampshire, and Georgia."

"You're kidding? Listen, college is overrated, baby doll. It's not for you."

"I want to try," she said. For the first time, the idea seemed to present itself as a reality, something she might actually do.

"So you want to go off somewhere?"

"Maybe."

"It's just a pipe dream," Sean said, feeling annoyed by the obvious. "Why waste time and money?"

"I want to see what I can do."

"What about me? What am I supposed to do while you're off in Georgia?"

Lauren shrugged. "I haven't thought it all out yet."

"No, you haven't thought it out at all. Why study something you'll never get a job at? Broadcast journalism? Business management? Give me a break. You'll never make money at that." The new information seemed to penetrate now. Lauren not only applied to schools out of state; she was also considering attending. In an instant, Sean slowed the car to a stop and pulled to the side of the road. He sat and said nothing as cars continued to pass with a rhythmic swish.

"What's wrong?" Lauren asked. "Why are we stopping?"

"It's just a pipe dream," he said.

Sean's words were the same, but Lauren saw the shift in his mood. "What's wrong?

"Say it," he ordered her.

"Say what?"

"It's just a pipe dream."

"No," she answered. It was a defiance Sean would not accept. This was not a cute, little girl tantrum. This was something else. This was now a betrayal.

Sean turned toward Lauren. Reaching across, he pushed her back in the seat, pinning her shoulders so that she could not sit up. "Are you trying to be better than me?"

"Of course not." The abrupt action surprised her; his hands pressing against her shoulders hurt and she wanted to sit up, but she wouldn't bend that easy. He would not get his way this time.

"Then say it," he said.

"Come on, Sean, I don't want to."

"Say it." He did not yell, but his few words were precise, razor sharp.

"No, I will not say that."

"Enough now. I think your Ma might be right. You're getting snotty."

"Let me up."

"Say it first."

"No, and you cannot force me."

"I'm not letting you go until you admit it."

"Admit what?"

"That you're dreaming." The game had gone on too long for Sean. It was no longer a back-and-forth struggle. Lauren recognized a new fierceness in his eyes, a determination that cautioned her not to proceed, to let it go. She knew it was best not to respond and to let him calm down. She dropped it.

"Okay. It's just a dream," she said. "I'll never make it through college."

Sean did not hear her change in direction, did not recognize her retreat. "Say it," he repeated.

"I did say it," she said, and then to appease him even more, she added, "I'm not smart enough for college."

Lauren's response was too late. She had pushed him. He was no longer hearing her; his thoughts traveled elsewhere. Her ongoing complaints and plans, once easily dismissed, were piled up like heaps of clutter, trash that he had to clear out. "I think the real reason you want to go is so you can meet a bunch of Southern college boys," he said, as if he finally understood her motives. "You want to fuck a Georgia college boy, is that it?"

"No. Why would you think that?"

"That's it. Isn't it?" Sean placed both hands around her throat. He could feel Lauren's small bones against his fingers, her neck stiff and tense. "If you even look at one of those college types, I'll kill you."

Lauren closed her eyes. She was in over her head. She had pushed him too far and now she was lost.

"You got it?" he asked.

She was unable to speak, so she nodded. Perhaps it was the terror in her eyes, the realization that her boyfriend would harm her, the draining of her dreams, or her total submission. Whatever it was that did it, it was the promise Sean needed. He opened his fingers wide, shaking his hands to release not only his grip from around her neck, but the tension between them.

"Then say it," he ordered one last time.

"I would never even look at anyone else, Sean."

"Okay then, as long as we are clear."

"We're clear, Sean."

Lauren spoke the truth. She was very clear.

CHAPTER 33

Nonno appeared at the house the next day to discuss Lauren's college acceptances. Without emotion, Lauren told them all—Nonno, Tony, and her parents—that she was breaking up with Sean. Nonno was the first to speak. "No more. No more will my granddaughter spend time with a hoodlum. She's too good for that. Good. You're done with him."

"I don't know why he would behave like that," Ma said. "I'm sure he didn't mean anything by it. Besides every knock is a boost."

"No. That's it now," Nonno said to Ma, with a warning that was not to be crossed. "It must be finished."

"Absolutely," Lou said to his father. Ma looked at Lou and saw him as a little boy, agreeing with his father without question.

Nonno stayed for supper, and Ma phoned in their usual Sunday meal from the local Italian restaurant, Milano's. Lou picked it up and spread the food out over the table. No one ate much and everyone quickly found a way to scamper away from the table. The phone rang five times during dinner and they all knew it was Sean, the rings shouting into their supper. Ma rose to answer and Nonno stopped her.

"We are eating," he said. "There will be no phone calls."

Sean called Lauren later that evening, but she refused to take his call. "Be patient," Ma told him. "Every couple has these little tiffs." He tried again one hour later and was told that Lauren had gone to bed. "Call again tomorrow," Ma said.

Early the next morning, it was Nonna who called, wailing into the phone at Lou. Nonno had been taken to the hospital. He had collapsed on the bathroom floor. Lou, Ma, and Lauren joined Nonna at the hospital, and by the time Sean called the house, only Tony was at home, sleeping off a cocaine-induced stupor. The phone rang and rang and rang. Sean's calls were left unanswered.

If the Napolitano family had been looking, they might have seen the signs, but they hadn't and were not prepared for the news. Nonno died. The doctors theorized about internal bleeding, past blood transfusions, cancer, depression—the whole mix. No explanation would comfort Nonna. The rituals around the death took several days. Lou wanted the family to stay with Nonna. She was inconsolable, and Lou did not want his mother to be alone.

Sean called the house several times, reaching Ma only once when she was there to collect some extra clothes. "Nonno passed," she explained. "Be patient with Lauren; it will take a little time." But Sean was not a patient guy, not someone who waited, and certainly not someone who waited for an eighteen-year-old girl grieving for her old Italian grandfather. He repeatedly phoned Lauren's girlfriends, Katie and Layla, to bully them or ask them out, whichever worked first, but soon grew tired of their goofy, indirect answers. Within a week, Sean was sighted with someone new.

Lauren was glad to be forgotten. High school graduation came and went without any fanfare, and she did not meet the response deadline for any of the three colleges. She didn't notice when Ma moved the acceptance letters from the kitchen table to the trash, or if she did, she didn't care. Katie and Layla planned their futures: Katie at New York University and Layla at Rutgers. Lauren was weary. Her friends prodded her to come out with them, enjoy a bit of summer, take a trip to the Shore. She refused for weeks, then finally gave in and agreed to meet at Katie's house to drive them all to the Shore. As Lauren closed the door to her room, a bathing suit and the keys to her Chevy Camaro in hand, Ma appeared from her own bedroom and joined her in the hallway at the top of the stairs.

"Are you running out without cleaning up your room?" Ma asked.

"Sorry, I forgot," Lauren said. She knew that her room was a mess, but she didn't have the energy to do anything about it lately. Clothes spilled out of the open dresser drawers; the bed was unmade, with sheets that were rumpled and dirty. The waste can was tipped on its side; used tissues dotted the carpet. The old college catalogues lay open, strewn about, but no longer beckoned or inspired.

"And you were just going to leave it for me?" Ma asked. "The maid. The maid of the house!" Lauren sensed a rumbling in Ma. She could feel Ma's anger rising.

"I'm sorry," Lauren said. "I'll clean it up."

"Forget it now."

"I'm sorry, Ma," Lauren repeated, hoping to stop any issues between them. "I'll clean it up."

"So now you're parading off with those foolish friends," Ma said— a statement, not a question. "You could have had a very different life." The subject of Sean had not been discussed between them, not since Nonno died. The breakup discussion was left hanging, like a needed house repair that went ignored because the fixing would take far too long or could potentially open up greater damage with unexpected and crippling costs.

"I don't know why you had to push him away," Ma said.

"Ma, he tried to choke me."

"I imagine you provoked him."

"Ma? He put his hands on my throat. He threatened to kill me."

"I'm just saying you must have pushed him to the edge," Ma continued. "There are two sides to every story."

Lauren considered her mother's accusation. "Ma, I didn't do anything." The comment begged for understanding.

"That's the problem," Ma said without a fleck of sympathy. "You didn't do anything. A man like that needs attention. And you just threw it all away. He was the most handsome man you're ever going to meet."

Lauren was tired of hearing about Sean's looks, as if being good-looking gave him a pass for bad behavior. "Who cares if he's handsome?" she snapped, and then she told her mother what she had felt for a long time. "He was a jerk. A big loser."

Lauren's message struck a sour chord, a message so off-putting and dissonant to Ma, that she instinctively raised her hand to strike her daughter. "What an ungrateful bitch you are." The slap was swift and unexpected for them both. Lauren stood stunned and still, but the action propelled Ma into a storm of rage.

"Get the hell out of my house," she said, giving Lauren a shove that sent her tumbling down the first five stairs. Lauren grabbed onto the banister and stood up, reaching to pick up her dropped car keys, abandoning the bathing suit that had fallen from her hand.

"Leave your keys right there," Ma screamed. "You can't take your car. That belongs to me."

Lauren dropped the keys and made her way to the bottom of the staircase while Ma stood at the top, hurling bombs—sentiments intended to crush her daughter, to stop her in her tracks. "You only care about your life. Your friends come first to you and not your family, and that's why you are and always will be selfish. That is why Sean dumped you."

Lauren walked through the foyer and did not look back up to her mother. "Selfish whore," Ma screamed. "Slut. You deserve nothing." Ma's last words stopped Lauren from moving forward, her legs frozen before the door. Was her mother really saying these things to her? Ma started down the stairs and when she reached halfway she reached into her pocket and pulled out a pill bottle. She hurled the bottle at Lauren. The cylinder hit the marble floor and rolled against Lauren's foot. "Pick it up," Ma demanded. "Pick that up." Instinctively Lauren did as she was told and reached down for the bottle. As soon as Lauren held the prescription pills in her hand, Ma started up again. "Put those to good use," she shouted, her voice regaining its full force. "You're a slut. Take that Xanax and get a grip. Maybe then you'll come back around. Maybe then you'll know how to respect your mother."

Lauren placed her hand on the doorknob, her fingers twisting it to the right. Just in case Lauren hadn't understood, Ma hollered out one final time with all her might.

"S-L-U-T!"

Lauren left the house, walking the blocks out of Belle Haven as Louie had before her. She had no idea what to do. So she walked without intention or direction, dumping the bottle of pills in the first Dumpster she passed. She walked until she reached a pay phone and dialed Layla, asking her friend to borrow a car and pick her up. She had Layla take her to the only place she could think of to go—to Nonna.

CHAPTER 34

Queens, New York

LIFE AT NONNA'S WAS QUIET, A CONSTANT SADNESS IN THE AIR. The two women nursed the wounds that numbed them. They were a comfort to each other and slowly, bit by bit, they inched through each day. The house was nothing fancy: a red brick split-level dwelling that Nonno built in the early years of their marriage. Nonna raised her two sons in the house. There was a large yard, at least by Queens's standards, and an extensive herb garden, where Nonno used to nurture dill, thyme, coriander, parsley, rosemary, and basil. Nonna couldn't bear to care for the garden, couldn't bring herself to dig in the same dirt that crumbled in Nonno's hands only weeks before. In less than a month, the garden was strangled by weeds, neglected and overrun.

Lauren was placed in the guest room upstairs. The room had a large window overlooking the street, where she could draw the weighty brocade drapes for quiet and dark. The room felt safe. Although it wasn't a secret that she was staying with Nonna, it was a place where she could hide.

Ma did not call, but sent Lauren a note inside a flowery pastel card. Across the back of the sealed envelope, Ma wrote S.W.A.K. Lauren recognized Ma's signature touch—the acronym was something Ma learned from her own mother, and it was the final touch for all of Ma's special correspondence. "What does S.W.A.K. mean?" Lauren asked her mother years ago. "Sealed with a kiss," Ma said. "It's a way to send love through the mail."

```
Dear Lauren,

Something you may want to know. Your car was
stolen out of our driveway last night. The
police found it in the cemetery this morning.
Blown up. It was burnt to a crisp. Go figure.

God Bless You,
Ma
```

There was little discussion between Nonna and Lauren about Ma. They both sensed that it was best to remain silent. Keep still. But when Ma's note arrived, it prompted Lauren to tell Nonna the details of why she left home, information she had not yet offered her grandmother. Her silence was partly because she had no idea how to explain the event, an argument that came up so unexpectedly, and partly because she could not figure out her role.

"Your mother is my son's wife," Nonna said at first. "I will always respect that." Lauren listened, hoping for a bit more, and slowly, with hesitation, Nonna continued. "Your mother can be difficult. She's unpredictable." Lauren thought this was the end of the conversation and was about to give up when Nonna continued. "It was always that way. It's how she is. I remember once when you were just a tiny thing and the boys were running wild outside in the backyard you started crying. You were a noisy crier. You had big lungs and could really scream. She never knew how to handle your crying. I think it made her nervous, made her think she was a terrible mother. We were standing in this very kitchen when you started to wail and she slapped you, which made you cry more, and she kept slapping and you kept shrieking. I went to grab you out of her arms and she slapped me too, so hard across the face it left a handprint for the next few days. I guess you can imagine that your mother and I are not friends."

Lauren took in the information without comment. The news didn't jar her like Nonna worried it might. Lauren only wished that she and

Ma had not gotten off to such a rocky start so very long ago.

∞

Dear Journal,

I like it here. Nonna cooks for me. My favorite meal is her stuffed red peppers filled with breadcrumbs, yellow American cheese, and the best pasta sauce. I guess I request this dish way too much but Nonna doesn't mind. There is homemade gravy, meatballs, pizza, and pasta fagioli. She serves bread and salad too. And there is always cake. Chocolate Duncan Hines cake. It is the absolute best. Nonna washes my clothes too, folds them in a nice pile and sets them on the bed in the guest room where I stay.

Nonna's three sisters make sure we have plenty of company and come to visit often. They sit in the living room like a circle of love, like angels. There is so much talk and laughter. The sisters knit Afghan blankets in bright colors, but Nonna does some kind of Japanese embroidery called Bunka. She uses a punch needle and silk thread to embroider still lives of apples in bowls and landscapes of Italy. The work is so delicate, shaded like paintings.

The sisters quiz me about my friends and my plans. They seem genuinely interested. I am looking for a job and maybe will attend school one of these days. I think there must be something for me. Still, I cannot stop thinking of Nonno. And Louie. And Wylie. All lost to me forever.

Lauren

CHAPTER 35

Nonna REFERRED TO HER THREE OLDER SISTERS—MARIE, ROSE, AND DINA—as simply The Sisters, like they were one and not three individuals. Lauren referred to them as her Aunties. Truth be told, her Great-Aunties did resemble one another with dark, coarse complexions, big-boned frames, and once-black hair threaded with white—long, snowy ribbons twisting through the darkness. The women were wide and strong, women who worked hard all their lives, and who carried themselves as if they were satisfied, not slumped and wanting.

If you cared to look closely at each Auntie, there were some distinguishing features. Marie was the tallest, Rose had the loudest laugh, and Dina had the most ample bottom. Combined, they amounted to The Sisters, the Aunties. They hovered over Nonna, the baby of the group, and their attentions to Nonna spilled over to Lauren. They were a cradle of warmth descending on Nonna's heartsick house. The presence of The Sisters, along with Nonna's tender care, agreed with Lauren; she gained a bit of weight and her nosebleeds and hives remained absent.

The aunts were skilled in the art of telling fortunes by tea leaves. "Reading the Cup," as they called it. The old English practice had been taught to Auntie Rose, the oldest, who left Italy as a young woman to marry an Englishman. It was her English mother-in-law who passed on the tea-reading skills. The husband and mother-in-law were now gone, but Rose's reading talents remained. Rose shared her knowledge with Dina and Marie, but Rose possessed an extra insight. She could easily make out the shapes the tiny leaves created at the bottom of the cup. She understood their hidden meaning.

Many afternoons, Rose made Lauren drink black China tea. She poured the loose tea into a plain white teacup instead of the patterned cups that Nonna usually used. "It's too busy to see the shapes," Rose told her. The cup had a wide opening for better viewing.

"Drink," Dina said to Lauren, having great confidence and pride in her sister's abilities, "just leave the leaves at the bottom." When the liquid was almost gone, the Aunties instructed Lauren to take the cup by the handle in her left hand and swirl from left to right. "Swirl and concentrate on your future, keep it in your mind," Marie told her. Lauren was then to pour the last puddle of tea into the saucer so that all of the liquid drained away.

The tea leaves clustered into formations at the bottom of the cup, shapes that Rose called significations, and she scrupulously examined them, looking for symbols and letters.

In Lauren's cup, Rose almost always saw flowers and hats. Once she saw a harp. All were strong signs for good fortune, success, and a happy marriage. This made the Aunties laugh. "In time," they said.

Auntie Marie said, "Change will come." It was also Marie who said that Lauren needed to start that change with her hair by returning to her natural beauty. Since the age of thirteen, Ma encouraged Lauren to color her darkening hair to a shade close to Ma's blonde. But Lauren was not a natural blonde, and the Aunties insisted she needed to look like herself.

"Marie is right. Cast off this blonde," said Dina.

The next evening, Marie returned with a box of hair color labeled Honey Chestnut. Rose applied the dye, while Dina monitored the process with the kitchen timer. When the timer sounded, the three Aunties hovered over the sink and Lauren was lathered, rinsed, conditioned, combed, and dried. The touch of their fingers working through her hair and massaging her scalp soothed her, gave her a sense of miraculous renewal and refreshment.

When they pushed her to the mirror, Lauren was afraid to look and closed her eyes.

"You look so fresh," said Nonna, admiring her sisters' efforts.

"Pretty," Dina confirmed.

And Marie added, "Open your eyes."

Lauren did. There she was, every bit of blonde gone. Her new brown hair looked right, like something she had misplaced for a long time. With that one little adjustment, Lauren felt her life was truly on the verge of change. She had no idea what that change might be, but she was on the edge. She only needed to leap forward.

Chapter 36

THE MOMENT LAUREN MET HIM, she didn't realize that there was anything unusual afoot. She didn't suspect that the brief exchange would alter her life. Michael knew. For the first time in his life, he was certain without question, without a complete analysis or debate with himself. He would only have to wait for Lauren to know too.

The Aunties were right. Change had found Lauren. It found her in Nonna's modest house in Queens and lured her out. First with small, untraceable steps and then longer, bolder jaunts until she found herself sprinting in a direction she never thought possible.

Lauren found a job as a telemarketer for a company that sold closet organizers. The job was straightforward: get the caller to sign up for a complimentary in-home demonstration. The company's strategy was to place the salesman in the home so that the potential customer would be more inclined to spontaneously purchase its closet kits and organizing accessories. Because of Lauren's amiable demeanor, she managed to engage those who picked up the phone—mostly the elderly, and young mothers confined to their homes during the day. There was something about Lauren's voice and speech, its timbre and inflection, a carefree cheeriness that put people at ease and enticed them to talk and stay on the line. Strangers revealed daily frustrations to her—a fussy toddler, an elderly husband with Alzheimer's, a bad back. Most of all, they chatted with Lauren because of boredom, a pervasive loneliness that plagued them day to day. Lauren listened with compassion and empathy, which encouraged the potential customer to engage more, and she would respond with concrete no-stress solutions: the chance to triple storage space with easy-to-install closet systems, uniform cubbies for chaotic toys, convenient wire pullout baskets for stray socks and underwear, clear compartments for t-shirts and sweaters. Lauren instinctively knew when to listen and when to offer the suggestion of adopting an easier, more organized life. By the close of the conversation and with an in-home consultation scheduled, her phone companions thanked her. In a short time, Lauren became the employee who garnered the most sign-ups. After one year, her supervisor was more than disappointed to see her go.

On a lark, Lauren took another job as an assistant for a woman who owned two restaurants called L'Esprit, the original located in Queens, not far from Nonna's house. There were plans to open a third eatery in Manhattan and to begin to bottle their popular salad dressings and jams. L'Esprit reflected the new eclectic American palate.

The place was bistro style, filled with worn kitchen antiques, teapots, beveled mirrors, rustic pine furniture, and an assortment of chandeliers. The sparkly lighting hung from a ceiling of pressed tin. The bar was fashioned from zinc. The look was funky flea market and everything was for sale—a customer could literally purchase and walk out with his dining chair.

Despite the antiques and French name, the restaurant was unpretentious and possessed a casual sophistication—a neighborhood gathering spot where a foodie could find a European soda, a healthy snack treat, or a good-tasting meal made from fresh and seasonal ingredients. The young, enthusiastic staff served up countless orders of café au lait in white ceramic bowls; omelets (never browned) were complemented by ratatouille and artisan breads; and swelling burgers (never smashed to speed up cooking) shared brightly colored plates with homemade Belgian frites. Organic mixed greens were the foundation for a large selection of salads, and hundreds of California-style sandwiches moved from the cozy, nimble kitchen into the dining room, followed by dark chocolate desserts. Dinner choices changed daily. There was almost always a line out the door.

The owner, Amy, was driven and creative. She gave up a lucrative but unloved career in finance to attend The Culinary Institute of America. Once she graduated from the renowned program, she didn't follow her younger classmates into fine dining—the Upper East Side corporate kitchens—and instead opened the creaky, multipaned doors to a long-held dream. Still, her Queens-based dream arrived with a burgeoning list of tasks, and Amy struggled to keep the details of her growing businesses and thin personal life on track.

That was when Lauren appeared, knowing nothing about restaurants or L'Esprit except that she liked to stop there with Nonna for a special pot of loose-leaf tea. Ten minutes into Lauren's interview, Amy was—like the potential closet customers—charmed and calmed by Lauren. High-strung Amy offered the earnest young woman the job before the interview was over.

Amy was a good fifteen years older than Lauren, and had an energy and determination that Lauren studied. She was inspired by what Amy accomplished, her dedicated willingness to succeed. Amy was hands-on, involved in every detail of her business (staff hiring, menu planning, customer relations, ordering, and ongoing maintenance) and as Amy's new sidekick, Lauren was exposed to it all—marketing, food costs, tip credits, new venue scouting, health department regulations, insurance, and bookkeeping.

Amy worked and then worked more. There was no downtime, and she quickly came to rely on Lauren, who had trained all of her life to work well under pressure and did not get rattled by the restaurant's commotion or hectic pace. In fact, Lauren thrived. She loved the high energy, the customer interaction, the meticulous attention and urgency that went into making each dish consistent, delicious, and promptly served. The pace was nonstop for sure, but it also demanded camaraderie and teamwork to make it function. The dishwasher was needed as much as the chef. Everyone played an integral role. This Lauren loved.

And she adored Amy. The two clicked, balancing and supporting each other through the long hours, confronting any challenge thrown their way. The older Amy kept a watchful eye over her new protégé, in and out of the restaurant. She knew Lauren was smart and also needed a wider understanding, so she offered Lauren college tuition reimbursement and weeknights off. It was the nudge Lauren needed and she enrolled in the evening community college program the very next week. She took baby steps—only one or two classes per semester, but they were steps forward all the same.

Ma heard bits and pieces of Lauren's success through Lou, who quizzed Nonna on a regular basis. Even though Lou's visits to Nonna's had lessened since the incident between Lauren and Ma, he made up for the lack of physical presence with calls almost daily. Months passed before Ma caved and began mailing Lauren cards—clichéd greetings decorated with floral illustrations and effusive sentiments. And S.W.A.K. written across the back of the envelope—they were always Sealed With A Kiss.

To A Special Daughter,

I Am A Mother Whose Heart Is Filled With Love...

Oh, the memories that we have shared,

a cherished treasure trove.

We have had our ups and downs,

but I hope you always know what I feel for you —

an unwavering commitment.

```
For our mother-daughter hearts are joined
forever,

bound in love.

God Bless You!
Ma
```

The chain of cards were an apology of sorts, always mailed in an ivory envelope dotted with small heart-shaped stickers and a special LOVE postage stamp placed carefully in the upper right corner.

The first several cards went unanswered, but then with the encouragement of Nonna and Lou, Lauren weakened and forgave her mother. "She's your mother," Nonna said. "She means well," Lou said. And while she took to visiting her mother in New Jersey when she could and speaking with her frequently on the phone, Lauren remained at Nonna's.

Amy's job demands and Ma's reinstated expectations for attention left little time for Lauren's college studies. In theory, she loved the depth and variety of her courses, but at night, sitting in overheated classrooms, she strained to concentrate, struggled to absorb the biology professor's slideshow of molecular evolution, and fought to retain the renowned art historian's verbose and lengthy lecture on sixteenth-century Italian art. She pushed, but as classroom windows reflected the night, her eyes closed, her back slumped and her mouth slacked quite against her will, until she felt a jolt of energy and sat back up again, stiff and upright.

On the cusp of her twenty-first birthday, the Fourth of July, Lauren brought her most recent grades to show Amy. There had been an A in Journalism, an A in Biology, and one B—a result of an Art History examination that required the students to identify and date a series of Madonna paintings. Amy was thrilled with Lauren's accomplishments, but not surprised. "That's just what I expected," she said.

Lauren consciously adopted Amy's no-nonsense work ethic and did not mention to Amy that it was her birthday. She begged both Nonna and Ma to let the day pass without special consideration. Nonna agreed to a point, but still prepared a special lasagna dinner with the Aunties. They were ready and waiting when Lauren arrived home, donning festive hats and blowing party horns. The sounds of neighborhood fireworks complemented dessert. Ma insisted Lauren stop by the house in Belle Haven. When she arrived, she was surprised to find that Ma had bought her a new car —a Mazda Miata. Lauren had been driving Nonno's old car for three years and had not expected the generous gift. But that was Ma, always full of surprises.

A few weeks later, Amy asked Lauren to come into work on her day off. It was a frequent request that Lauren didn't mind. Late that afternoon, Amy presented her with two large and heavy boxes wrapped in matching gold paper. "This is for you. I'm sorry I missed your big day."

Lauren blushed, surprised at how touched she was by Amy's personal gesture. The boxes contained a new computer with a large screen. "This is only for your studies, not to be used at work," Amy explained. "So don't set it up here."

Amy suggested that they get away from the restaurant for a drink at a local Queens bar, two blocks from L'Esprit. Lauren balked a little, but Amy insisted. "After all, you're legal now," she said to Lauren, "and I need a new drinking buddy."

And so Lauren, barely 21, found herself in Flanagan's Pub with a margarita in front of her. The bar was dark and quiet, occupied by only a few neighborhood customers. The women were discussing Amy's upcoming culinary trip to Paris and Rome—a journey Amy referred to as research, but Lauren suspected was more about a new adventure than any gastronomic enlightenment—when a group of seven young men walked through the bar's foyer and settled mid-bar around the television, where a game between the New York Yankees and Boston Red Sox played.

Like any group of young, single men out on a weekend afternoon, they were loud and noisy. Lauren recognized the type as quintessential yuppies: young stockbrokers trying to make their mark or ambitious lawyers vying for partner. They most likely commuted into Manhattan for their all-consuming jobs, or lived in the city during the week, coming home to Queens for a homemade meal and clean laundry on the weekends. Perhaps they gathered to see childhood buddies from the old neighborhood. Maybe one or two had purchased sleek lofts in the up-and-coming Long Island City—hip and spacious bachelor digs—until the time came to move on to the trendier dwellings and soaring prices of Tribeca.

Lauren's assessment wasn't far from the truth. In fact, Michael was heading out with old friends and cousins, a group of young professionals, for an evening in the city. They had stopped by the neighborhood bar to catch some of the game before heading to lower Manhattan. Michael had not wanted to make the stop, but was outvoted by the group, and so he sat off on the edge of the group, restless and ready to move on.

Lauren had not paid attention to the men, other than sizing them up as they entered; they provided a background rumble to the formerly empty bar, and she and Amy raised their voices to hear one another. After two margaritas, not something Lauren had consumed before, she excused herself to the bathroom. The sweet drink left her pleasantly relaxed, almost giddy. She passed by the men and the one seated on the end looked up and smiled. Lauren smiled back. When she returned he was there, with his chair turned away from the television, waiting for her.

"You're not watching the game," Lauren said to him.

"I'm not," he answered, a simple statement of fact. "You're not either," he said.

"I'm not," Lauren said, copying his tone and matter-of-fact style.

"So what are you doing in this dumpy bar on a Saturday afternoon?"

"Celebrating," she told him. She noticed his soft black T-shirt and black linen pants. His attire seemed to suit his demeanor, straightforward and comfortable even in July, but sophisticated.

"What might you be celebrating?" he asked her.

"Good grades and a birthday." Normally, she would not have

confided something so personal, but the drink made her spontaneous, ready to respond to his direct and affable style.

"Good reasons to celebrate."

"The best," she said.

"I'm Michael."

"Hi, Michael," was the only plausible answer.

The words were simple and insignificant, like filler, an excuse to say something out loud while they sized up the other. Michael felt the attraction first, but he was stopped short. His companions settled the bill and gathered by the door, fortified and ready for their evening in the city. "Mikey, let's go," a cousin shouted.

"Can I give you a call?" Michael asked Lauren. "I'd like to wish you a belated happy birthday." The question was tossed out without a foundation to support it. The small exchange between them did not justify his request, but she was light-headed and he seemed pleasant.

"Sure," she said and wrote her number on the back of his Heineken coaster. Lauren never expected to hear from him. She had never handed out her number to a strange man, and hadn't intended to do so her first time in a bar, but he appeared in such an unexpected and timely moment and that seemed to change everything.

Michael did call her. When he arrived in a smart beige summer suit the following Saturday night, the Aunties were alert and waiting. Michael was introduced first to Nonna and then Rose, Marie, and Dina. He made a slight bow to each woman before clasping an extended hand.

"It's a pleasure," he told them, and they all felt he was sincere.

Michael surprised Lauren from the start. First, he picked her up in a compact navy blue car. The vehicle was nondescript and understated, nothing like Sean's loud and showy wheels (her only point of reference). The car belonged to his mother. In fact, Michael didn't own a car, didn't want one in Manhattan—a lifestyle choice that would have been incomprehensible to Lauren's New Jersey friends. Second, she hadn't expected anything much for the date, but Michael drove her to lower Manhattan and they traveled up to the 106th floor of the World Trade

Center's North Tower, to a restaurant that was situated at the top of New York City's tallest building. She stood before the floor-to-ceiling windows, marveling at the sight before her—a spectacular view of the Manhattan skyline, dazzling and glittering below them. She felt both astonished and completely out of place.

"Happy Birthday," he said to her.

Lauren had never dated a man who wore a suit, particularly in summer, and she liked it. Michael blended with the other men, all in suits and subtle ties, all secure and grown up—confident that they were meant to be seated at a table in such an outstanding venue. The suit didn't seem to be a cover for Michael, not something he threw on for a special occasion as a disguise to make him appear acceptable. He seemed at ease in both the clothing and the restaurant. When the maître d' appeared to escort them to their table, Lauren was careful to follow Michael's lead.

Michael talked to her. He was older by seven years and behaved like an adult, one who was sure and satisfied with his direction. She learned that he was from an extended Greek family and had grown up in Queens, not far from Nonna's. He told her that his mother raised him for a while, on her own. The circumstances were difficult for her and them, but they were firmly bound as a result. There was no bitterness or resentment in the telling; he was merely laying out the facts. Michael had been interested in politics since he was a boy. He graduated from New York University and then earned a master's degree in political science from Rutgers. He currently worked as chief of staff for a state senator. Lauren was impressed and intimidated by the information. Michael didn't tell her these things with arrogance or bravado, but how could she tell him about herself and her limited accomplishments? How could she follow those facts?

When she hesitated to divulge anything about her own life, he prompted her, and once she began, she was surprised to find that it was not difficult to continue. He asked about her work at L'Esprit and about Amy over bluepoint oysters and foie gras, and about her favorite classes over lobster-and-mushroom raviolis. The combination of exquisite food and paired wines, the stupendous starry sky, and Michael's attentions made her open and vulnerable—her unleashed words rushing forth without inhibition. Never-spoken dreams were revealed over beer-braised short ribs for Michael and rack of lamb for Lauren. They drank from the renowned Kevin Zraly wine list as they brainstormed her future possibilities. And they laughed, one at a time and together, overlapping and harmonious—chuckles, giggles, and contented sighs—a musical riff of merriment that complemented the wonderful fruit sorbets and chocolate soufflé. Michael lingered over her comments, digesting her thoughts as if she were not only worth hearing, but as delicious as the gourmet fare. His behavior drew her out, encouraged her, and before they finished the soufflé, the dark chocolate fresh on their tongues, she had whispered to him untold things. They discussed her father, his accident at the garage, and the depression that now dragged him down; how she missed Nonno and Wylie; and how she had not heard from her brother, Louie, in years. She confessed that Tony was a growing worry for the family and had now, by order of the court, been placed in a rehab center for a significant cocaine habit. Her parents hoped the treatment would stamp out not only his addictions, but also his predilection for crime. She said that she loved her mother, but that her mother could be unhinged, their relationship combustible at times. She warned him about her health issues. She let him know that she wrote in a journal almost every day. Michael soaked it all in, not only without judgment, but with admiration.

On the long elevator ride back to the ground floor, descending from the starry galaxy, they were languorous and satiated. Michael reached for her hand as if it was a habitual gesture, one he had repeated for years, an action born out of longtime intimacy. When she turned to smile at him, to acknowledge the connection, he kissed her. At first their lips brushed lightly, skimming the edges. He waited for a cue, and when she did not resist and left her lips settled against his, he pressed, fervid and impassioned for more. As with their long and lively conversation, she now answered him with confidence, an honest yearning. They both felt the rise in temperature, a heat circling through the elevator, leaving little doubt about their mutual desire. As they passed the eightieth floor, she tightened her arms around him. She wanted to hold the two of them there, intertwined and suspended between sky and earth. By the time the elevators parted on the ground floor, they emerged with arms linking, dazed and content.

"Happy Birthday," Michael said again. As they walked to the parking garage, Lauren felt somehow altered. The concrete city streets and the harsh, vivid lights surrounding them seemed different too. Her perceptions were revised—it was now a world with Michael in it.

The evening ran long and Michael returned her late to Queens. It was well past midnight when Michael pulled up in front of Nonna's darkened house. Nonna had gone to bed and Dina and Marie had gone home, but Rose had stayed put, knitting, snoozing, and watching for Lauren's return.

"Well?" Rose asked when Lauren entered the quiet house.

"He's nice," Lauren answered into the dark room, her aunt's face lit only by streetlight.

"Yes, he's nice. Yes, he's handsome," Rose challenged her. "He wears a sharp suit too. Who cares about that? I want to know if you like him?"

"I think I do," Lauren told her Great Aunt.

"I knew it," Rose said, triumphant and satisfied. "I read it in your teacup."

Chapter 37

THE PAIRING OF LAUREN AND MICHAEL TURNED OUT TO BE DESTINY. For weeks, Lauren held her breath, waiting for Michael to reveal a temper, a criminal past, a propensity to hit—some hidden factor that would rise up and force the union to crash and burn, leaving their intimacy a charred remnant. But Michael stayed constant and Lauren came to trust him bit by bit.

Together, the couple seemed inextricably right. They were a team: both integral to the whole. Michael Stefanakis was not a tall or brawny man, but he possessed an intrepid confidence that made Lauren feel protected. His determination, accompanied by black hair and eyes and a Grecian complexion, made him appear serious, even stringent, but once he spoke, his animated manner made it clear that he was amiable and kind. Lauren noticed that he took an interest in everyone—Nonna, the Aunties, the waitress at the diner, Amy and L'Esprit, and Carlos, the superintendent of his small Manhattan apartment building. Michael remembered not only names, but personal details (a bad back, children's ages, an ailing wife, an important business deadline) and he relished a good chat, whether it was with Karrie Riedel, the popular senator who employed him as her chief of staff, or with a late-night taxicab driver delivering him to his Perry Street stoop after a sixteen-hour workday.

Michael was raised without ostentation in a family where material goods were overshadowed by books, study, contemplation, and a devotion to spirituality. His mother Anastasia was left a widow when Michael was an infant—Michael's father been taken from her when an unexpected heart attack struck him at the age of thirty-two. Both Michael's parents were Greek immigrants, and the young Anastasia turned to the Greek Orthodox Church for guidance.

Anastasia Stefanakis, a young mother without means, charted a plan, and after some tenacious years of balancing motherhood and study, found work as an elementary school teacher. No one in the church community was surprised when following three public outings, Paniagotis Kosta, the church's middle-aged chanter twenty years her senior, asked Anastasia for her hand in marriage. It wasn't a union based on passion. Rather it was a good-sense partnership with the advantages of common interests, respect, and a deep love for church, study, and community that eventually bloomed into love. Paniagotis Kosta took the young Michael as his son, keeping a watchful eye over the rambunctious boy, and one year later the newlyweds were blessed with a daughter, Evangeline. Paniagotis Kosta was indifferent to money and unnecessary possessions. The family lived without decoration while Paniagotis studied to become a priest. There was an exception to their frugal life—Michael's and Evangeline's education. That had been rigorous and first class for both. In time, the chanter did become an ordained priest in the Greek Orthodox Church. Everyone, even his family, called him Father Kosta. It simply suited him.

When Michael and Lauren met, Lauren's schedule was challenging from working at L'Esprit and putting herself through college at night. Nonna had offered to help with her expenses several times, but Lauren declined. She wanted to do it herself. Lauren made a strong effort to balance it all. She was making up for her spotty education, attempting to fill in the gaping holes in and out of the classroom, and that required her to work harder than most. She had not known the difference between a Republican and a Democrat, had not tasted aioli or sipped Bordeaux, and had not understood Aristotle. Lauren's courtship with

Michael was taking her on a romp through a new world—food, politics, philosophy, travel, museums, foreign films, and espresso specialty beverages. Lauren was an earnest student, amazed at what Michael knew and grateful that he chose to share his knowledge with her. It was Michael's "think big" sensibility that pushed her to imagine herself in other circumstances, to break out of the limited confines of her past. And while Michael never judged her, there was one bit of knowledge that Lauren did not grasp and only came to comprehend years later—she was also teaching Michael, influencing him with a fresh perspective, a positive outlook, and a curious mind. She quieted his all-out approach and taught him to be still in the moment.

Both Lauren and Michael worked long hours. Amy kept Lauren immersed in L'Esprit business and Michael's career was gaining steam. He was recognized by *New York* magazine as one of the "Top 30 Under 30" in New York politics. But the couple made a point to go out together on Sundays. They walked Central Park, ventured in and out of tiny NoHo boutiques, and shared Little Italy's best gelato. Michael loved to roam the streets, looking for a delicacy, discovering a new treat. He acquainted Lauren with his old haunts: pizza topped with artichokes and feta cheese on Eleventh Street; fresh, hot bagels on the Upper West Side; attending the Brooklyn Academy of Music for theater or a matinee performance at Avery Fisher Hall. At the American Museum of Natural History, Lauren stood among butterflies.

When Lauren smiled, which was often, Michael felt uplifted, joyous. He marveled at her graceful and delicate neck, the small curve of her waist, her slim, fine fingers. Years of illnesses had left their mark on Lauren, a scar here and there from chronic hives, and Michael sometimes noticed a stiff joint when she walked. But that only increased her undeniable loveliness, the blend of vulnerability, strength, and gratitude with which she embraced each day.

At night, when Lauren held Michael, her toes wriggling and burrowing between his, she would look out the window of his basement brownstone studio to see the traffic's waving ribbons of light and overhear dabs of dialogue exchanged between the passersby. This was not the basement window of her childhood, of Country Club Lane, and she snuggled into Michael, where there was no trace of heavy cologne, just Michael, fresh and clean. It was a place where she no longer fretted about rats, or fires, or accidents.

In his platform bed, which took up most of the small Greenwich Village apartment, she felt more like herself—not like a confused child, but a woman who knew what she wanted. She wanted him. If she were to give voice to these feelings, say them out loud, they would sound like stale lovers' clichés: he took her breath away, they spoke the same language, she felt giddy when she saw him, and she suffered pain when they parted. She did not have the vocabulary to make their union sound unique, but she knew they were, whether she could string the right words together or not. And so she found another way. After Michael fell asleep, fulfilled and satisfied, Lauren traced letters with her neatly painted fingernails across his back. "My beloved" she wrote. She hoped that the sentiment, etched into his flesh with the lightness of a feather, would remain in his heart too, and not erode over time, because for her he had become as essential as air.

After two years, Michael took her to Paris. They walked Montmartre, the Tuileries Gardens, and up the Champs-Élysées. They visited Musée Rodin. And finally, at nightfall, he brought her to the oldest bridge in Paris, Le Pont Neuf, where they stood over the river Seine, before a spectacular sight—the Institut de France, the Louvre, and the Eiffel Tower, all glowing in the distance. It was here that he requested she spend her life with him. "I would be honored," she said without a speck of hesitation. They walked Paris for hours, then found their way back to their small hotel and tumbled into bed, making love until the shouts of French farmers setting up the morning vegetable market across from the hotel broke the amorous spell. They giggled to each other before drifting into a dreamy slumberland.

⌒∞⌒

Dear Journal,

Tonight was the best night of my life.

Some interesting news (actually a miracle).

Marrying Michael.

I love him.

I love him.

I love him.

*If only I could tell Louie.

CHAPTER 37

Westfield, New Jersey

THE ENGAGEMENT WAS ANNOUNCED TO NONNA first and then to the Aunties. Michael phoned his mother, Father Kosta, and Evangeline. Telling Ma was all that was left.

Over the last two years, Michael met Lauren's family on several brief occasions. Lauren kept the intensity of her relationship a secret from her parents, and most often visited them without Michael. She worried about the contrast between the two families. Michael's mother was religious, soft spoken. Her words were measured and thoughtful. Anastasia was occupied with her job as a fourth-grade teacher, and she and Father Kosta created a home where dinner was the platform for lively philosophical and political discussions, and Plato was enjoyed with dessert. Lauren could not imagine her father and mother seated at the table with Father Kosta and Anastasia.

On Michael's first visit to Belle Haven, Lauren called ahead to caution Ma that Michael was not comfortable around dogs and asked that she confine Jack, the attack-trained cockapoo, in a bedroom. Ma wondered what kind of a man didn't like dogs and chose not to stow Jack away. Ma was not fond of touching strangers, but she greeted Michael with a loose embrace, tapping him on the back with her fingers, little codes of a half-hearted welcome, while Jack circled around Michael's feet growling at the intruder.

"Careful of my little Jack," Ma said sweetly to Michael. "I'm afraid he doesn't like men. He's small, but don't be fooled. He could rip your face off." Jack seemed to take Ma's warning as an invitation, and charged ahead for Michael's leg.

Michael smiled at Ma, but Lauren, embarrassed already, knew he was uneasy. She scooped up the yapping cream-haired menace and ran up to Ma's bedroom, where Jack was deposited, and where he barked himself hoarse. Lou offered a soft hello but said little, turning the long list of questions over to Ma. Through dinner, Ma quizzed Michael about his background, and when she uncovered that Michael's stepfather was a priest, she made a face, pulling down her lips and scrunching her nose like there was an odor, putrid and foul.

"Priests can be married in the Greek Orthodox Church," Lauren reassured her mother.

"Sounds creepy," Ma said.

They continued on to other topics, pertinent information a mother would want to know about her daughter's suitor. When it came to Michael's employment, Ma did not understand or care what a senator's chief of staff might do. "I am sure this is all very impressive," she said, "but in my experience, politicians are blatant liars, not to be trusted. Of course, that's no offense to you."

"None taken," Michael answered.

With Jack locked away, Michael wasn't rattled. Ma spoke her mind and he welcomed that—he was used to Father Kosta's frank talk. Michael appreciated that Ma was an attractive woman, with a younger appearance than most women her age, and it was apparent where Lauren got her pretty looks and slight frame. There were also definite differences between mother and daughter. Ma was sarcastic, her movements quick and sharp, and their eyes were dissimilar. Lauren's brown eyes were open and wide like her father's, her effortless smile was his too, voluptuous and full. When Ma stared at Michael, her ice-blue eyes were squinted and unfocused, searching for a place to settle. Her examination kept him on his guard, but Michael made a private vow to win Ma over, for Lauren's sake.

But now, long after that initial introduction, Michael and Lauren arrived in Belle Haven to announce their engagement.

"I would like to marry your daughter," Michael told them. "I would like your blessing." Without a pause, Lou surprised them all with an ebullient shout. "This is wonderful news!" he cried, embracing his daughter. Lou then turned to Michael, wrapping his arms around his daughter's love with a gesture of fierce approval. Ma was left to follow Lou's lead, opening her arms, limp and light, as this Greek stranger, her future son-in-law, clutched her close.

"I know Lauren will want a wedding," Ma said to Michael. "There will be a ton to do. Lauren better move back home with us so that we can plan a proper wedding." Lauren had not expected her mother's request, and she worried about leaving Nonna alone in Queens. Nonna encouraged the move. "It's a time to be with your mother," she said.

Even though Lauren knew she would deeply miss Nonna and her Aunties, and her commute to school and her job at L'Esprit would be longer, Lauren took the plunge and returned to Ma's home, to her childhood room.

The first night as she unpacked her belongings, her parents stood in her bedroom doorway.

"I'm glad you're home," Lou said.

Before Lauren could answer her father, Ma pointed into the room and asked, "What's that on your bed?"

"Michael gave it to me," Lauren told her mother with pride. "I've named it Magic." Lauren held the stuffed animal, a bear, against her chest. "You'll think it's silly, but the name is a tribute to Michael's magical presence in my life."

"Magic is another name for dust magnet," Ma said. "Here we go again. I would have hoped that Mr. Stefanakis would be more mature."

"It's a gift of love, Ma. Michael gave it to me when we visited the Hamptons. And I do think this is all quite magical."

Ma was not convinced. "I don't trust him as far as I can throw him. Just remember that your mother's instincts are always right. Politicians are liars. Not to be trusted. If you ever run into trouble with him, you can come right back to this house."

"I'm glad you're happy," Lou said. "Michael seems like a fine man. But Ma is right, sometimes you can't trust those political types."

Encouraged by her father's words, Lauren told her parents her and Michael's most recent wish. "We want to be married there," she said. "We want to be married in the Hamptons."

Ma heard the words, but upon impact she could not digest their meaning.

Lou jumped on board without a second thought. "If that is what you want then that is what it will be," he said, speaking up, before Ma, for the first time in years.

"Really?" Lauren said.

"Yes," Lou's voice was solid, determined, a voice Lauren recognized from her early childhood.

"A wedding in the Hamptons," he proclaimed. Lauren ran to her father, bathing him in grateful kisses. As she clung to him, she turned her head to Ma.

"I'm so very happy," Lauren told her. "What's happened to me is wondrous."

"What's wrong with New Jersey?" was all Ma could squeak out.

CHAPTER 39

MA INSISTED THAT THE NAPOLITANO FAMILY WAS ROMAN CATHOLIC even though it had been years since she visited the Chapel-at-the-Mall. With the onset of her engagement and much contemplation of her future as Mrs. Stefanakis, Lauren began to consider conversion to the Greek Orthodox Church. While her daughter examined the question of conversion, Ma researched group discounts for plastic surgery.

"You've got your father's nose," Ma told Lauren. "I think we ought to do something about it before the wedding."

"Michael wouldn't want me to change anything," Lauren said.

"And you believe him?" Ma asked.

"I do."

Ma let it go by, but had not given up on having Lou improved. Ma had long been embarrassed by Lou's damaged face. Never handsome, Lou's looks were always defined as rough and rugged. Since the accident, his face was misshapen, off-kilter, and dented.

Lou was against the idea. Ma pushed. She thought they both needed to look their best, especially in front of the snooty-tooty Greeks and all their never-ending prattle. She would make sure that the Napolitanos held their heads high. She would make sure that her only daughter's wedding was magnificent. That would give them something to blab about. And, as the mother of the bride, she would be the standout.

Ma did have her way, and while Lou had his nose and cheeks re-shuffled, even though there was not much that could be done, Ma had her forehead creases erased, her eyes lifted, and the little sag under her chin tightened.

Lauren passed on the correction of her nose, but willingly agreed to a conversion. "I don't know why you're not good enough the way you are," Ma said. "These Greeks only want to change you. We're Catholic. Seems like a perfectly fine religion to me."

The conversion was to be a small private ceremony in Queens with Michael, Anastasia, Evangeline, Ma, and Lou in attendance. Father Kosta would officiate. The morning of the conversion, Ma felt poorly, her bleeding ulcer acting up. It burned, searing her middle, the pain spreading through to her back and radiating out. She could barely stand. Lauren thought her parents should stay home, but Ma refused. "I will try my damnedest to make it through," Ma promised Lauren. In the car ride from New Jersey to Queens, Ma folded over with her head tipped forward like a scrap of white paper. Lauren suggested several times that they turn back. Ma wanted to soldier on. When they arrived at the church, Michael met them and helped Lou remove Ma from the car. She was blanched and weak. Supported by the men, she set out to climb the steps of the church, each forward movement causing excruciating pain.

Once inside the church, Michael politely asked his stepfather if he could speed things along, and they began the first Catechism prayers immediately. Lauren was directed to turn her back from the altar.

"Do you renounce Satan, and all his works, and all his worship, and all his angels, and all his pomp?" Father Kosta asked.

"I renounce him," Lauren answered.

"Have you renounced Satan?" recited Father Kosta.

"I renounce him."

"Have you renounced Satan?"

"I have renounced him," Lauren declared for the third and final time.

"Then blow and spit upon him," Father Kosta instructed, and Lauren spit three times to the West. Father Kosta then positioned Lauren to face east, toward the altar, and as she turned she saw Ma, her arms folded over her stomach, bolstered by Lou and Michael. She worried for her mother and wondered if it was right to continue.

"Do you join yourself to Christ?" Father Kosta asked her.

"I do join Him," Lauren answered.

"Have you joined Christ?"

"I have joined him," Lauren answered for the second time.

"And do you believe in Him?"

"I believe in Him as King and as God."

Lauren tried to concentrate on the additional prayers, but agonized that she would complete the conversion rituals only to find her mother, withered and collapsed, on the church floor. Ma held on as promised. When the ceremony was complete, Lauren and her parents made hasty apologies and skipped the celebratory lunch that Michael's mother planned. "We're so very sorry," Lauren told Anastasia, "but my mother is ill." Michael suggested that Lou take Ma home to rest and that Lauren come to the luncheon as planned, since several of his relatives were arriving and eager to meet her. "I can't leave her like this," Lauren told him. Ma was jockeyed back to the car, where she lay down across the backseat, and once they were safely home she went straight to bed without a word.

Chapter 40

The wedding guest list included too many Greeks and very few Napolitanos. Ma thought this made zero sense since the Napolitanos (meaning Lou, Ma, and Nonna) were footing the big, fat bill for the Hampton-Shmampton, hoity-toity hotel reception, hours from home.

Most of the members of Ma's family were unavailable. Jimmy was in prison yet again. This time he stuffed his mother in a basement closet, locked her in, and left her. The act drove Ma's brother, Bill, further down his non-stop, binge-drinking path. Jack Anthony was dead. Pat was still in the institution and Liam was still missing. Ma's estranged mother, Bessie, the matriarch of the O'Donnell clan, passed from liver failure in 1995, leaving "slow" Nora to fend for herself, and Nora refused to leave the rickety, old Bronx house.

Ma had not heard from Louie in years.

There were a few from Lou's side who would come out for the occasion. Nick, Lou's spoiled brother, would attend. Of course, so would Nonna, and that gaggle of old ladies. Lauren called them the Aunties. They would be there too. Ma's only comfort was that Tony was being released from his second stint in court-appointed rehab and was expected home in time for his sister's wedding.

Lauren and Michael selected the Oceanbleu in Westhampton for the reception, a waterfront venue with soaring ceilings, grand pillars, and an oversized, jeweled chandelier. More importantly, the ballroom could accommodate 175 dancing Greeks.

There was much to do. On top of planning for the wedding, Lauren was racing to complete her remaining courses for a degree in business before the nuptials. "You'd better drop all that college nonsense," Ma instructed. "Forget about it now; you're getting married." Lauren ignored Ma. Living with Nonna and the Aunties had built Lauren's confidence. The love, nourishment, and support they provided helped her gain the strength and drive to stay the course and finish school. Eclipsed by the upcoming wedding, there was no pomp and circumstance for the accomplishment, but Lauren felt pride in the degree. Michael did too.

Ma attacked the wedding arrangements with full force. She wrestled and haggled with the hotel's whiny party planner over the buffet menu, wedding cake choices, party favors, and seating arrangements. She rented Lincoln Town Cars to ferry guests from the Greek Orthodox Church in Southampton to the reception in Westhampton. She auditioned countless bands. The wedding was extravagant, but Ma devised ways to cut costs. She insisted upon a Sunday wedding rather than the more expensive Saturday night date. The bridesmaids, in pale gold dresses, carried one rose instead of a full bouquet, and the photographer was limited to one hour. Lauren's dress, a white strapless princess ball gown with a skirt of tulle, was a discounted sample, but Ma splurged on her own couture outfit, a low-cut, floor-length, beaded gown in soft champagne.

"Are you sure you want to wear this shade?" the saleslady at Happily Ever After asked Ma. "It reads white."

"I am very sure," said Ma. "We will look beautiful." And it was true. Standing before the fitting room mirror, mother and daughter looked like two brides. Both were stunning.

Amy agreed to be Lauren's maid of honor and she was joined by Michael's sister Evangeline (who had become Lauren's close friend and kindred spirit), and Lauren's high school chums, Katie and Layla, as bridesmaids. Father Kosta was honored to marry them.

Every guest came from out of town and most stayed at the lavish Oceanbleu. The Napolitanos did not. Ma felt it was too expensive and that she had already emptied her bank account to pay for the affair. She would not give them another penny. Lauren, Ma, Lou, and Tony spent the eve of Lauren's wedding in a budget motel nearby, sharing one standard room. "Let the Stefanakis family see how they have drained every last nickel out of us," Ma said. "Let them stand by while the bride goes budget and they are in the lap of luxury. Let's see who cares about that."

Everyone did care. Countless guests offered Lauren their room, including Anastasia, who was sharing with Michael, Evangeline, and Father Kosta. Nonna, the Aunties, and Amy offered to trade rooms as well, but Ma preferred to drive the point home to the stingy Stefanakis clan, to publicly out them before their guests, and insisted that the four Napolitanos stick together—for one last time as a family—even if it was to be in a no-frills motel.

Ma was happy that she stuck with her decision, particularly after Anastasia made them all trot out for what she dubbed the rehearsal dinner, but as far as Ma could tell, the so-called dinner was no dinner at all. Anastasia, mindful of her ongoing financial restraints, offered a simple meal at the hotel: a pasta dish, penne with sweet summer vegetables, a salad of arugula and raspberries, and chardonnay. She felt the food was good and fresh, nothing too heavy before the big day. When the waiter placed a glass of white wine in front of Ma's setting, Ma said, "I don't drink wine."

The waiter bent closer to Ma to whisper, "This evening your hostess invites you to enjoy a glass of chardonnay."

"I told you, I don't drink wine," Ma snapped. "What I want is a vodka and tonic."

The waiter leaned in again so that he would not draw the attention of the other guests. "Madam, your hostess is offering wine this evening."

Ma was irritated. After all she had done, could she not just have the drink of her choice? "I do not want a glass of cheap wine." Her comments echoed throughout the room.

"Please," Anastasia interjected, "bring Mrs. Napolitano the drink of her choice." Ma raised her wine glass to Anastasia. "Thank you," she said, but the sarcastic tone did not make either woman feel like the issue was resolved.

The dinner resumed without further event until Michael said to Lauren, "Sweetie, I think your nose is bleeding." Lauren dabbed her nose with the white linen napkin. Before she could press and close up her nostril, the blood rushed fast, soaking through the napkin, flowing past Lauren's lip and chin and onto to her grey linen suit.

Lauren left the table without explanation and headed to the restroom, where she slumped to the marble floor. Both Ma and Nonna recognized the problem and moved to scramble after her.

"I can't believe this," Lauren wept. "Not on my wedding."

"It's just nerves," Ma said. "So much commotion—and you didn't get a proper meal tonight."

"Your Ma is right," Nonna said, backing Ma. "It's a lot of excitement."

"We'll go back to the room and rest," Ma suggested. Ma wet the thick white paper towels found in upscale restrooms, and held her daughter's head back. She knew just where to pinch the nose to make the bleeding subside.

"Don't you worry; it'll be fine," Nonna said.

"You know that every knock is a boost," Ma said. Lauren looked at her mother and Nonna. Seeing them together, hovering over her, mothering her, made her hope that she could believe them. That it would be fine.

The dinner broke up early and Michael stood outside the ladies' room waiting for Lauren. "I'm so sorry," she told Michael. "I'm afraid I've ruined dinner."

"Not at all," he answered and kissed her on her forehead. "Are you okay now?"

"Yes, I'm just so disappointed. This hasn't happened in months. I thought it was behind me. And I'm worried about Ma. I don't want her to be upset."

Michael sighed as he looked from Nonna to Ma and back to Lauren. "I saw what happened with your mother. She was out of bounds."

"I know Ma can seem edgy," Lauren interjected, noticing Ma's eyes flash in response to Michael's words. "But she has done so much for us in organizing and planning this wedding. We should be grateful for all her help."

"Okay," Michael said. "It doesn't matter now. I can't wait for tomorrow. I can't wait to call you my wife." And when he spoke the word *wife* in front of her mother and Nonna, Lauren no longer cared that her new grey suit was stained with blood. She didn't care that she made such an ungracious exit from dinner.

∽

Tony didn't let the inferior accommodations stop him from appreciating the private beach, cabanas, or tiki bar at the Oceanbleu, nor did propriety keep him from entertaining some of the single guests attending the wedding. One particular attendee, Michael's cousin, found Tony quite charming. When Tony returned to the motel after midnight, he found Lou asleep and Lauren and Ma watching infomercials.

"I just made f-r-i-e-n-d-s with one of the Greek cousins," Tony bragged as he came into the room. From the way Tony said the word "friends," there was no doubt what he meant.

"Oh Tony, you didn't," Lauren said.

"She was begging me." Tony laughed.

"What did you do that for?" Lauren hoped her brother was not telling the truth.

"I'm telling you, she was moaning for more." Ma began to laugh with Tony, and they both began to moan, accompanying each exaggerated cry with a writhing wiggle.

"Ma, cut it out," Lauren pleaded. "It's not funny. He can't do this here. He cannot behave like this at my wedding."

But Ma was having fun. "Oh come on," she said. "It's no big deal."

"What will Michael's family think?"

"Party pooper," Tony taunted his sister, pouring gin from Ma's bottle into a plastic cup provided by the motel.

"Party pooper," Ma repeated and she began to sing, with Tony joining her in a loud, off-key harmony, "Every party has a pooper; that's why we invited you, Party pooper! Party pooper!"

Lauren did not answer the singing duo and hoped her father would stop them. Lou wasn't roused by the noise. It was evident that he was out for the night.

Lauren did not sleep that night. She sat with her head propped up high against a stack of pillows, hoping to prevent any potential nosebleeds on her wedding day, and spent the next several hours listening to Ma and Tony yuk it up, mostly at the expense of the Greeks.

The next morning was sunny and clear, with a faint ocean breeze. It was a quintessential summer day, perfect for a wedding. Lou went out early to get coffee for the bride and the wee-hour revelers. Tony cooperated and so did Ma. They seemed to have exorcised their juvenile antics, and when a handsome Tony escorted his mother down the church aisle that afternoon, they appeared refined and proper, with Ma wearing a beautiful wrist corsage. Ma looked elegant and young; her newly renovated face did not betray the ruckus from the night before. It was Lou, who slept through the night, who looked the worse for wear. The father of the bride stepped slowly down the aisle with his daughter, an ebullient and ravishing Lauren, with his shoulders caved, his eyes bloodshot, his mouth slightly open.

Several months of planning had not prepared Ma for the ceremony. She did not understand how her daughter had come to stand before the altar with this man. She couldn't reconcile the fact that her daughter was now a grown woman. Ma focused on the back of Lauren's head. She wished she could see her daughter's face, but Lauren would not be turning toward her. So she tried to imagine it, feature by feature. Her nose, her mouth, her eyes. Ma tried to imagine herself.

Father Kosta seemed to be chanting in monotone for an eternity. Would he ever stop? And just when Ma believed he would, there was more he had to say. She began to fidget in her seat. And Father Kosta kept on, and on, and on.

The wedding guests heard Father Kosta say, "That He send down upon them love perfect and peaceful, and give them His protection; let us pray to the Lord." Then, there had been a shriek; a loud, drawn-out cry.

Lauren did not turn her head at first. Father Kosta kept speaking, so Lauren, not wanting to be disrespectful, kept her head forward.

"That He may keep them in oneness of mind, and in steadfastness of the Faith; let us pray to the Lord," Father Kosta said.

"It's stabbed me!" This time, the shriek had words. This time, Lauren knew it was Ma. Ma in distress, calling out into the church on Lauren's wedding day. Amy was the first to step away from the wedding party, to move to the first pew and attend to Ma.

Father Kosta kept on. "That He may keep the course and manner of their life blameless; let us pray to the Lord," he said. Lauren did not know if Father Kosta continued because it was imperative never to interrupt a prayer in motion, or if his concentration had been so deep that he had actually not heard the cry. Michael now turned and so did Lauren, afraid of what she might see. Every guest in the church was concerned for Ma.

"This damn thing has stabbed me," Ma shouted to Amy in horror. "I can't get it out."

Amy whispered that she would remove the long corsage pin that had wedged its way into the underside of Ma's wrist.

"Be careful," Ma told Amy. And then she said to Lou, "Make sure she's careful."

Amy was fastidious, withdrawing the needlelike pin without a hitch, leaving only a faint rose impression on Ma's skin. Amy sat down in the pew, between Lou and Ma, and reassured Ma that she was now fine.

"How do you know if I'm fine? You're not a doctor, are you?" Ma wailed, still agitated from the shock.

"No, I am not a doctor," Amy said, "but I think you're okay. Look, I've got the pin out; you're really okay."

Every guest was awaiting Ma's response and even Father Kosta stopped his prayers and spoke directly to Ma. "Are you all right?"

"I've been stabbed," Ma answered. "I may need to go to the hospital."

"I think she will be fine," said Amy to Father Kosta.

"Are you hurt?" the Father asked.

"She's fine," Amy repeated. "I'll sit here with her to make sure."

"Good," said Father Kosta. "Shall we continue?"

"Yes, please, continue," Ma said. "I just hope I will not get lead poisoning, but please go ahead."

And Father Kosta winked and grinned at Lauren. The action caught her by surprise, but it had the effect he intended. Lauren's worries about her mother began to melt.

"Shall we continue?" he said to Lauren and Michael, who looked at each other and exchanged smiles. Lauren was concerned for Ma, but there was no doubt they should continue.

"Bless Michael and Lauren," Father Kosta said raising his voice in an effort to reengage both the couple and the guests while Ma raised her arm, making sure that she did not turn blue. As Father Kosta proceeded, Ma made small breathy sighs of distress.

"Bless this marriage and grant Lauren and Michael a peaceful life, length of days, chastity, love for one another in a bond of peace, offspring long-lived, fair fame by reason of their children, and a crown of glory that does not fade away."

Amy held Ma's hand until the ceremony was over and Lauren was whisked down the aisle, smiling and joyous, crowded by well-wishers and love. The couple was ushered into the Lincoln Town Car Ma arranged, bound for the reception in Westhampton.

"What a nightmare," Ma announced. "That was the longest wedding, the biggest bunch of gobbledygook I have ever heard in my life."

"You did a great job," Amy said to Ma, as if congratulating a small child. "How are you feeling now?"

"Okay, I guess," Ma told her. "I was so worried that the pin had struck a nerve."

When Ma and Lou reached the reception, Ma put on her best face. She was gracious when the Greeks circled around her, inquiring about her injury. She thanked them and said she prayed there would be no further problems with the wound. And they thanked her for the beautiful champagne gold-themed reception. They thanked her for the fine food and dancing. Some complimented the golden linens, and others the panoramic views of the majestic Atlantic. "It's a splendid wedding," they told her. "Perfect."

In fact, it was a splendid wedding. Ma knew that she had made the Napolitanos proud. She had spoken little to her daughter, except when Lauren and Michael came to her, arm in arm, and said thank you. Michael grabbed Ma's hand in his and led her out to the dance floor for a spin, then he turned her over to a great uncle who did not speak English, and who proceeded to push her round, and round, and round.

But now, seated in an expensively draped organza chair, Ma felt deflated and numb. She watched her daughter, still full of vibrant energy, shake and shimmy and cuddle with her new husband. She watched Lauren kiss him. She watched them shout "Opa!" Ma could see that Lauren loved Michael profoundly and would now adopt his ways and his family. She could not fathom her daughter's choice or a life without Lauren. Michael seemed so foreign to her, and she wondered who he really was. Who was this man who had swooped in and carried her daughter away without any regard for her mother?

PART THREE

You just gotta ignite the light
And let it shine . . .

—Katy Perry, singer, Firework, 2011

CHAPTER 41

Greenwich Village, Manhattan, New York

LAUREN AND MICHAEL RETURNED FROM THE GREEK ISLANDS of Santorini, Mykonos, and Crete as husband and wife. The ten-day honeymoon, away from family and job responsibilities, at first celebrated and then cemented their union, and they arrived at JFK International Airport golden and blessed by the sun, longing to face their future.

Without fanfare, the taxi from the airport brought them to what was now home—Michael's Greenwich Village studio apartment. Its 450 square feet seemed smaller now. There was one closet, which was neither wide nor deep, and it did not accommodate Michael's clothing, much less the addition of Lauren's wardrobe. The kitchen stretched across five feet of the apartment's back wall. It had two cabinets and two wobbly drawers, a half-size refrigerator, a hot plate, and a toaster oven. Lauren couldn't have been happier to be there. Over the next few weeks, she bought fresh flowers at Balducci's, two bright orange coffee mugs, a purple duvet cover, and plastic bins shallow enough to scoot under the bed to hold her clothes. She framed photographs of their adventure in Greece and hammered them into the bumpy, cracked walls. It felt happy. Their first home.

Michael jumped right back into his duties as chief of staff for State Senator Karrie Riedel. The senator's no-nonsense, moderate philosophies and bipartisan approach to politics resonated with hardworking

New Yorkers, and she was currently vying for the United States Senate. Michael, immersed in the campaign effort, helped the senator craft messages of collaboration.

Lauren was also back to work and began a reverse commute from Manhattan to Queens, where Amy and L'Esprit kept her racing. Amy was in the middle of opening two new locations in Manhattan (one on the Upper West Side and one in the East Village), which brought the restaurant count to five. Lauren was overseeing the construction and hiring for the new operations, helping with marketing of the salad dressings, and keeping Amy on task.

The first Sunday after their return, the newlyweds went to see Lou and Ma in Westfield. Lauren brought several envelopes bursting with glossy photos, which she dealt across the kitchen table for Ma and Lou to admire. Here they were on Aegina with its picturesque church of Agios Nektarios (Saint Nectarios), and in Crete on the beaches of Agios Nikolaos and Elounda and the ancient family village of Mahera outside of Iraklion. Here they were at a Greek tavern dining on octopus and ouzo. Here they were in Santorini, boarding a vessel named *Pegasus* that took them to Nea Kameni so they could make their way up the volcano for a view of the caldera. And here they were again in Crete at the Palace of Knossos, standing in the home of the half-man, half-bull creature—the mythical Minotaur.

Ma skimmed the snapshots with a superficial overview as the couple reminisced, but she could not focus and was distracted by Michael's behavior. He would not stop touching her daughter—his hand on Lauren's shoulder, his arm around Lauren's waist, his fingers sliding through Lauren's thin hair. He was like a snake coiling around her daughter. Tightening his grip so that no one else could come near.

Lauren looked different to Ma. In just a few weeks, her small, childlike body had seemed to swell, giving her more distinct curves, a fullness that was not there before. It made her look womanly and grown up. It made her look like Mrs. Stefanakis.

"Must have been wonderful to see something of the world," Lou said to them as he examined each photograph. "I've always wished to do that."

"Sounds like a nice trip," Ma said, "if you like that sort of thing."

Michael smiled at Ma. "It's paradise. What's not to like?" he said.

Ma answered as if she had been biding her time, waiting to gain permission to speak her mind. "Since you ask," she said, "it seems to me that running around the world is not only dangerous, but a waste of money."

"The trip was priceless," Lauren told Ma.

"It's none of my business, of course," Ma said, continuing to make her point, "but I would have thought that you would want to save your money."

"It was worth every penny," Lauren said.

"I would have thought you would have wanted to save your pennies to give my daughter a proper place to live," Ma said to Michael.

Lauren grabbed Michael's hand as if to protect him from the insult, and Ma caught the gesture, felt the change in Lauren's loyalties. Michael was undaunted; Ma didn't get under his skin. "You're right," he said to Ma. "Lauren deserves much more and I intend to provide it."

Ma opened her mouth to wield a sarcastic comeback, but nothing came to mind and she kept quiet as she watched Michael lean into her daughter, watched him hold Lauren's delicate face in his hands—gracing her with three soft kisses.

Lauren and Michael did not return to Belle Haven again until Thanksgiving. It was not an intentional slight to her parents, but a juggling of Michael's work—the stresses of the Riedel campaign, which had ultimately resulted in victory. Riedel was elected with an unprecedented 88 percent of the vote. It was easier to pop by Nonna's house on the days when Lauren worked from L'Esprit's office in Queens. Michael's parents also resided in Queens, and Father Kosta and Anastasia joined the couple twice for dinner at Nonna's. Lauren did not mention this to Ma. Since the wedding, Lauren wasn't comfortable putting Ma and Anastasia at the same table. It was a mix that would never blend, and would most likely leave a bad taste in everyone's mouth.

Lauren did phone her mother every Sunday evening, and even if it was a brief conversation, Lauren never missed the call. Feeling that she was due much more, Ma was not impressed with the effort. Each Sunday's call began the same. "Lou, it's your daughter on the line," Ma shouted. "Placing her weekly pity call."

"How have you been feeling this week?" Lauren queried, ignoring her mother's jab. This was a question that was too tempting for Ma to resist. She would emit a long and loud sigh and relent, launching into sick-talk—bleeding ulcers, migraines, high blood pressure, fatigue, and nerves. She feared that worry over Tony and his suspected heroin habit was causing and prolonging her irregular heartbeat. Of course, the doctors were good for nothing. Worthless. Ma nursed herself with assorted prescription pills, but nothing relieved her ailments. On her worst days, Ma suspected that something more serious was lurking inside of her. "I can feel my organs under attack," she told Lauren.

∽

As Thanksgiving approached, Lauren knew she needed to spend time with her mother. Michael's parents had gone to visit relatives in Greece and Evangeline was left alone. Evangeline planned to stay at Yale, where she was completing her master's degree in forensic psychology. "You must be with us," Lauren told her new sister-in-law. "You can't stay in New Haven alone on Thanksgiving. Besides, we miss you." Lauren didn't get to see Evangeline often, but they liked each other from the start. Lauren admired Evangeline's confidence and determination. Evangeline would decide to take an action and then without delay, without belabored analysis—whether she had declared to change the style of her wardrobe or pursue a graduate degree—she would head toward the goal, on a direct and efficient course. Evangeline was outspoken and full of life. Lauren loved her. Ma did not, and referred to her as "that bossy know-it-all."

In an effort to please everyone, Lauren asked Ma to start fresh and host Thanksgiving, which meant Ma would have to open her door not only to Evangeline, but Nonna and the Aunties too. Ma never entertained at the house in Belle Haven. The thought made her woozy. Lauren pressed every day for a week until Ma said, "Okay, but opening up my house to a bunch of ninnies might kill me."

Ma was to provide the turkey. She instructed Lou to bring the fresh twenty-pound bird home the afternoon of Thanksgiving Eve, and when he returned home thirty minutes late, lugging the bird into the kitchen, Ma was mad.

"I suppose there was traffic," Ma said, her sarcasm polished sharp.

"No, no traffic," Lou answered her. "Just a long line to get the turkey."

"I suppose Lori was in the line too," she said.

"What?"

"Lori!" Ma repeated.

Lou hadn't heard Ma mention Lori in years and was bewildered by the question and the force behind it. "Lori wasn't there," he said.

"Well, she's been here."

"Lori was here?" Lou was confused and felt trouble brewing.

"The rats. They're back. I saw them out on the picnic table," Ma told him.

"They're back?"

"The damn things were crawling all over the table," Ma said, with her arms flailing to demonstrate the rodent activity. Up and down. This way and that. Under and over. "When I hollered at them, they just looked at me. Looked me right in the eyes. They didn't run off."

"You saw rats?" Lou asked.

"They'll be getting into the house in no time. What's everyone going to say about that? What's your son-in-law going to say about that when he comes for his Thanksgiving dinner?"

"You saw rats?" Lou repeated.

"You told me you took care of the rats," Ma accused.

"I did," said Lou.

"Then Lori must be at it again." Ma was shrill, her voice climbing to its highest pitch. "She's bringing rats into our home again. I blame you. I blame you. I blame you. You and your whore."

Lou raised his hand to strike her and as his palm positioned to cross Ma's face, Lou clenched his fist instead and slumped to the floor. "I've told you," Lou cried. "I've told you. There is no girlfriend. There never was. Not Lori or anyone else."

"You've told me lies," Ma shouted as she stood over her deflated husband.

"It's the truth," Lou said, but his brief moment of fire was stamped out and he lay lifeless on the kitchen tile.

"Because of you the rats are back," Ma repeated as her left foot kicked Lou in the side. She withdrew the foot and then rushed it into her husband again. He flinched when the tip of her shoe jabbed his ribs, but he did not attempt to rise or protect himself.

"Do something," Ma raged. Lou would not move.

Ma picked up the plastic-covered turkey and hurled it down onto Lou. When the big bird first struck Lou on the leg, he felt the moisture from the wrapping soak through his pants; he could see the giblets slide from the hollow cavity to a brown clump at the corner of the bag.

Ma bent to the floor and retrieved the fallen bird. She struggled to raise it back to the counter and repositioned her feet to gain strength. She wrapped her arms around the heavy Thanksgiving ball until she was secure and then bludgeoned Lou again, this time aiming the turkey at his head, and then again on his arm. With the fourth and final turkey blow, the fowl hit Lou's boot, propelling the turkey to fly one last time and then land with a considerable plop at Lou's side. The impact forced the plastic wrap to break open—releasing the gizzard, heart, and liver, the watery blood spilling out in a puddle around the organs.

"Do something!" Ma yelled. Lou turned onto his side, raising his knees to his chest. The turkey, no longer Ma's weapon, lay dormant next to him.

Chapter 42

Westfield, New Jersey

THANKSGIVING MORNING, MA CAME DOWN to the kitchen to find that Lou had stuffed the turkey and it was cooking in the oven. Nonna and the Aunties arrived with manicotti, olives spiced with orange and fresh basil, homemade pear cider, and dessert—Auntie Rose's pecan pie, Auntie Dina's ricotta cheesecake, and Auntie Marie's chocolate ganache. Jack yapped as each guest came through the foyer, but when the dog realized the large pans and glass containers were filled with the Aunties' ample treats, he stopped—silenced by a great hope that he, too, would have the opportunity to rummage through their contents.

Evangeline, Lauren, and Michael did not cook, but carried bags from Dean & DeLuca—assorted soft and hard cheeses, toffee brittle, and a Sumatra coffee. The mélange of aromas lured even the lost and rumpled Tony out of his room and to the table.

Ma set out an autumnal-flowered paper tablecloth and filled a ceramic pumpkin with orange and red mums. The family took their places around the table and Ma, with Jack secured in her lap, offered to read a blessing, which was neatly printed on a parchment card. The card had come with the turkey, one for every customer. Ma looked at her guests before she began and then she read the words, loud and clear.

We Give Our Thanks

For food that stays our hunger,
For rest that brings us ease,
For homes where memories linger,
We give our thanks for these.

"Amen," said Rose, which was echoed by Dina and Marie.

And Ma added, "And on this day of thanks, we also remember my beloved brother, Jack Anthony, who was stolen from me by death before his time."

Lou stood, the turkey before him. From the bird's cavity, he scooped out a sausage-and-polenta stuffing. Everyone made the obligatory oohs and aahs at the sight. Lou then sliced through the crispy skin and into the meat.

"Lou, it looks so nice and moist," Nonna said. "Not dry at all."

Evangeline and Lauren giggled, like schoolgirls, the tops of their heads touching, tittering, until Evangeline began to snort for air.

"What's so funny?" Ma asked.

"Nothing, it's just silly," Lauren said, unable to quiet her delighted squeals.

"I guess it's something," Ma said.

"You had to be there," Evangeline said, dismissing Ma. She looked to Lauren with a smile.

Their giggles were innocent, ignited by a remark concerning a boy Evangeline fancied, but Ma could see the girl was nothing more than a rude weasel, not someone Lauren should associate with, and certainly not someone to trust. As Lou continued to slice and stack the meat onto a platter, the girls grew quiet mid-giggle. The Aunties looked to Lou.

The turkey was not like any they had seen before. The browned skin and dark meat looked delicious enough, but there were thin lines of blue and tinges of green splintered across the white meat.

"It's a big bird," Nonna said, complimenting her son.

The platter was passed around and each guest eyed the odd-looking meat.

"Why is it green?" Tony asked, with an unfiltered disgust.

"Probably a bit too much garlic," Nonna said. "Sometimes too much garlic will do that."

Everyone was quiet.

"I'm sure it's fine, Lou," Nonna encouraged. "It smells wonderful." And the turkey did smell good, but not one fork lifted meat to mouth.

"Well, I am embarrassed to tell you the truth, but here goes," Ma said with a shy smile. "Yesterday, after Lou brought this big thing home, and by the way, I did tell him not to get such a big bird, but he wanted something special for you all, so we had it on the counter and I guess we hadn't pushed it far enough from the edge and it fell off. Just dropped right off the counter and onto the floor. Can you imagine?"

"That shouldn't have hurt it," Rose offered.

"Wouldn't have hurt it at all," Dina said, joining the effort to make Lou feel better.

"Of course it's fine," Marie agreed.

It was Michael who changed the subject for good, brought the attention away from the blue-turkey business. "I've got some big news," he announced.

Everyone turned toward Michael to hear the news. Rose guessed they must have found a bigger apartment. Dina hoped it was a baby. Even Ma thought Lauren must have come to her senses and insisted that she and her new husband move back into her parents' house.

"Senator Riedel has asked me to join her and head up her transition to the United States Senate," Michael told his expectant family.

"Hear, hear!" said Evangeline, and she raised her glass, first to her brother and then to Lauren. Evangeline's congratulatory response was so quick that Ma was sure that this information was not news to Evangeline. How long had she been privy to this secret?

"Hear, Hear!" Everyone followed Evangeline's lead.

"That's wonderful," said Nonna.

"Congratulations," cheered the Aunties.

"It means we will be moving to Washington, D.C.," Lauren said, making sure everyone understood what the new position would mean.

Ma clutched her fork and stabbed it into the slice of turkey before her.

"Hear, hear," Evangeline repeated, and the group followed. Glasses rose into the air again, clinking against one another in shared joy.

"To the newlyweds," Evangeline toasted. "To Lauren and Michael."

Chapter 43

Lauren moved her clothes and boxes to Belle Haven. Michael gave up his apartment in Greenwich Village, and the couple moved into Ma's house, back to Lauren's childhood bedroom for the last two weeks of December. Michael was to begin work for Senator Riedel on January 2, and they planned to drive to Washington, D.C., on New Year's Day.

Ma tried her best to make Lauren see the light about the move. "It's so far away," she protested. "There's more crime in that city than most," she pointed out. "You'll be so lonely," she taunted. "Why don't you stay with us until Michael is sure this is what he wants?" she reasoned. "You've worked so hard. Why give up a job that you love?" she scolded.

Lauren countered all of Ma's arguments with the same answer: "Ma, I'm married now. I want to be with Michael."

To make matters worse, Michael parked a rental truck in their driveway. It was the smallest size available, as the couple did not own much, but Ma thought it was offensive—a loud announcement of the couple's disrespectful decision. Lou helped Michael load the truck and arrange the contents so that they wouldn't slide about during the drive. The packing didn't take long, and as they moved boxes of clothing, three suitcases, Louie's boyhood dresser, and Louie's old desk out of the house and into the truck, Lou cautioned Michael not to bump or jostle the two propane tanks that flanked the front path.

"Such an odd place for those," Michael said, noticing the two metal containers near the front door.

"I know. They're an eyesore. I always intended to have them moved around to the side of the house," Lou told Michael, "but somehow I never get around to it. One of these days I will. Maybe in the new year I'll actually do it."

The upcoming new year seemed to be symbolic for most. To Lauren and Michael it marked a new life as man and wife, a jump into the future. In the five years that Michael lived in Manhattan, he never once ventured to Times Square on New Year's Eve, never wanted to navigate the crowds or witness the overindulgences that the holiday encouraged. He preferred to stay home, warm in his bed—away from the noise, the pressure to have fun, and the absence of available taxis. This New Year's Eve, with a wife and a new career opportunity, Michael had a different attitude. He wanted to take Lauren and watch the ball drop. He wanted to join the crowds and greet the New Year. He wanted the two of them to be part of it as they moved toward their future together.

Ma thought the idea was crazy. "You'll be mugged or worse," she warned them through flu-like sniffles. When Michael explained his reasoning, she said, "I'm much too weak to argue with you," and went back to bed, hoping to conquer the winter bug that assailed her.

Lauren and Michael didn't give Ma's warning any thought. They were ready to squeeze into the crowd of midnight revelers. Michael even bought silver-and-blue noisemakers. A few hours before they were to leave for the city, Lauren felt an uneasiness come over her, and soon after she began to vomit. She checked herself for hives and found none. Then Michael detected the same queasiness. He tried to deny his body's sudden warmth and shaky stomach, but it was no use. For several hours, they alternated running down the hall to the bathroom. At one point Lauren stayed put on the bathroom floor, hugging the toilet basin.

"Are you kids okay?" Lou asked.

"We've got the flu," Michael said.

"Ma's got it too," Lou said. "Let me know what I can do," he offered, but he knew only time would make the bug pass.

Dick Clark counted down the seconds. Ten . . . nine . . . eight . . . seven . . . six. Lauren and Michael lay in bed, oblivious to the New Year's celebrations, hoping for a reprieve from their rioting bellies.

By early morning, they were sweaty and frail, but neither had succumbed to the nausea for a couple of hours. Michael rubbed the back of Lauren's shoulders.

"Let's get going," he told her.

Lauren moaned in protest.

"I think it's important that we go today," he whispered. "It seems significant somehow. Like our happiness depends upon it." Lauren rolled over and stared at her husband. She could tell he was serious.

"I don't want to spend the first day of the year sick in bed," he said. "I know this sounds nutty, but I think it will be a bad start if we stay under the blankets feeling miserable."

Lauren nodded.

And on the first day of January 2003, as they entered their sixth month of marriage, Lauren and Michael dragged themselves up and out of Lauren's childhood bed. They dressed and pulled themselves into the rental truck. They headed to Washington, D.C.

CHAPTER 44

Capitol Hill, Washington, D.C.

Ma and Lou were coming to visit. It had been two years since the newlyweds made their home at 133 First Street. Senator Riedel helped them find a place to live, arranging the Capitol Hill rental from a retired Senator. The townhome was quintessential D.C. Victorian, a red-brick row house. The space inside was warm and harmonious, with a fireplace, exposed brick walls, and a renovated country kitchen. French doors at the back of the kitchen opened onto a small outdoor patio where Lauren placed pretty blue pots filled with seasonal plants and flowers. Now in early November, the pots held yellow chrysanthemums. Upstairs were three bedrooms and two baths—more than enough room for the young working couple and plenty of space to make Ma and Lou comfortable guests.

Lauren had been pestering her parents to visit, and after almost two years of persuasion, they were due to arrive. She wanted to show them her new D.C. life, how far she'd come. She wanted them to feel proud of her and her husband. The relocation had been more challenging than Lauren expected. After the initial excitement of settling into the townhome and being offered a staff position with a renowned former congressman at his newly established nonprofit organization, Lauren's enthusiasm for the adventure began to fade. As her life normalized into a routine, she could not shake the uncertainty that it was not a perfect fit. She missed familiar foods, the neighborhoods of both New Jersey and Queens, and the loud and direct way people spoke. She missed her father, Nonna, the Aunties, and even Tony. Lauren was surprised to find that she missed her mother most of all.

Ma kept Lauren close for as long as they had been joined as mother and daughter, and now that Lauren had scrambled away, disentangled the ties, and set out on her own, Lauren felt the tug of Ma pulling her back. It was true that Lauren wanted to see how far she could venture toward her own pursuits, and she wanted to stand by Michael's side, but she also did not want to lose touch with the past, did not want that to drift too far away. Lauren knew Ma had many troubles over the years and the Napolitanos had seen their fair share of the bad times compared to the good ones. But Lauren was grateful for Ma and knew that some people were in worse situations than hers (Ma's words echoed in her head—daughters without mothers, without any family whatsoever). There were times when everything Lauren knew seemed so far away. Over the last years, Lauren would think she was moving forward, only to find that an indescribable longing would settle over her, dampening her spirit. She began to feel as if she was treading water in a wide river, and while she knew she must swim, she was confused and conflicted. Yes, there was a lush shoreline that loomed in front of her, but the solid land that rose up behind her beckoned as well. Lauren knew if she didn't choose a direction soon, she would be dragged downstream. Drowned.

"Give it some time," Michael said to her. "let's give it three years. You're in transition, and getting used to that doesn't happen overnight."

For Michael, it did happen overnight. He felt an instant affinity for his new city and was proud to be part of the historic fabric, to follow those who had come before, those who had come to make a difference. Senator Riedel kept him in rapid motion, a pace that thrilled him. There were meetings, meetings, and more meetings, topped off by seemingly endless events. Michael was moving toward a target, his direction straight and clear. Surrounded by Washington's movers and shakers, he was propelled into the constituents' awareness by the multifaceted hands-on doing that his position required. Working side by side with the senator in Washington gave him the opportunity to put his studied, abstract theories into practice. He relished it all, and hoped his wife would soon come to feel that same sense of belonging.

It wasn't that Lauren was out of touch. Ma telephoned daily, but Lauren could feel that the distance made Ma unsettled, and that mood was infectious. Every night, Ma would dial up her daughter. And despite the frequency of the calls, Ma always had news. She collected bad and sad accounts of D.C. trouble—reports of inclement weather, a recent armed robbery, murder, a burgeoning crack epidemic, or the latest political scandal. She encouraged her daughter to visit the police station for a crime map, because after all, Lauren was choosing to live in a place that had once been dubbed "The Murder Capital." If Ma did not have a local tidbit to pass on, she moved her scope nationwide.

"Does she always have to be so negative?" Michael would say to Lauren as she quickly covered the receiver so Ma could not hear the critical comment.

"She just gets nervous," Lauren would whisper to him. "She worries about us."

"She's crazy, is what she is." Michael would push his hands through his hair and walk into another room, sparing himself from Ma's string of mishaps. Lauren sympathized with Michael's point of view, though sometimes she wished that he would be more tolerant toward Ma and support their mother-daughter relationship.

Michael did make the effort to join Lauren in visiting Ma in New Jersey. Since their departure, the couple returned to Belle Haven five times. Lauren brought photographs with her in an effort to illuminate their D.C. life, hoping to convince Ma that the city had much to offer, but Ma always seemed preoccupied, giving only a half glance to the photographs and saying, "You couldn't pay me to live in that place."

Ma saved newspaper clippings from *The Washington Post*, one of three newspapers she now purchased so that she could make it her business to be informed about her daughter's environment. The clippings were stored in a red folder marked CRIME AND MORE, which she would pull out of the kitchen cubby and hand to Michael within minutes of his arrival. The folder contained descriptions of fires, burglaries, rapes, rabid dogs, brutal attacks, and homicide. "Just thought you would want to be aware of the kinds of things that surround you and my daughter," she said, pushing the fat folder toward Michael for his review.

Michael had come to dread these sojourns, not because of the bad-news folder, but because once he stepped inside his mother-in-law's home, he felt trapped. Ma was a homebody, while Michael, a doer, an out-and-about kind of guy, had trouble staying put. Lauren still hoped to please them both. Most of all, she aimed to keep Ma calm, careful not to tip the balance and cause upset, and if that meant being confined to Ma's territory, drinking and talking crime, that is what she felt obligated to do.

The upcoming trip was a radical shift. Ma and Lou were coming to D.C. and Lauren wanted everything to be perfect. Ma, who rarely traveled, issued instructions for their first visit. Lauren was to have on hand several bottles of rum and Coca-Cola for Lou, and three one-gallon jugs of pinot grigio, which Ma recently took up. "I don't want to do much," Ma advised Lauren. "I'm looking forward to just relaxing with a glass of wine."

Michael had other ideas. Lauren's parents were coming to the nation's capital, and he hoped to pull out all the stops. He hoped to impress them by planning the best city tour possible—one they would never forget.

Ma and Lou flew separately from LaGuardia, arriving at Reagan National Airport on separate carriers. Their planes touched down in the District of Columbia one hour apart. "God forbid the plane should go down," Ma said. "How could you manage losing us both?" she asked, not waiting for Lauren's answer. "Anything could happen. The plane could burst into flames. A terrorist could be on board. The plane could plunge into the Potomac. It could happen," Ma warned. "You would lose both of your parents in one fell swoop. Tony would never ever survive it."

Ma arrived first that late November afternoon. She wheeled a striped suitcase with bands of bright primary colors. It looked like a child-size rainbow was trotting behind her. Lauren watched her mother come toward her and was surprised to notice that Ma's face looked puffy and she had gained weight that settled in her middle. One hour later, Lauren was even more surprised to see her father radiant as he emerged from his flight. The day was clear and sunny and as the plane flew up into the pale, pastel sky, through the huddled clouds, Lou imagined first leaping effortlessly from cloud to cloud, and then hiding amongst the wispy fluffs where no one would ever find him. The meditation left him with remnants of great joy, which manifested in a big smile and lively steps as he moved to greet his beloved daughter.

After they arrived at the townhome, Lou was impressed as he examined each room of his daughter's new quarters. Ma skipped the tour and went off to the guest room to attend to the task of unpacking her suitcase, which was filled with gifts. Michael arrived home from work and they gathered around the coffee table in the living room as Ma handed out presents, elaborately wrapped with colorful, curly ribbons. There was a royal blue cashmere sweater for Lauren. A mahogany jewelry box with Lauren's name engraved in gold. Twin crystal teddy bear figurines whose chubby, glass bodies reflected the light (the cute pair was also meant for Lauren). There were Lauren's favorite cannoli and Italian cookies—an assortment of biscotti, pizzelle, anise, and butter cookies—which had not traveled well and were either soggy or crumbled. And a heap of dish towels with coordinating refrigerator magnets. The dish towels came in matching sets of two, with red- or green-checked backgrounds. Each set was embroidered with a patch of cheery flowers and alternating slogans about love: "The Greatest Love is a Mother's Love" and "God Made Hugs, Smiles, and Daughters." As Ma bestowed each gift, Lauren felt touched by her parents' generosity. She was glad to have them close, sitting in her living room.

There was one last gift crumpled at the bottom of the suitcase.

"I brought this for you." Ma handed Michael a soft, flat present wrapped in no-frills tinfoil, across which ran an excessive amount of Scotch tape to keep the contents enclosed. The tinfoil had become dented and torn, presumably due to travel. When Michael ripped the tape apart, a dress shirt fell into his lap. The shirt was solid black.

Michael didn't know what to make of the gift. After an acknowledgement of thanks, he said, "We've got a big day planned for tomorrow."

"I just want to relax," Ma said.

"Relax?" Michael said. "We're going to show you the town."

Michael took the day off to be part of the big tour. As the chief of staff to Senator Riedel, he would often take visitors and officials to tour the Capitol Building, and this was their first stop. For Michael, the building symbolized democracy, and he delighted in escorting his family trio upstairs to the grand rotunda. Here, he highlighted some of his favorite and lesser-known facts. He called their attention to the 1865 fresco, *The Apotheosis of Washington*, by the Greek-Italian painter Constantino Brumidi. Michael directed Ma and Lou to look overhead into the eye of the Capitol Building's rotunda, 180 feet above the floor, where they would see the only work depicting George Washington as a God—glorified, rising to the heavens, and surrounded by the female figures of Liberty and Victory. Lou was mesmerized and moved in a slow circle, straining his neck to take in every inch of the 4,664-square-foot masterpiece.

Michael never tired of the building, and while in the presence of the one hundred statues of the National Statuary Hall, standing with the figures honoring notable citizens from all fifty states, Michael recalled the words of Senator Riedel. They were driving up Constitution Avenue, with the majestic Capitol Building in full view, when she stopped their discussion abruptly and told him: "If you ever look at that building and it does not inspire you, it is time to leave Washington." Michael had seen the Capitol Building numerous times, both inside and out, and it always left him breathless.

As an additional treat, Michael arranged for a private tour of the

West Wing of the White House. "And now on to the White House," he informed Ma and Lou.

"Really? That too?" Lou asked his son-in-law. "Who would have thought that we'd ever get to see all this?"

"Will we see the president?" Ma asked.

"Probably not," Lauren told her mother.

"Just wondering, because I am not a fan," Ma said.

For Lou, the West Wing of the White House was as remarkable and absorbing as the Capitol Building. The friendly White House staff escort brought them through the Rose Garden, Cabinet Room, Oval Office, and lastly the Press Briefing Room. Their escort explained that the small, theater-style room was built on top of what was once FDR's swimming pool—a necessity for his polio rehabilitation. After forty years, as more space was needed for the growing press, President Nixon arranged for the room's construction directly above the pool. "It must make everything very moldy," Ma said.

Lauren nodded to Michael that it was time, and he approached the podium, standing in front of the blue curtain, next to the American flag, and before two microphones. He was poised to speak.

"Excuse me," Michael said, addressing his in-laws over the microphone. As Michael's words echoed out to them, Lauren clutched her father's arm with expectation.

Ma stood in disbelief. What was Michael doing standing at the podium just like a White House press secretary ready to give a daily briefing to reporters, or just like the president addressing the nation, positioning his face at just the right angle so that the microphones could give his words great power?

"I have an official announcement to make," Michael said. Lauren looked at her husband and smiled. She knew what was to follow.

"From this extraordinary spot where I now stand, I would like to announce something quite momentous." Michael was not able to conceal either his joy or his pride, and he waited to savor the moment before he released the news into the room. "My wife and I are highly honored to inform you that we are expecting our first child."

Ma and Lou stood quiet, digesting the unexpected and very public news. The few others in the room, on a separate tour, were also made privy to Michael's amplified words, and they heartily applauded.

Lou turned to his daughter. "Wonderful news," he said, before embracing her. "This day just keeps getting better and better." It was a fact he said more to himself than to Lauren.

Michael stepped off the podium, putting any reservations about his mother-in-law aside, and drew her into his arms.

"When?" Ma asked him.

"July," Michael told her.

"Just like Lauren," Ma said.

Michael had made reservations at the storied Willard Hotel, where they were to have a celebratory lunch at the Round Robin Bar, a spot few tourists frequented, as it attracted those who were involved in the business of politics. Michael was excited to give his in-laws a flavor of in-the-know Washington, and the Willard Hotel was just the place. The hotel hosted not only politicians but a long list of authors and poets who spent time drinking, socializing, and even writing: Walt Whitman, Nathaniel Hawthorne, and Martin Luther King, Jr., who stayed in the hotel while writing his "I Have a Dream" speech.

As the family headed to the Willard, stepping out to cross Pennsylvania Avenue, several police cars sped up to the intersection and stopped traffic, cautioning pedestrians to stand back. The traffic and those on foot halted, waiting in expectation. Ma could see several police motorcycles making their way down the avenue.

"What's going on?" Ma asked.

"It's a presidential motorcade," Michael told her. "What luck."

The police motorcycles came first, riding in unison, followed by a procession of twenty vehicles. The all-black armored convoy drove through the street with lights flashing; an additional cavalcade of ambulances, police cars, and police motorcycles brought up the rear.

"It's like something out of a movie," Lou said.

"It's a lot of fuss, if you ask me," Ma added. But despite her words, Michael noticed that she raised her hand, offering the passing black limousine that carried the nation's leader a small wave. Michael witnessed the gesture and felt instant victory. Even Ma was impressed.

They arrived back at the townhome, the long day now a significant memory. Ma was worn out. But Lou was still elated. "Today was one of the best days of my life," he told the expectant couple.

Ma slumped into the large white couch that faced the fireplace. "Get your father a drink," she said to Lauren.

Michael jumped to fill the order, happy to do so, pleased that the day worked out not only without incident but as a great success. As he presented Lou with a special whiskey, Ma stopped him. "What kind of drink is that?" she asked.

"Just what the doctor ordered," Michael teased Ma, placing the libation in Lou's hand.

"That glass must be for some kind of midget." Ma was commenting on the small crystal glass, which was part of a set, a wedding present from Michael's parents. "Get him a real drink in a proper glass. Man-size."

Ma had taken to giving Lou rum and Coke each evening to help him relax. Lou liked Ma's evening ritual; the remedy made him sleep right through the night. This evening, after a perfect day, he also liked the taste of Michael's whiskey. The drink started out smooth, without too much flavor. He could only detect a bit of sweetness and a trace of charred oak. There was no real bite and it soothed him.

Michael followed Ma's directions and made Lou a rum and Coke in a large soda glass. Lauren was in the middle of laying out a light supper when the loud whirring sound of several helicopters caught Ma's attention.

"What's that racket?" Ma asked.

"We're so used to it we barely notice the noise," Michael told her. "It's Marine One."

"How do you know that?" Ma asked, doubtful. "There must be four or five of them." This was a realization that stunned Ma.

"It's Marine One," Michael explained. "The United States Marine Corps carries the president."

"We just saw him a few hours ago," Ma challenged. "I doubt he's flying around now."

Lauren noticed the tense catch in her mother's voice and was on alert. "As a security measure, they fly in a group. They're decoys, and sometimes the president isn't even with them."

"How do you know that this is not a terrorist attack?" Ma challenged.

"It happens all the time," Michael assured her.

The disturbance continued to hang over the conversation, and Ma began to shout. "How do you know that they are not terrorists spraying Agent Orange or something far worse?" Ma's voice began to run into the realm of hysteria.

"This can happen a few times a day," Michael insisted.

"It could be herbicidal warfare," Ma argued.

Michael's patience was coming to an end. He would not let Ma ruin a perfect day, the day that they first announced their pregnancy, a day that he had planned for weeks. "That's not possible. Our townhouse is under the path of Marine One."

"Did you know that Agent Orange can cause cancer?"

"Ma, it's okay," Lauren said. She turned to her father for assistance, but Lou remained silent, sipping his oversized drink.

"And birth defects!" Ma said, with great emphasis. "Did you know that it can cause birth defects?"

Now Michael was fuming. "There is nothing to worry about."

"Can you say that 100 percent?" Ma was ready for battle.

"I can and I do." Michael returned his answer with some force, in a tone that he had never used with his mother-in-law.

The stern message was received and Ma did lower her voice, but she did not completely stop before squeezing in one last comment. "Well I still don't believe that you know that 100 percent." Rather than fight further, she reached into her purse and retrieved a Xanax, which she washed down with a glass of pinot grigio and a chug of Benadryl.

Lauren plated some of Ma's soggy cannoli and the Italian deli an-
tipasto that she had purchased to make her parents feel more at home.
They gathered around a shared meal for the second time that day, but
Michael's enthusiasm was stomped into sullen silence.

"Not bad," Ma said to Lauren as she picked over the food. "But
we get much tastier food at home." Lauren nodded in agreement, relieved that the Agent Orange argument didn't escalate into a full-blown
tantrum.

Michael excused himself from the table and headed upstairs to the
bedroom to review some paperwork.

"I think I'll go get into my pj's," Ma said to Lou, and she also headed
upstairs to the guest room.

Lou, realizing that only he and Lauren were left in the room, said,
"Well now that Ma's off to bed, I think it's time for me to go up also."

"You can stay up and chat with me," Lauren suggested, hoping that
her father would visit with her, something she could not recall doing
privately since she was a young girl.

"It's nine thirty," he said. "I'd better hit the sack." He got up to leave
the kitchen, but not without saying, "Thank you for today. I loved every
minute and I can't wait until the little one arrives."

With her mother more than likely passed out upstairs and her father soon to follow, Lauren proceeded to clean up the kitchen and get
things in order for the breakfast she would serve in the morning. Michael read a book in bed. For the most part, Lauren thought the day
went well. Her parents had seen some of the best of D.C., and Ma had
behaved well until dinner, when her nerves got the best of her.

Two hours later, as Michael drifted in and out of sleep and the pages of his book, the double doors to the bedroom slammed open. The
impact caused the right door to rattle against the doorstop. His mother-in-law stood before him in purple floral pajamas. She scowled. Her
blue eyes appeared black in the dimly lit room, but Michael could see
enough of her to know that she was consumed with rage. Michael sat

up straight against the pillow. Ma did not move forward to the bed, but her tongue flew around her lips once, and then twice, trying to soften the dryness that aggravated her, trying to remove the caked saliva that had hardened in the corners of her mouth. Her thin hair stood up on one side, the carefully covered bald patch raw and exposed.

"Where are my nuts?" The sound Ma emitted was an acid, warlike scream, a screech far too eerie to be defined as simple anger. It was as if she meant to annihilate her enemy, to slay the evildoer propped up on his pillows and expose him of his heinous crime.

"I'm not sure." Michael was gentle and steady so as not to invoke any further trouble. "You may want to look for them in the kitchen."

Ma cocked her head to the side, considering the suggestion, and then she turned and exited the bedroom. Michael watched her leave his room, until she became a patch of noxious flowers gusting down the hall.

Lauren was flipping through some new cookbooks when Ma entered the kitchen. Ma walked to the right and then to the left. She seemed unsure of where to go, until she spied her purse on the couch in the adjacent living room. The sight of the purse seemed to fill her with determination, and she began to dig through its contents. "They gave me a package of nuts on the plane and I can't find them," was all she had to say to Lauren.

"I haven't seen them," Lauren told her mother.

"I need to refill my cup," Ma said. "Where's that bottle of wine?"

There would be no contest now. No reasoning. No war of words. Lauren simply opened a new jug of pinot grigio and poured it into a ceramic mug for her mother, abandoning the pretense of a fragile wineglass. She placed the mug on the coffee table, within her mother's easy reach.

Lauren watched Ma hunch over her handbag, rooting through to the bottom in a frenzied effort to excavate the petite package of nuts. Lauren's hand instinctively flew to her own chest. With fingers splayed, she pressed hard against the breastbone—a meager attempt to contain the great dread lodged in her heart.

CHAPTER 45

BABY. BABY. BABY. The upcoming arrival of baby Stefanakis was joyful news for both sides of the family. Nonna, the Aunties, Michael's parents, and Evangeline were all eager to welcome their newest relative. Even though Tony rolled his eyes when he heard, he also felt the anticipation. It was Ma, the mother of the mother-to-be, who was giving the utmost attention to her first grandchild's pending entrance. Ma was ready and waiting. She mailed Lauren books about pregnancy, fetal development, and motherhood. She wrote lengthy lists of tips for Lauren, including her own views: first on pregnancy and then supplemental directions for infant care, which encompassed feeding schedules (breastfeeding was tabled as an unnecessary nuisance), burping, diapering, and multiple naps. She sent a crisp white crib, changing table, and rocking chair to the Capitol Hill townhome for the nursery. Now Ma's daily phone calls to Lauren were discussions of the difficulties of motherhood and the elaborate baby shower that Ma intended to throw in New Jersey.

Ma had one other very particular philosophy: a new mother should not work. And here, Lauren and her mother were at odds.

"You know how fragile and sensitive you are," Ma cautioned. "I think it's best if you take it easy now and after the baby is born." Ma even suggested that Lauren move home to New Jersey, where Ma could take care of her daughter during pregnancy, eliminating any discomfort or worry caused by her busy and dangerous D.C. life. "Any stress the mother feels will be passed to the baby," Ma argued. Ma worried about all kinds of potential pregnancy catastrophes and preferred that Lauren, for the sake of the baby, be housebound. Lauren did her best to appease Ma. She always treated her with respect. She listened to Ma's ranting and consoled her during times of stress. And as much as Lauren hoped Ma would come around someday, she never once considered the invitation of returning home. Even so, as Lauren carried her unborn child, felt its swift movements inside the womb, she recognized an ongoing and continued tug to be close to her mother.

With such frequent communication, there was little Lauren could keep from Ma. When Michael took Lauren for an early spring hike in the nearby Shenandoah Valley, Ma was beside herself. "I want to know what kind of husband would take his pregnant wife hiking in the dead of winter?" Lauren explained that the hike, which was more of a wooded stroll along a novice trail, was best at this time of year, when trails were less crowded and overgrown, and there were fewer bugs and no bears. In Ma's continuous scolding, the possibility of a bear had never entered her mind. Once Lauren brought the information to Ma's attention—the incredible danger that the possibility of a bear presented—Ma gasped multiple times, her breath sucked inward, repeatedly inhaling any stray remnants of fear. "It's too much for you," Ma wheezed. "You must be careful."

Despite Ma's concerns, Lauren had no intention of being housebound, no intention of treating herself like an invalid or taking the dozens of prenatal vitamins Ma constantly recommended, and certainly no intention of leaving her job, now or after the baby was born. Lauren considered her current employment a blessing, a gift of good fortune.

In fact, the job had been not only auspicious, but also unexpected. When Lauren and Michael first arrived in D.C. three years ago, Lauren was at a loss for where to look for employment. She began by circling a few help-wanted ads in *The Washington Post*. She then retraced the same positions until the pen poked through the newsprint, making the ads unreadable. She wasn't inspired to call or apply for any of them. It was Senator Riedel who put her in touch with Carl Hill, a revered congressman who retired after thirty years of service, the first fifteen-term member of Congress, who currently ran America's Future Professionals—a nonprofit organization for children from disadvantaged backgrounds. Lauren applied for a job as his administrative assistant. It was her one and only D.C. interview, but after the meeting she didn't feel the need to pursue a job search. She liked Carl Hill from the start and felt the feeling was mutual.

Carl was unlike anyone Lauren had ever met. He served fifteen consecutive terms in the U.S. House of Representatives and played a major role in the quest for civil rights. He was gracious and impeccable and always presented a demeanor of calm and aplomb, especially with the contentious personalities he encountered in his work. Even on weekday afternoons, after long days at his desk, he remained pressed and composed, never wrinkled or crumpled. His wardrobe consisted of dark suits, which he brightened with light blue shirts and accented with solid maroon or navy neckties. He spoke with a rotund and measured voice. The tone was not intimidating or pompous, but open and thoughtful. Carl, who was approaching his seventy-third year, was an old-fashioned gentleman.

When they met for the first time, Carl explained to Lauren how important the association was to him. He told her how he grew up in poverty and lived in public housing with a hardworking, widowed mother who had little education. He told her that he and his brothers attended the segregated public school in their battered neighborhood. He told her how he was able to rise above his adverse circumstances, and that he wanted every child from a similar background to know that he or she could do the same. He did not relay these personal details with any trace of bitterness, arrogance, or regret, but rather as a profound commitment to his life's great hope.

And if Lauren found herself perplexed on the job as she learned the ins and outs of D.C. political culture, Carl was accessible and patient, even fun, a trait she was amazed to witness in a man of his reputation and serious stature. At America's Future Professionals, Lauren met people from all kinds of professions—teachers, nurses, counselors, social workers, ministers, politicians, and fundraisers. Despite Ma's worries, the demands of the job did not tire Lauren's constitution or cause her ailments to emerge and erupt. On the contrary, her workdays made her energized. They nourished her.

Ma was not impressed by Lauren's job. Ma was raised in a neighborhood similar to Carl's and she married Lou as a quick means of escape. Ma had no intention of falling back into the past, and did not see why her daughter needed to know about any of the unpleasantness associated with poverty-stricken neighborhoods. As far as she was concerned, Ma said good riddance to that life ages ago. No good could come from Lauren dwelling on other people's misfortunes. And now there was her grandchild to think of as well.

Yes, she was pregnant, but no matter what her mother said, Lauren was not giving up her treasured job. Carl surprised Lauren even further. When she had been in the position for over two years, Carl offered Lauren a promotion to America's Future Professionals' spokesperson. It was a gigantic opportunity. "Are you sure this makes sense?" Lauren asked, testing Carl, offering him a way out. Carl said, "Yes, I am very sure."

Lauren was honored and overwhelmed by the confidence and trust that Carl placed in her. She was dazzled at the prospect of taking on such a prestigious and high-profile position. While she wanted to accept the responsibilities with a loud and adamant *yes*, she also felt harnessed and restrained, unable to move forward and claim the job as her own. Lauren was all nerves. She worried about her lack of experience. She fretted about her lack of a fancy education, which she saw in those around her. More than anything, she brooded about the possibility of letting Carl down.

It was in this state that Lauren confided the opportunity to Ma. Unlike Lauren, Ma had no doubts. Ma was sure. "Are you crazy?" Ma's question came through the phone like a sharp and prolonged pinch. "You can't do that. You're pregnant. And Lauren, let's face it . . ." Lauren knew what was coming. She immediately recognized the introductory setup for the words she hadn't heard in years. But there they were, ready to be trotted out again, as strong and hurtful as ever.

"I know. I know," Lauren yelled at Ma. "You don't have to remind me. Let's face it. Let's be honest. I'm not all that smart. Not the sharpest knife in the drawer. Right? Is that what you want me to face?"

Ma realized the tactic wouldn't work and changed course. "It's not that. I just believe that motherhood is the most important job of all. Out of my three children, Louie was the bookish one, and that never helped him. He was stuck on grandiose dreams. You understand reality, which is what is really smart. Louie didn't know his place and look how he ended up." Lauren was surprised that Ma summoned Louie's name, a moniker they never uttered. After all these years, to hear the name spoken out loud made Lauren feel bruised and battered all over again. How *had* Louie ended up? Lauren didn't know. She only knew that she still missed him.

Ma's clear dismissal of the job proposal eroded any sense of accomplishment or competence, erased any earned pride for years of hard work and study. Lauren stumbled, tripped, and fell. No matter how much Michael or Carl encouraged her, offered her a hand to stand up and move forward, Lauren's self-assurance dwindled to nothing. "I'm sorry, I just don't think I am ready," she told Carl with finality.

The episode irked Ma, and she was relieved when Lauren came to her senses and turned down the position so that they could return to discussing the upcoming shower and, more importantly, the baby's name.

The baby was a boy. Once that fact was revealed to Ma, she had definite opinions about what to call him. "His name should be Sean," Ma said. Lauren instinctively trembled at the suggestion. It was yet another word from the past. Sean, her high school boyfriend, was nothing she cared to remember or honor. "It's a good, solid Irish name," Ma told her.

"How can you even suggest it?" Lauren asked her mother. "Besides, we were thinking of something Greek for Michael's family, or Italian to honor Nonna and Nonno."

"Sean," Ma said, "has a good ring to it. You have to admit it's manly. The baby boy names today are wussy. I want my grandson to be a man. Just think about it," Ma pressed. "That's all I'm asking—just think about it."

Lauren did mention Ma's peculiar suggestion to Nonna, but Nonna was no longer receptive to analyzing Ma, not like they used to when Lauren lived with her in Queens. Perhaps it was because Nonna was getting older and felt too weary for any conflict or upheaval from Ma, or perhaps it was because Nonna's son was back in her life and she wanted to keep him there at all costs. Whatever the reason, she no longer entertained discussions about Ma, and made every attempt to avoid negative remarks about her daughter-in-law. Nonna simply said, "Lauren, you have such a wonderful husband. Name your baby after his father."

Ma pushed for an early baby shower. She did not want Lauren to travel close to her due date, and in case the baby should arrive early, Ma wanted to make sure that there was ample time for a proper shower. The celebration was set in Lauren's sixth month. Ma booked a New Jersey venue, Santelli's. She meticulously selected the buffet brunch menu, and sent over fifty invitations to friends and relatives, including a suggested baby gift registry. She purchased decorations and party favors. Unlike the wedding in the Hamptons, this was Ma's event, on her territory, and Lauren gave her mother full planning reign.

In April, Michael and Lauren arrived in New Jersey the day before the shower and stayed at the house in Belle Haven, moving into Lauren's childhood bedroom for the night. Ma ushered Lauren upstairs right away. "No boys allowed," she said, leaving Michael downstairs with Lou. Tony, who was supposedly home, did not come out to say hello. Upstairs in Lauren's bedroom, Ma reached into the empty closet and pulled out a dress, which she held up before her daughter—a maternity dress, in pale cerulean, with a ring of complementary sapphire-colored rhinestones dotting the neck.

"It's beautiful," Lauren said.

"I wanted you to have something special to wear tomorrow," Ma told her.

"I can't imagine anything prettier."

Ma was pleased with Lauren's response. Just before she headed back downstairs, she stopped at the doorway.

"There's one more thing I wanted to mention," Ma said with un-characteristic hesitation. "Dad bumped into Amy at Home Depot near Nonna's. He was buying some things to take care of a problem that's come back into the house."

"Amy? You saw Amy?" Lauren asked, delighted to hear news of her former boss.

"Well, it's kind of an embarrassing story," Ma said. "We found a rat in the kitchen a few weeks ago. Actually, in the silverware drawer. I thought we were done with all of that and I am too old to dredge up the past with your father, but we wanted to let you know because Dad felt so uncomfortable when he ran into Amy. I wanted to make sure we got rid of the problem in case any guests wanted to come out to the house before or after the baby shower. It's just that I am so humiliated about it, but your father has everything under control now."

Lauren listened to Ma, who seemed fidgety as she dashed through the content of her message. "Why would you be embarrassed?" Lauren quizzed.

"Well, if you must know the truth, I didn't want anyone thinking that I keep a filthy home. That we're dirty."

"Ma, no one will ever think we're dirty." Lauren was confounded to find herself in the role of reassuring Ma. "Ma, don't worry so much. The shower will be perfect."

"I know; you're right," Ma said. "Sometimes stress just gets the best of me." Lauren could not deny that Ma was looking colorless and bloated, which seemed to have become a permanent state, and Lauren had also noticed that the number of prescription pill bottles lined up across the kitchen windowsill had doubled. When she listened to her mother, flustered and disconcerted, Lauren felt she was in the presence of a young girl and could see the face of that child, vulnerable and lost. She knew her mother to be odd and dramatic, even impossible at times, but as Ma stood in the doorway, Lauren felt a great urge to console her. She knew that Ma had clawed her way out of a rotten beginning, and with Lauren entering a newfound maturity, she came to understand it as the reason why Ma always played it tough. Lauren wanted to protect the little girl she saw in her mother; to wash the shame away, envelop her, and tell her that she was so sorry for what happened long ago.

Of course, Ma would not have allowed any such demonstration of tenderness. Instead, Lauren said, "Ma, thanks so much for doing all this with the shower, I know how much effort you've put into this party. We are so grateful to you."

"Of course, I want to do it," Ma said, shaking off the brief bout of exposed weakness. "What do you think? You're my daughter and we're talking about my grandson."

The next morning, Lauren woke to find blood on her pillow. She wiped her nose and felt the usual crusted and dried blood. She went downstairs to tell Michael, who was already up and drinking coffee with Ma and Lou in the kitchen. "I'm sure it's nothing," Ma assured her. "The dry air on the plane can give anybody a nosebleed. And the excitement of seeing everybody today probably didn't help." Michael and Lou agreed.

Lauren dismissed any anxiety she had in favor of her mother's diagnosis until the family stood in the marble foyer ready to leave for Santelli's. As Michael went to drape his wife's coat over her shoulders, he saw a formidable spot, a bloody patch on the back of Lauren's pretty new dress.

There was a hustle to get Lauren into the car as she began to cry. "You'll be okay," Ma told her. "It's nothing to worry about; I know it's nothing." And Ma kept repeating the phrase to herself long after Lauren and Michael drove off, headed to the emergency room of the hospital.

Ma and Lou did not go to the hospital, but thought it was best to drive to Santelli's to greet the shower guests, who would be arriving momentarily. Ma did her best to welcome the bevy of relatives, to offer each invitee a single white rose—the hard stem flying a delicate blue ribbon, which said, "Precious Baby Boy."

Ma tried to stay chipper and keep the group calm, especially Michael's parents and Evangeline, who were alarmed and wanted to go to the hospital. "It's best you don't bother them right now," Ma said. "It will be fine. Stress can cause so many ailments, so many strange things to happen in your body. And unfortunately, life in D.C. is hardly stress-free. But my daughter has been through a lot and I know she can handle this, too."

When Michael's relatives were out of earshot, Ma whispered to Nonna and the Aunties, "Did you know that her husband took her on a mountain hike? I don't want to place any blame, but I think it was a terrible idea. If I'd been around, I never would have allowed it."

Ma kept in touch with Lauren by phone, calling out regular updates to the anxious group:

"They have her hooked up to monitors."

"The ultrasound machine is checking the baby's heartbeat."

"They can't find any reason for what happened."

"The bleeding has stopped."

"She's resting now."

In between updates, Ma tried to run the celebration as she had envisioned for months. An elaborate brunch banquet was served complete with omelet, carving, and waffle stations, but no one had much of an appetite, and the chopped omelet ingredients, waiting to be sautéed in butter, stayed raw. The expertly sliced ham and tenderloin remained untouched. Ma's organized games, guaranteed to enliven any baby shower, were not met with enthusiasm either. No one felt like playing.

Ma brought photographs of Lauren and Michael and asked guests to cut out their favorite features of both—nose, eyes, lips, ears, and hair. They were then instructed to combine the best parts of the individual together, forming a vision of what baby Stefanakis might look like. Amy, Evangeline, and the Aunties tried to be good sports in an effort to appease Ma, but as their scissors began slicing through the glossy face of Michael and then Lauren, removing an eyebrow, an upper lip, and a nostril, the players' spirits dampened further and all abandoned the game, leaving the baby's potential visage unfinished. The discarded photographs sat in a pile—the images of Lauren and Michael severed and dissected.

The bottle race failed miserably as well. Ma filled baby bottles with white wine and each guest was to drink the libation as fast as possible. The first person to empty the bottle won the prize. Tony and Lou were the only guests who cared to indulge in the amusement, and Tony spent his remaining time at the shower nursing a plethora of untried bottles.

Two hours later, Ma was able to get the remaining guests gathered around a telephone, which was stationed at the restaurant's bar. Lauren was put on speakerphone. "The baby's heart is beating normally," Lauren told her nervous family. "It looks like everything is okay. I'm so sorry to have worried you, but it's all okay. They are going to keep me here for another couple of hours just to be sure. Please enjoy the party. My mother went to so much trouble to organize this." The guests all sent their good wishes back into the phone: "We are so happy for you," "We miss you," and "We love you both so much."

Ma was stunned at the extent of the outpouring; she never received one ounce of that kind of attention.

The good news was a tremendous relief. Still, no one felt like socializing. Guests found excuses to bid Ma, Lou, and Michael's parents good-bye, emphasizing that they were so happy that all had turned out well. Ma insisted that each guest take away the untouched food, and some acquiesced, carrying off a little bag of cake, or a muffin, or a thin slice of tenderloin along with their white rose.

The generous stack of presents, mostly wrapped in blue, sat unopened. Later at home, to help cheer Lauren, Ma thought she would prop Lauren up in the rocking chair, a favorite family heirloom that provided so much comfort over the years, and place the presents at her daughter's feet. She would set a salvaged white rose in Lauren's lap; she would coax Lauren to smile for a photo; and they would press and dry the rose for a keepsake, commemorating such an eventful day.

But for now, the parents of Michael and Lauren gently placed gifts in the backseat and trunk of Ma's newest Cadillac. Michael's parents and Evangeline mostly helped in silence, except to repeat, "Thank God."

Ma was offended by the Stefanakises' relentless solemnness, their lack of assistance to liven up the party after Ma's months of planning, and their deficient gratitude for her efforts. But as fellow grandparents of this baby, she thought they should be privy to one other unknown detail. "Now that we have good news, I would like to confidentially share with you something important," Ma told them in a whisper meant for secrets. "The baby's name will most likely be Sean."

Evangeline and her parents paid little attention to Ma's "big news." They weren't so interested in names at the moment, only that their son, his wife, and their unborn grandchild were going to be all right.

CHAPTER 46

LAUREN AND MICHAEL RETURNED TO D.C. hoping for answers, but Lauren's doctors could offer no definitive explanation for the enigmatic bleeding. Words like "rare" and "unusual" were tossed back in response to Lauren's questions. The doctors admitted they were perplexed, but since there was no further sign of bleeding, their concern was minimal. Lauren was told to stay well rested and to report any new incidents.

Michael's stepfather was certain about what he should do. Father Kosta prayed. As he approached his seventieth birthday, he felt a renewed and profound connection to God. He prayed in church for the safe and healthy arrival of his unborn grandson. And he prayed at night so often that it was no longer alarming for Anastasia to wake in darkness to find her husband kneeling next to their bed, bent and concentrating, his long silvery beard fluttering, the coarse hair puffed forward by the breath of his reverent petitions.

Ma stayed with her theory and was convinced she identified the source of the bleeding long ago. "I'm telling you," she told Lauren over the phone, "it was that hike. I'm not pointing any fingers, but with your weak constitution, Michael had no business taking you out on some wilderness trek. And what about the vitamins? I told you to take vitamins." She repeated her diagnosis so frequently that Lauren demanded that she not mention it again. Still, Lauren was only able to draw her mother away from the hiking hypothesis by inquiring about Ma's new set of wheels.

Ma's amethyst Caddy had, like the one before it, met with misfortune. The car was crunched and disfigured in the parking lot while Ma shopped at Bargain Chic Warehouse. Ma's intuition made her wonder if Lori Molinari was at it again. It was not something Ma could prove, but the suspicion was strong. Something Ma knew. With the insurance money, Ma bought not one, but two cars from a broker in Greenwich, Connecticut. One for Tony and one for Ma. Ma stuck with a Caddy for herself, but purchased a pre-owned silver two-door Jaguar for Tony. The luxury vehicle had only been driven 30,000 miles, and had been the property of a wealthy investment banker with an affinity for fine things. Since the banker perished in the World Trade Towers on September 11, and no one else cared to adopt the car, Ma managed to negotiate a deal for almost nothing. She queried the car broker for the details of the man's death. Had he been in the North or South Tower? Had he tried to escape? Jumped to his death from the burning building? Been caught unaware by the first impact? Was he trapped before dying of smoke inhalation? Had he been panicked and then killed in the eventual collapse? The broker could not give Ma any particulars, so she spent a good bit of time imagining the affluent man's final minutes.

Lauren thought Ma's obsession with the Jaguar was ghoulish, but she was even more troubled by the fact that Tony would be driving, especially since he had two recent DUI convictions. "Ma, I don't think Tony should be driving at all right now," Lauren said.

"Of course he needs to drive," Ma maintained. "He needs to feel like a man. Let him feel good about himself so that he can make something of his life. This car will give him a taste of what it's like to live the good life, and he can be grateful that he is the one who is alive."

What Ma didn't tell Lauren was that she had recently declared Tony mentally incompetent so that she could collect disability checks, and that Tony had taken to self-mutilation, slicing intricate images of skulls across his rough, dry flesh. Tony also added a tattoo across his chest—a skeletal figure holding a large scythe, clothed in a black cloak with a hood. The newly inked image was labeled "Angel of Death."

As Tony careened into the lower depths of wretchedness, following the sullied footsteps of Ma's father, brothers, and nephews, Michael soared. His hard work and determination singled him out, and his potential was immeasurable. A fortuitous and providential opportunity, which had yet to be announced, had been in the making for months behind the scenes, and the couple's dream of moving to tony Georgetown was emerging into a real possibility.

"Your father and I are coming to D.C.," Ma announced. The decision caught Lauren by surprise. She had seen her mother six weeks ago for the baby shower, and after their visit last November Lauren assumed that her mother would not set foot on the streets of the nation's capital anytime soon. "It's Mother's Day, and we should be together," Ma said.

This time, Michael didn't plan to tour his in-laws around town, and he prepared to stay out of Ma's way as much as possible. Lauren's parents were only coming for one night and leaving late on Mother's Day. More and more, Michael dreaded Ma's company, dreaded her sour energy in his home. This trip, Ma surprised him. While Ma and Lou came with and snacked from their perpetual pill bottles and drank from the required stock of alcohol, Ma was rational, almost chipper. She tended to Michael's clearly pregnant wife with the utmost dedication. Ma made tea, offered Lauren pillows for her sore back, positioned the ottoman to raise her daughter's swollen ankles. She brought a stack of gossip magazines and a suitcase full of food. The usual fare—Lauren's Italian favorites. "You should not be cooking and I don't want you to fuss over us," Ma said. "You deserve all the attention. Just take it easy." The day-old food was bountiful, but despite Ma's good intentions, the meals never traveled well—the trays of eggplant parmesan and lasagna were dry, the lettuce in the salad turned brown and became soggy from settling in too much dressing, the spaghetti was stiff and glutinous, and the cookies crumbled.

Still, the following day, they gathered at the dining room table as a family for a midafternoon Mother's Day meal. The couple's dining room walls boasted several framed keepsakes from Michael's work and travel, which could be viewed from every seat at the table. There were photos of Michael standing shoulder to shoulder with well-known Washingtonian highflyers and international dignitaries, with the president's wife and Chinese officials in front of the Great Wall, and with the Pope in Vatican City. There was a certificate and a couple of menus from flights on Air Force One.

Lou admired each frame and its notable contents, while Ma seemed annoyed by the display. "It's too much flaunting for my taste. It looks 'show-offy' to me," she said. "I guess I just don't believe in tooting your own horn." Michael, who was proud of his adventures and honored by his momentous opportunities, and who was deeply moved when Lauren took the time and care to organize and frame the memorabilia, let Ma's jab slide out of respect for his wife.

It was Lou who smoothed things over with a toast. "On this Mother's Day, I would like to recognize the two incredible mothers sitting with us at this table, and let us toast to our first grandson, whom we hope to meet very soon." And the family members raised their glasses to celebrate mothers and babies, clinking and smiling while they set their differences aside.

Ma began to stack the dishes and clear the table, and when Lauren made an effort to stand and help her, Ma insisted that she stay put. "You need your rest," Ma told her. "I have a feeling this baby boy wants to come early."

"Let's not even say that out loud," Michael cautioned.

"You can't always control everything," Ma said to Michael. "Nature has its ways and I have a feeling."

Nonsense and negativity often tumbled out of Ma, but Lauren grew up trusting Ma's intuition and she wanted to ask her mother for guidance. Michael shut the prediction down. "I don't want to hear another word about it," he warned them. Lauren felt the familiar twang of homesickness: the tug of her mother was strong, and the contention between Michael and Ma made her upset. As she was getting ready to become a mother for the very first time, her heart ached for her own mother to be present and to help her through the momentous occasion. Doubt and worry crept into her mind that Michael might be the cause of the tension and nerves that came with Ma's visits.

Before Michael's in-laws departed late that afternoon, Ma presented her daughter with a slim volume of poems commemorating the joys of motherhood called *A Mother's Love*, which Ma had purchased at the local Hallmark store in New Jersey. Ma brought a second gift too. It was a silver bracelet for the baby. Lauren began to thank her mother, handing the miniature armlet over to Michael so that he might do the same, but as Michael turned the band over, raising it into the light, he caught the engraving—the name *Sean* was delicately etched into the sterling. Michael was unable to stay silent. "I'm sorry," he told Ma, "but our son will not, under any circumstances, be named Sean. Do you understand?" Michael acted as a stern parent might—offering the recalcitrant child one last chance before punishment—and Ma looked to Lauren, baffled and hurt.

∽

Lauren snuggled into bed early. She made a small fort out of pillows, comforting her back and legs. Michael joined her under the soft down comforter, determined to get some reading done for Senator Riedel. But he fell asleep moments after settling in next to his wife, content and happy that his in-laws were en route to New Jersey. With her husband snoozing, Lauren felt free to indulge in a favorite romantic comedy, *Sweet Home Alabama*, a film she watched many times before. It was a story she adored—the pretty, smart, and spunky Reese Witherspoon couldn't see clearly, couldn't figure out what was right under her nose, and had trouble finding her way back to her true love, her true destiny. Lauren was enchanted by Reese's Southern family, with their quirky ways—a family that appeared odd and unrefined to outsiders, but who loved each other all the same.

About three-quarters through the film, just as Reese was standing at the altar, realizing that she still loved her first husband and had to send her new fiancé packing in front of hundreds of wedding guests, Lauren began to feel a gush of warm liquid. Lauren was bleeding. Again.

CHAPTER 47

THE BABY WAS BORN THAT NIGHT. Seven weeks before he was scheduled to arrive. The unexpected delivery had been rushed, chaotic, and immediate. The available doctor, the newest to the practice and fresh from his residency, walked through the door of the hospital with barely enough time to remove his leather bomber jacket and get into his scrubs before performing an emergency cesarean section. After a swift delivery, the baby was rushed to the neonatal intensive care unit, where he was placed in an incubator for evaluation.

Baby Stefanakis's first few days were not what his parents envisioned. He weighed three pounds and ten ounces; his thin body remained in the plastic box where he received regulated air to keep him warm. Monitors followed his heart and breathing rates and the oxygen levels of his purplish-red skin. He could only be removed to be breast-fed, and then was quickly snatched from Lauren's arms and returned to his sterile and controlled environment.

Lauren was a jumble of moods and emotions. She felt great joy and immense gratitude that her baby had not been lost. For this, she would feel forever blessed. But then she would be burdened by equal inclinations toward fear and self-pity. What would happen to her baby now? Why her baby? Why did he have to endure this? Why couldn't she scoop him up and hold him in her arms? And then there was the guilt, crushing and paralyzing, so oppressive at times that she lay prostrate in her hospitable bed, unable to speak to anyone, including Michael. No one could relieve the self-condemnation and sense of failure she felt for not having carried their child to term.

The doctors, looking for clues, sent the placenta to the lab. It was concluded that the placenta had suffered a stroke—a placental hemorrhage. There was no clear reason for this. "These things can occasionally happen," the doctors told the couple. The inconclusive explanation did not make Lauren feel any better.

During her better moments, Michael offered Lauren the phone, where she heard from a continuous stream of well-wishers—her parents, Michael's parents, Nonna, the Aunties, Evangeline, Amy, Carl Hill, and Senator Riedel, all offering their support, relief, and happiness.

After five days, Lauren was released from the hospital. It was necessary for the baby to stay behind. Lauren's first steps away from her son were leaden and dispirited, and she was only able to make her way out of the hospital and into the car with Michael's alternating and repeated reassurances: "He will be okay. We'll see him soon. He will be okay. We will see him soon." Michael did not let his wife know that his confidence in his promise wavered, and that he had called his own father and begged for the priest's continued prayers.

The baby stayed in the hospital for six weeks. When he came home, it was still necessary to have him hooked up to a monitoring system that would alert Lauren and Michael should his heart stop beating. And if such a thing should occur, they had been trained to revive him.

Lauren sat for hours at a time in the nursery, rocking her newborn son in the white chair Ma had gifted them months before. She felt unadulterated rapture when she held her son in her arms—the baby boy who gained strength daily, the little boy who was named for his father: Michael Stefanakis Jr.

Chapter 48

Michael Stefanakis Jr. was a blessing from the start. Since his arrival, the Stefanakis's household received a host of good fortune. For starters, Michael Sr. was recruited by the U.S. Department of State to join the secretary's team as chief of protocol. It was a position Michael was honored to accept, and he moved on and up with the support of Senator Riedel. Because Michael would be traveling abroad regularly and Lauren intended to keep her position with Carl Hill, the couple employed a full-time nanny. They were anxious about the prospect until they found Christine, an experienced and warm childcare provider who emigrated from Brazil several years ago, and more importantly, who made an immediate connection with baby Michael. Christine also made Lauren recall her childhood babysitter on Country Club Lane—Christina. For Lauren, the name coincidence seemed like a sign, a signal to embrace the new Christine. Sure enough, she slipped into the Stefanakis family without a snag. Lauren felt comforted by Christine's nurturing presence and instinctively trusted her with her son.

Ma was not happy about Christine's foray into the family. She and Lou came to meet their new grandchild, but the visit was also designed to check out the much-talked-about, much-praised-and-admired Christine. Although Christine was Ma's same age, the resemblance stopped there. Christine was tall and lanky, with broad shoulders and muscular arms. Her skin was smooth, not a blemish or scar in sight. Her black hair was coarse and wavy. She was Brazilian, with coffee-colored skin and light hazel eyes. She kept her face scrubbed clean, without a trace of makeup. Her beauty was natural and striking. When they stood side by side, Ma seemed even smaller, paler, and sicklier.

"I don't see why you have to have help in the home," Ma criticized Lauren. "I never would have allowed it. I wouldn't want a stranger caring for my baby."

But Christine was no stranger to Lauren and Michael, and she quickly became an integral and vital component of their family. She settled into the Stefanakis home, almost like a mother would. She brought flowers for the house, magazines for Lauren, and Brazilian hard candies for Michael. She doted on the baby, and while he napped she kept the house mopped and polished. And she loved to cook. Cooking was not one of her responsibilities, but she insisted.

Ma watched Christine assemble a simple recipe of white rice, black beans, bacon, sausage, and garlic, and Ma was quick to point out, "That is not the kind of food my daughter and son-in-law will eat. I can tell you that Michael won't like it. He's a picky eater."

"I think he likes it very much," Christine told Ma with her lilting Portuguese accent and a trust in her native dish.

At dinner, Michael complimented Christine's meal countless times, gobbling up every bit of food on his plate and then requesting a second serving. Lou joined Michael's praise for the meal. Ma did not eat one bite. When Christine asked if Ma's food was to her liking, Ma embarrassed Lauren. "No, it's not the kind of thing our family eats," Ma complained.

Ma chose not to attend her grandson's baptism the following month. Little Michael was to be baptized in St. George's Greek Orthodox Cathedral in Washington, D.C., and Ma did not want to visit D.C. again. She also didn't want to be in the presence of Christine, the Brazilian hustler who weaseled her way into her daughter's life, and would no doubt be invited to the ceremony. Nor did she want to watch Michael's sister, Evangeline, become her grandchild's godparent. Most of all, she could not stomach her son-in-law boasting about his new promotion. The Big Cheese. Ma responded with regrets, citing her many ailments, which were not entirely untrue, and also used the excuse that she could not let Tony out of her sight, which she really could not. There was another DUI, a report of assault, and an arrest for shoplifting.

It felt odd for Ma to miss such an important event in her grandson's life. Ma was becoming more and more of a recluse, and Lauren felt the fissure between them widen.

The community of St. George's Greek Orthodox Cathedral embraced Lauren and Michael, and despite their busy schedules, the church was an essential part of their lives. They were delighted when Father Gabriel agreed to preside over the baptism and even welcomed Michael's father, Father Kosta, to assist him in the ceremony. Evangeline was appointed godparent, and Carl Hill and his wife honorary sponsors. Without any explanation, Amy understood the necessity of her presence and came to stand with Anastasia and Christine. Lauren had no immediate family in attendance—Lou wouldn't travel without Ma, and Nonna was too frail to make the trip —but this small group of extended family and close friends circled her baby with infinite love. The baby did not cry or squirm. He seemed content with the ancient ritual, soothed and comforted by the ardent devotion that surrounded him.

"Let us pray for mercy, life, peace, health, and salvation for the servants of God, the newly illumined Michael, the godparent, and all those who have come here together for this holy sacrament," said Father Gabriel, and Father Kosta joined him, "For You are a merciful and loving God, and to You do we send up all Glory, to the Father, and to the Son, and to the Holy Spirit, both now and ever, and to the ages of ages."

And baby Michael's family responded with Amen.

Father Gabriel poured olive oil into the hands of Evangeline, and she proceeded to anoint the child between his shoulders, and on his feet, hands, and ears. Father Kosta took the oil and made the sign of the cross on the baby's forehead before he spoke. "The servant of God Michael is anointed with the Oil of Gladness, in the Name of the Father, and of the Son, and of the Holy Spirit, both now and ever, and to the ages of ages."

And baby Michael's supporters responded with Amen.

With Little Michael's body blessed, Father Kosta baptized him, immersing him three times and then holding him erect to look toward the East. Father Gabriel spoke: "The servant of God Michael is baptized in the Name of the Father. Amen. And of the Son. Amen. And of the Holy Spirit. Amen."

As Father Kosta held his grandson high, Lauren could see that her baby was a miracle; she saw the pageant of heavenly angels looking down upon her son, watching over him, and Lauren knew that her child would be protected for the rest of his life.

CHAPTER 49

LAUREN RETURNED FROM WORK TO FIND A LETTER. She recognized the pastel floral print, the LOVE stamp in the upper right corner of the envelope, the S.W.A.K. tradition scrawled across the back, and assumed that Ma must have sent a card for her grandson's baptism. She opened it.

Dear Lauren,

I realize you no longer have any time for me or your father. Now you have your newly baptized baby, your husband, your servant Christine, and you insist on continuing to work. Your thoughts are focused elsewhere. Should I spell it out?

NO INTEREST IN YOUR REAL FAMILY

I guess we should all understand. Now that you are married and moved away, and a college graduate, and work in Washington, D.C. (a place where criminals run wild) and now that your husband makes a big salary and is such a Big Shot, I suppose you think you are

such a smarty pants and SO ABOVE IT ALL. And
now that you are working for politicians (who
are always liars so don't be fooled) I guess
you think it's just fine to turn your back on
your family.

YOUR OWN FLESH AND BLOOD

I get that. I don't mind that you no longer
give a rat's ass about me or your father. But
how about a little help for your brother???
While you have received the best, he's had a
hard time getting on his feet. He's had some
bad luck. Do you even care? Do you have one
ounce of compassion? How about giving HIM a
hand? Are you too good for your own brother?

Or will you turn a blind eye to him too?

From,

Ma (The person who brought you into this
world and cared for you, which you might recall was not an easy job!)

Lauren set the letter down and called Ma. It was a spontaneous and
instant reaction.

"It's the princess," Ma shouted. "The princess is calling from our nation's capital."

"What do you want me to do?" Lauren asked, ignoring her mother's
greeting. "I think Tony needs some kind of rehab."

"He doesn't need that," Ma snarled. "He needs a job."

"Ma, I can't recommend him for anything unless he gets some help
first," Lauren answered. "What I can do is help you find a place for him
to go and get better."

Ma stayed silent, seething. Her daughter's suggestion was insulting.

She was missing the point.

"He has to get himself together," Lauren repeated.

"He just needs something to do," Ma said. "Or some money to get going. I spent everything I had on that wedding of yours."

"Ma, I'll pay you back. I'll help pay for the rehab."

"I don't understand why that high-and-mighty husband of yours has never bothered to lift a finger for Tony," Ma said. "I should have known you wouldn't help your own brother."

"Ma, let's be honest—Tony wouldn't let me help him," Lauren said.

"That's rubbish. You never asked."

"The truth is he would never let me," Lauren told her mother. "He's never given me the time of day. I don't even know who he is and I never have. I only had one brother." Now Lauren said it, made it known that the only brother she knew was Louie and he was long gone.

Ma wasn't expecting Lauren's response, and she heaved one last assault, hoping to crush her daughter. To shut her up. "You have always been nothing but a stupid, stupid, selfish whore. When that Greek husband of yours realizes who you really are and walks out on you, don't bother to come running back to me."

Christine stood watching as Lauren put down the phone. "You are not okay?" Christine said to Lauren.

"It's nothing," Lauren told her.

"I think it's something."

"I'm okay," Lauren insisted.

"I think you do not say the truth." Christine held out her arms and Lauren did not resist the maternal embrace. Christine enveloped her like a small child, rocking her back and forth.

When Michael came home, Lauren told him about the phone call and showed him the letter. Michael knew it was enough. He recognized Ma as a crux in their life, but had stayed out of the situation as much as he could out of respect for his wife. He called Ma and told her that she was never to speak to his wife like that again, that if she could not control her temper, if she could not speak with respect to her own daughter, if she could not find something positive to say, then she would not be allowed to communicate with Lauren for a very long time. He let Ma's behavior slide for years, but he would no more. Lauren felt the strength of her connection with her husband and her heart swelled with emotion. For a while she had misgivings, felt doubt, and even questioned Michael's motives in regards to her relationship with Ma. All of that disappeared as she watched him stand up for her. Lauren had spent so long trying to salvage the relationship with Ma, she couldn't see beyond it. She felt the tug from Ma dissolving—as long as Ma was present, causing friction and unhappiness, Lauren couldn't thrive. Lauren knew she would have to move on.

∽

Three days later Lou called Lauren as she was driving to work. "Your mother had an episode," Lou told his daughter. At first, Lauren did not realize the magnitude of the situation, but as Lou continued to speak, with Tony in the background adding details to Lou's recounting, Lauren pulled to the side of the road and stopped the car. She slid into the passenger's seat and huddled over her phone, trying to make sense out of what her father and brother were spewing at her.

Early that morning, Ma drove the fourteen miles to Newark to the vocational school where Lou taught collision repair and caused a ruckus in the hallways. She started out by bellowing for Lou. "Lou, where are you, you cowardly son-of-a-bitch? You goddamned clown. Lou! Come out here and face your wife."

When Lou didn't appear, Ma pounded on lockers and classroom doors. "Lou, I know you're screwing every secretary in the place. Come out here and face your wife."

From inside the workshops, students who registered for eight o'clock classes looked up from their vehicle repairs and adjusted their safety goggles to see what the fuss was all about. What they saw was a tiny middle-aged woman hurling insults in the hallway. Her blonde hair was matted in the front and stuck straight up in the back; ill-behaved, the texture of straw. Her clothes were stained and wrinkled, her face splotched and red with a rash. The noises she emitted were not mere screams, but deafening maniacal warnings, which echoed and reverberated throughout the halls for all to hear. She followed and tormented a student who was late to his first class. "You'd better keep walking," she commanded the sleepy young man, "and don't turn around." The student followed Ma's orders until he managed to slip around a corner. Once he was out of sight, Ma lost interest. "That bitch is whacked," he muttered to fellow students once safely behind the door of his classroom.

Two male instructors emerged from classrooms to confront her. Lou did not appear. Ma could not find him. To begin with, the instructors tried to assess the circumstances, to reason with her, and a large number of mostly male students began to gather around. Ma would not listen and kept on with her unabashed rants. "There are rats in my home, and don't think I don't know what he's up to. He knows and so do I." Since Ma would not cooperate and was talking nonsense, the instructors escorted her to the entrance of the building, moving her along by the elbows, while she continued on in an incomprehensible frenzy. "Get your hands off me. Lou?! Lou?! Are you going to let that goddamned Greek ruin our lives?"

Lou had heard Ma's cries and chosen not to claim her. This school was his only private domain, a great solace, and now she was invading it. From the moment he heard her wails, Lou instinctively understood. This behavior was not Ma's usual shenanigans; this outburst went far beyond what he knew and had witnessed for years. This time, when she called for him, her cries were rabid, demented howls, like those of an abused dog who knew it was defeated, but would summon up the energy for a final and lethal attack. Lou knew Ma was in trouble, had tipped over the edge. He left the school without her and called Tony at home to warn him. Amazingly, Tony picked up the phone at that early hour. Then Lou called the police. His wife needed help. He was finally going to do something about it.

Lou's resolve didn't pan out as planned. Tony met up with his father at the school and together they tried to accomplish what needed to happen. It was an awkward coupling, as father and son rarely spoke, much less combined forces against the ruler of their family. Lou reported the episode to the police, reported that he considered his wife and the mother of his three children to be both suicidal and homicidal, both common traits in her family's background. Lauren never expected to hear her father speak against her mother, and what he confessed to the police was horrendous. She also knew it was true.

The strategy was for the police to go to Belle Haven, to the family home. They would send an ambulance as well. They would collect Ma and bring her to a local mental health facility where she could be evaluated. But plans never seemed to go Lou's way. Not in the past and not now. It was by coincidence that the police officer ultimately sent to the Napolitano home was Steve, the lumbering detective who had recently returned to the force. Ma's old buddy.

Lou, Lauren, and Tony stayed connected by phone as the dispatcher informed them that unless Lou had a court order, state law prohibited the police or paramedics from removing Ma from her home without her permission. They could not take her by force.

While they waited for the dispatcher to report the outcome, Lou confided to his apprehensive children, "Ma's very sick. Ill. She has been for years. She needs help and we're doing the right thing." Lou's stance, spoken out loud for the first time, was as much for his own benefit as for his children's. Lauren was torn. How could she plot against Ma? She wondered if Ma, once she found out what they were doing, would try to harm her father. Or Tony? Would she go so far as to hire someone to harm her or her family? Would it tarnish their reputation? Hurt Michael's burgeoning career?

Lauren crouched on the floor of her parked car. The space was tight, but she fit. Here, she felt a bit of protection, hidden from not only the passing cars but the world. She waited for the storm to pass. Waited for the police to capture Ma.

Tony took the phone from his father and spoke to his sister. Lauren could not recall when they last had a direct conversation, and his voice was unfamiliar. "What Dad says is right. You don't live here anymore. You don't know everything," he said to his sister. "You were the youngest, the only girl, and never understood everything." Lauren wanted to tell her brother to shut up. She didn't trust him and didn't want to hear what this longtime truant would say to defile her mother. She didn't want him to communicate one more awful thing. But he did, in a robotic, controlled voice, without anger or shame. "You don't know what she's done. You don't know what she's had me do. I don't even know how to read."

Before Lauren could respond to her brother, the dispatcher's static voice came on the line. It was confirmed that Ma was at home. "It has been determined that the person in the home is coherent," the dispatcher reported. "She has stated that she is okay and is denying any treatment. The officers and paramedics are leaving the property."

Chapter 50

Lou's resolve melted to nothing. He should have known better. He requested a police officer to escort him home for fear of what he might find. Tony chose not to accompany his father. Officer Steve met Lou at the bottom of their driveway and they parked their cars on the street, walking up the long, curly drive, and past the propane tanks at the front entrance. Lou opened the front door. It was unlocked. Ma greeted Lou and the police officer in the foyer and Lou was astonished to see that she had brushed her hair and put on clean clothes. She seemed gracious and composed, as if greeting invited dinner guests.

"Please," Lou pleaded with his wife. "Please go for help."

Ma gave a small smile to Steve, her old detective friend, the one who stood by her with Jimmy and who would be loyal now. "My husband is tired," she told Steve. "Ever since his accident several years ago, he has spells of misunderstanding. He gets confused."

"Please," Lou implored. "I've never asked you for anything, but I am asking you now. Please."

"Sweetie," Ma said, addressing her husband with a dash of foreign affection. "I don't know why you are so worried. I'm not going anywhere. Everything is fine. I'm fine and you're fine. Everything is going to be okay."

Early that evening, after Ma had fallen asleep, exhausted from the day's events and Tony still being away from home, Lou called his daughter. "I know Ma is very ill, but I promise you I will help her," he said, his voice weak and barely audible. "I will try my best to get her better. You have my word."

The day seemed surreal for Lauren. She had not yet assimilated the assault of information that had been heaved upon her over the last several hours. Once home, she looked in on her baby boy, who was sleeping peacefully. Christine was snoozing in the rocking chair next to the crib.

Lauren went downstairs to sit, to puzzle over what she now knew. To uncover the buried truth. To find an intelligible way to confide the circumstances to her husband, who was sure to walk through the door in a matter of minutes. She noticed the answering machine light was flashing earlier when she came home, but she had ignored it. Now, more out of habit than interest, she pressed PLAY. It was Ma. Her voice was cracked and singsongy; the inflections of her speech had gone awry, become twisted and knotted, the word "crazy" stretched far too long:

> **"You and your husband, you may work for the president, but you are pure scum. Lowlifes. Do you think I am crazy? I am not c-r-a-z-y. I'm not c-r-a-z-y. You think so? Fine thing to learn after all I've done for you. May you rot in hell, you psycho bitch. Look who's calling me c-r-a-z-y. Could it be that the pot is calling the kettle black?"**

⤫

Dear Journal,

I can't stop writing. This writing goes best by hand and once my pen begins to travel across the lined page, the black ink leaving a blotchy trail, my thoughts tumble forth. At first the words leak out bit by bit, random and irregular, but then move into a steady stream of organized letters until my hand cramps and I think there can't possibly be more. But there is. Hours and hours pass by. More and more and more. I am left to rub the sore joints of my fingers between sentences, feeling satiated and empowered. I am so grateful for your pages.

Lauren

CHAPTER 51

LAUREN DID NOT SPEAK TO MA FOR THREE YEARS. She was done. If her mother would not acknowledge her alarming and wretched behavior, if her mother would not seek help, then Lauren could no longer stomach the relationship. She would not, under any circumstances, expose her husband and little boy to Ma—to the ugly soul Ma had become. In three years, there were no messages from Ma, no small signs of promise for improvement, and no gestures of hope for reconciliation. Only silence—like dead air, black and suffocating.

Contact with her father was sporadic, with Lou sneaking off to make a whispered and rushed phone call to his daughter, a call that always ended in Lou promising, "I'm doing my best." These fitful communications had become almost nonexistent. Tony was no better, and Lauren feared that her brother spent most of his hours in a crystal meth nightmare, alternately anxious and indifferent.

Lauren's decision to terminate contact was firm. Ma frightened her. Still, not a day went by that Lauren did not think of her mother—pine for a relationship with her. It was as if an integral part of her identity had been savagely yanked away, leaving the raw, severed edge exposed and unable to heal. Lauren replayed Ma's mad rampage from three years ago, habitually turning and assessing every fragment of the event in her mind. It was inexplicable. She cast back to her childhood, trying to dig up a significant detail, a telling clue. Where had Ma gone off track, wandering off into a demented and barren wilderness? When had their relationship rotted beyond repair? Excavating the past plagued her. She was frantic, perpetually digging into a wound, sorting through the pus and lesions that refused to scab and mend. Lauren did not know how to ameliorate the affliction. She did not know how to survive a life without her mother.

Michael hoped that the anguish over Ma's condition and absence would diminish for his wife. He waited and watched, but it had not waned, and he pushed Lauren to receive counsel from the church. Together they went to St. George's Greek Orthodox Cathedral, and sat before Father Gabriel to describe Lauren's past, to lay it out before him. They went to question, to unburden, and to confess the bewildering facts, as well as to receive answers and find courage, but neither Lauren nor Michael expected Father Gabriel's diagnosis.

"It is the devil's work," he said with certainty. "You need to be as wise and guileful as the serpent and as peaceful as the dove."

Father Gabriel prescribed an exorcism. "We will turn to the prayers of Saint John Chrysostom and Saint Basil for protection."

When Lauren heard the word "exorcism," her fingers turned icy; her breath came short and shallow. It was as if the infected wound, which she had long endured, now festered into the ultimate consequence, an incurable, terminal disease. She imagined the Hollywood exorcism— a spinning head, screams of unspeakable profanity, green bile spewing from her mouth. Would she shake? Convulse? Fall to the floor? When the cross passed over her head, would her tongue slap and flap, forcing out rancid and unintelligible debris to anyone who would dare to bear witness?

"You need protection. We should not delay," Father Gabriel said.

Michael knew the priest was right. And deep down Lauren must have known it too—or at least welcomed someone to help carry the inveterate burden—because she let them lead her from Father Gabriel's office into the sanctuary.

When they entered the nave through the cathedral's central doorway, Lauren felt the scrutiny of a heavenly pageant of saints and angels. And although she had stepped through these majestic doors many times over the last five years, this time she felt drawn to His Throne in the cupola of the high dome—where concentric circles of blue, green, gold, and deep rose surrounded Christ. Sunlight bounced in irregular patterns through the stained glass, across the paintings and mosaics, highlighting each in an unearthly glow.

Without introduction or hesitation, Father Gabriel began his prayers, leaving no space for second thoughts. Michael joined his wife, standing at the altar with purpose, sheltered by the purple vestment that Father Gabriel raised above them.

"May the Lord rebuke thee, Satan! May the Lord rebuke thee, Satan!" The second command was louder than the first, the priest's words precise and sharp. Backed by the power of the Almighty, he sang out over their heads as if the sanctuary were at capacity and then paused, waiting for the dictum to echo through the empty cathedral.

"Shudder, tremble, be afraid," Father Gabriel charged. "Depart, be utterly destroyed, be banished!" Father Gabriel's demeanor did not suggest the outrage that the meaning of the words carried, nor did his small, thin frame exude the physical force or aggression that might have been warranted on such an occasion. He moved through the prayer recitation in a deliberate and methodical manner. His objective was clear and he was confident that when his task was complete, he would triumph.

Lauren lowered her head forward, in part from fear and in part from shame, as Father Gabriel itemized each offense. "Thee who fell from heaven and together with thee all evil spirits: every evil spirit of lust, a day and nocturnal spirit, a noonday and evening spirit, a midnight spirit…"

Lauren squeezed Michael's hand, his fingers interlocked with hers, and the moment he felt the pressure, he reciprocated, his grip so tight it caused their golden marriage bands to scrape against each other. Father Gabriel's words floated into the crevices of the cathedral, circling high into the dome. "Depart . . . Be gone . . . I adjure you . . ."

Lauren could not fully comprehend the priest's intentions. What was it that he suspected? What was it that Father Gabriel was certain had to be chased away? Out of her soul? Out of her heart? Driven away forever, so that she might become "whole and sound and free"?

Lauren tried to concentrate, succumb to Father Gabriel's commands, but she couldn't help but wonder what Ma would say about all of this. And Lauren could hear Ma's voice above all. "What a bunch of hoopla," she would say.

Or was it truly Ma that Father Gabriel was after? Lauren was still working it out in her head when Father Gabriel said, "Your mother is possessed; she is incapable of loving you. We need to protect you from her harm."

Lauren's eyes opened and she felt the courage to raise her head. Looking up, she saw them watching—the Byzantine icons that inhabited the cathedral, depicted in mosaic and paint, watching her from the walls and ceiling. Did they know? Could they explain? What was their judgment? What was wrong with Ma?

Father Gabriel pushed on. "I adjure you, most wicked, impure, abominable, loathsome, and alien spirit . . ."

As Father Gabriel moved through the prayers, Lauren began to feel suspended, dizzy—mesmerized by the medallion of Christ. The surrounding windows faded into a circle of unbroken, natural light.

She felt the priest touch her head and then her heart with his cross, gilded and imposing.

The light pressure of the cross made her expect the worst, and she opened her mouth so that she might release the inevitable, but nothing came out. Moments later she only felt immersed in relief, stripped of a thick and waxy burden.

Then Lauren looked up and noticed Theotokos, Mother of God, in the dome of the church ceiling. Theotokos, with arms extended, emerged in the light. Gathered around Her were nine medallions of Her heavenly attendants, the angelic hosts. All joined Father Gabriel with the business at hand.

"I adjure you," they seemed to chant. And Lauren bowed her head again, this time not out of shame or fear, but to join in the chorus of protective prayer. "I adjure you," she whispered. "For He shall come without delay to judge all the earth, and shall assign you, and all the powers working with you, to the fire of hell, having delivered you to the outer darkness, where the worm constantly devours, and the fire is never extinguished."

CHAPTER 52

DURING THE DAYS FOLLOWING THE EXORCISM, Lauren was filled with questions. Inquiries multiplied inside of her without answers or relief. The questions popped up like hives. First one, then another—petulant and not to be squelched. She kept thinking of Louie. The longing drove her to pull out an abandoned plastic box packed with bygone keepsakes, including her old journal, the last gift Louie gave her before he fled the family. Louie made the journal from one of his school composition books. The aluminum foil that wrapped the black-speckled cover was creased in several places. Lauren was surprised to see that it still remained silver and shiny, even after all of those years. The red strip of construction paper that Louie glued across the front of the book was now a faded anemic pink, but the title he wrote remained clear and strong: *Lauren's Private and Secret Thoughts.*

Lauren ran her fingers over the metallic cover. She could no longer recall Louie's face, but she could hear his words. She remembered what he had said when he presented the book to his little sister: "You can write anything. Anything you want. If you can't think of what to write, you can even make a list of questions. It doesn't matter."

The journal was well used and full of drawings, doodles, and words in pencil, pen, and thick color markers. A childlike depiction of rats appeared cartoonlike, almost cute, on an early page. There were also various self-portraits and an illustration of the family, including those who were now missing—Louie, Wylie (her father's favorite dog), and Jimmy, whom she had drawn wide with a block head. It also included her favorite poems, a sketch of her pretty prom dress, and secret confessions of her love for Vinny, her first ardent admirer. She'd hoped to be smart like him and like Louie. Lauren lingered over each entry, traveling through the years, reacquainting herself with the author—young Lauren, someone she had almost forgotten. She placed the journal on her nightstand, where, after the day's demands of work and motherhood, she could return to each page. Again and again.

On August 15, five days after the exorcism, Lauren woke to discover that the weather was as cool and breezy as it had been the day of the exorcism. That day had been an exception to the usual hellish days of summer.

August 15 also happened to mark the Feast of the Assumption on the Greek Orthodox calendar—the moment when the Virgin Mary ascended into heaven. To honor both the weather and Mary, Lauren suggested that she and Michael take the whole day off from work. They decided to attend church, making it a true family day by bringing along both Little Michael and Christine. After the service, they walked the block to the Washington National Cathedral, where they let little Michael toddle down the winding stone paths of the Bishop's Garden. Here, the family wandered under the shade of cedar, fig, oak, and magnolia trees.

The cathedral, which took eighty-three years to build, always impressed Lauren, with its solid limestone blocks, laid one on top of the other, and flying buttresses of solid stone. The brochures told her the cathedral weighed 150,000 tons and boasted 231 stained glass windows, 112 gargoyles, and 288 angels. To Lauren, it seemed as though the angels outnumbered the grotesque gargoyles by so many more.

She watched her son as he explored the gardens. She could see herself in him. Everyone remarked that Little Michael looked just like her, but what she recognized as familiar was his vivacious energy and tireless curiosity as he marveled at the texture of the boxwoods, the fragrance of each flower he encountered, and the leafy variations of historic herbs. Lauren identified with her son's wonder as he experienced the treasures of the garden, this haven of nature in the middle of the city. In this moment, on August 15, the Feast of the Assumption, she felt that there was no place she would rather be.

That night, she joined Michael, who was already in bed. The day had not been extraordinary by most definitions—church, garden stroll, lunch—but Lauren had basked in the hours spent with her family. She'd felt a strength and pride in the loving world she now inhabited. She was set to close her eyes, determined to rest. And yet, in the quiet of the night, she was once again struck by the persistent urge to cast back, to question. And so, like the other nights of the week, she reached for her old journal.

Lauren had been journaling more frequently in the last months, jotting down memories, random thoughts, and recaps of daily events. Over the years, journaling had become an irregular habit, and she had filled several diaries. This night, she found herself again drawn to her very first journal, and she reminisced with each page. When she turned to the final entry, she noticed that the last few pages remained empty. They looked stark compared with the colorful, packed contents of the book. She thought she should write something—offer some finale, some grand closure to that very first journal—but she could think of nothing to add.

"Don't think about what to write; just push the pen across the page," Louie instructed her so many years ago. "Repeat, and repeat, and repeat any word combination until the words break free and carry you on to new and deeper thoughts. To important discoveries."

Even in her recollections, Lauren trusted Louie. She picked up her pen, and, following his suggestion, wrote a list of questions.

1. Why?

2. Why has this happened?

3. Why do I bleed?

4. Why do I bleed when I'm near Ma?

5. Why?

There was no answer ready and willing to reveal itself, and so she wrote the questions again. And again. And again. Just as Louie prescribed.

1. Why?

2. Why do I bleed?

3. Why do I bleed when I'm near Ma?

4. How can someone make you bleed without physically touching you?

Still, there were no answers. Lauren closed the journal, giving up. It was almost midnight and she needed sleep. She closed her eyes once more, but her mind kept on, roaming through the contents of her childhood journal. She had committed the pages to memory and could call them up with eyes shut tight.

The pages held the typical messy, carefree drawings of a young girl: hearts, butterflies, flowers. But there were also rats. The journal was full of rats. In sketches and in words—always rats. The worry of rats. Ma's longtime trouble with rats. It was a book of rats.

Lauren opened her eyes. She rose again. She opened her journal and turned to the very last empty page and wrote:

Rats in the beginning, rats in the middle, and rats in the end.

There had always been rats. Sneaky rats in Lauren's basement bedroom on Country Club Lane, dirty rats in Lori Molinari's house, invading rats on the picnic table at Belle Haven, and hidden rats in the moving boxes. There were rats in Ma's silverware drawer. Ma ranted about rats when she stormed through the halls of her father's school.

How very odd to have rats in the silverware drawer, Lauren thought. It made no sense. She had not paid attention before. Now, she revived the conversation she'd had with her mother right before the baby shower.

"Dad bumped into Amy at Home Depot near Nonna's," Ma had told her. "He was buying some things to take care of a problem that's come back into the house." Lauren could hear her mother's voice. The overlooked memory now seized her with its lucidity. "It's kind of an embarrassing story," Ma had said. "We found a rat in the kitchen a few weeks ago. Actually, in the silverware drawer. I thought we were done with all of that and I am too old to dredge up the past with your father . . ." Ma had continued with the explanation. "It's just that I am so humiliated about it, but your father has everything under control now."

Lauren stared at her recent words in the journal. With her pen she repeated what she had just written.

Rats in the beginning, rats in the middle, and rats in the end.

The letters, mere black lines on a ruled white page, began to wiggle and vibrate. They began to scurry around the page. Just like rats. Lauren bolted from her bed, letting the rat-infested journal fall to the floor. She ran downstairs to her computer.

She opened a search engine and typed: *Effects of rat poison on humans.*

In an instant, her computer screen filled.

. . . Warfarin or Coumadin, a blood-thinning compound used in rat poison . . . in poison, the dose is high . . .

Lauren read more.

Rat poison reduces Vitamin K levels, which affects clotting . . . can result in abnormal bleeding . . . bleeding from the gums or nose . . .

And more.

Anticoagulants, such as Warfarin, commonly found in rat poisons can cause bleeding after ingestion.

Lauren typed again, rearranging her questions, demanding confirmation.

... frequent nosebleeds ... bruises ... internal bleeding, which can cause pallor and low blood pressure ... deplete red blood cells, leading to anemia, fatigue, dizziness, headaches ... bleeding

The night hours passed and she interrogated her computer, a self-styled inquest. The answers came. They flooded in. She gulped in the information the computer spit back to her, gorging herself, binging on facts. It just couldn't be. She wanted more. She needed more. It just couldn't be.

Coumadin (such as Warfarin), if present during pregnancy ... pass through placental barrier ... can cause bleeding in the fetus ... associated with spontaneous abortion, stillbirth, neonatal death, birth defects, preterm birth ...

Lauren was gluttonous, feeding on details, reports, definitions, descriptions, and data throughout the night. In her frenzy to amass testimony, she wouldn't allow herself to analyze or digest what the new knowledge meant. Those thoughts were unthinkable. Not possible. She was dizzy and confused, but the insatiable quest to probe pushed her on. At 6:58 a.m. she stopped, barely able to drag herself upstairs and into her bedroom, where Michael slept. The alarm would sound at 7:00 a.m.

She sank to the floor next to the bed, holding on to the edge for support. If one had not known how she had spent the last hours, she might have appeared to be a young mother in prayer. In just two minutes the alarm would cry out into the present silence, and she would have to regurgitate the findings of the night. Findings that could deci-mate her life, demolish everything she knew to be true.

Michael spent that day buried in research, following up on his wife's late-night groundwork. Probing, delving, searching, investigating. His findings concurred. He checked again. He doubled back. Reviewed and retraced. He had no doubt.

Over the next few days, they called and visited Lauren's doctors, who were astonished by the couple's questions and assumptions. They revisited and reviewed Lauren's baffling pregnancy, the cause of the pla-cental hemorrhage, and the premature birth. The doctors strayed from the purpose of the current consultation and mentioned again that most women who suffered from the circumstances of Lauren's pregnancy were cocaine users, but even for this group a placental hemorrhage was rare, a .001 percent chance. The doctors knew full well that Lauren did not fall into this category, and the discussion seemed like filler to Mi-chael, words that meant nothing. "Sometimes these things just happen," they confessed.

The medical experts, each in his or her own manner and on sepa-rate occasions, danced away from the original question of possibilities, preferring not to dwell upon the unspeakable accusations the Stefa-nakises brought up. Michael wouldn't let it drop, brought them back to the unsettling accusation. What about warfarin? Was it possible?

In the end, the experts confirmed *yes*. It wasn't out of the realm of possibilities. Not just the pregnancy. All of it: Lauren's constant health problems, fragile constitution, nosebleeds, and lethargy, as well as the hemorrhaging and her baby's premature birth. The doctors conceded, "Yes, warfarin could have caused . . . definitely could have . . . But no, there were no blood tests at the time. No, there wouldn't be proof, as the poison would leave the system within 48 hours. But, yes . . . yes, she was lucky . . . there could have been much more damage. Lauren's death? Yes. Birth defects? Yes. Stillborn? Yes. Yes, and much, much more. Yes, it could be. Yes, it was possible."

Yes. Yes. Yes. Yes. Yes. Yes. Yes. Yes. Yes. Yes. Yes. Yes. Yes. Yes. Yes. Yes.

The information stayed stacked and hoarded in Lauren's mind until it became impenetrable and mountainous. The colossal knowledge towered over her, unmoving and menacing. There was no way up or around or through. Now she was face-to-face with meaning. Conclusions must be formed. Evidence recognized. Truth acknowledged. What had her mother done? Had Ma poisoned her? Wanted to hurt her only daughter? For how long? Had Ma tried to harm her baby? Desired to destroy her own grandchild?

Her own flesh and blood?

So there Lauren was, the information pressing against her. One small move—a tiny whimper or infinitesimal breath—was all it would take for the mountain to crumble, inciting an avalanche of unspeakable horror.

Chapter 53

The cankerous information lodged in Lauren's soul was unfathomable. She had come to bear witness. She wished she didn't have to know, that she could live in ignorance, even danger, rather than face these unconscionable facts she uncovered. But she couldn't. The sinister truth stood before her, like a fast-growing, malignant tumor, demanding regard. Now she was sentenced to a diseased life, dominated by an incurable and perverse knowing—the encumbrance surely required more strength than she could ever manage. She felt weakened, fallen limp from the crush of understanding.

The vomiting came violently and was prolonged, as if she wished to expel a lifetime of poisons, expunge her mother's intentions by heaving every memory that remained inside of her out. With each retching, she worried that even more truths lay hidden within her. Had it been poison all along? Right from the early days? The rashes? The stomachaches? The chronic bleeding? The missed days from school? Her first school formal? The blue turkey? Her baby shower? The night before she and Michael moved to D.C.? Had she tried to poison Michael as well? Wylie? What about Nonno? Had her beloved grandfather fallen victim too? What about the explosions? The torched cars? The near burning of their home on Country Club Lane? Had they all been subject? Had anyone known? And why? She was riddled with whys. She could never look Ma in the eye and ask her, why did you try to harm me? So how would she ever evacuate that pestilential question?

Each morning, Lauren doubted if she could manage to steady her feet on the floor and rise up. She might not have done so, might have given into the feverish fatigue for good, if it were not for the fact that Little Michael, ignorant of the reasons for his mother's despair, would come to the edge of her bed and smile. "Mama, it will be okay," he'd say, his wee fingers patting her hand with unadulterated reassurance. For him, Lauren would try. She would stand and hold her hairbrush. For him, she would eat. For her son, she would get dressed.

She began to tell those close to her. Christine—who served her healing teas. Evangeline—who joined her on the floor and held her after Lauren slumped down and wailed, clutching at her sister-in-law's ankles like a pleading child. Father Gabriel—who prayed to the Virgin Mary. And because she could not work, she asked Michael to tell Carl Hill. The reactions were all supportive and loving, their stunned horror concealed, but Lauren felt that she was dragging a putrid pile of refuse, placing it permanently before each person she told.

She attempted to divulge her findings to Nonna. Nonna—her grandmother, confidant, and cheerleader. But Nonna, who spent her days drifting in and out of clarity, could not or would not understand the magnitude of Lauren's accusations. "I begged my son not to marry that girl," was all she repeated. "Lou is a good boy, a good son."

In the end, Lauren contacted only one other family member. She telephoned Tony on his cell phone. She thought that Tony might argue with her, convince her that she was delusional, offer an alternative theory, or even threaten her for slandering Ma. Lauren was wrong. Tony listened and did not contradict her. After that, he began to call Lauren daily and even confided troubles of his own. "I know I'm a failure," he confessed to his sister, "but maybe I didn't have to be."

Lauren began to hope that out of this misery she might gain a relationship with her brother and she encouraged him. He disclosed fragments of the past. He speculated how he might have been different, how he might have made something of himself if Ma had pointed him in the right direction, had not pegged him for a life like Ma's brothers, had not guided him along the O'Donnell family tradition. And he recalled a question Ma once asked him years ago. "How can you poison your enemy?" Ma asked. "Antifreeze," Tony guessed. Whether Ma followed his suggestion he did not know.

Lauren tried to provide a road map for Tony's turnaround, for his escape. She plotted with him, offered him a place to live, offered help with reading and studying for his GED. She offered him money for rehab. She advocated for him to leave Ma's home and come to D.C. to start a new life. Tony indulged his sister, puzzling over what he might do, how he might get there. How she might help him. Then the calls stopped. Their hopeful discussions were finished. He refused to answer her. Tony was lost again.

The envelope arrived in the mail with a familiar seal: S.W.A.K. Lauren recognized the penmanship, the address written in her mother's hand. She expected a nasty missive, but hoped for a long-awaited communication, an extraordinary explanation that would make everything all right. When she pulled the plain white paper from the envelope, she found that it wasn't from Ma. It was a typed letter from her father.

```
Hello Lauren,

Please Stop.

    1. Stop blaming Ma for everything.

    2. Stop talking negative nonsense about
       Ma, especially to Nonna.

    3. Stop stirring things up with Tony.

Three years ago, I should not have called the
```

cops on Ma. It was most definitely the wrong thing to do. I should have listened to Ma from the very first and gone home to comfort her instead of calling 9-1-1.

We always tried to do the best for you and your brothers, especially Ma.

I was no angel and caused a lot of the situations. Your mother is the one who kept me in line and had to do it forcefully to get her point across. Her focus was always on you, Tony, Louie, and me.

Stop dwelling on just the negative things Ma has either said or done. Start comparing them to some positive things. Ma seems to always be the one that takes the blame for everything but never seems to get any credit for the good things.

Like I said in the beginning, please stop.

I better not ever hear anything negative about Ma from you or your husband.

Love,

Dad

CHAPTER 54

LAUREN WAS SURE THAT TONY TOLD HER PARENTS ABOUT THE DISCOVERY, and this letter was all that her father offered her. She questioned whether he even wrote the letter. Had Ma dictated it and forced him to sign? Did it matter? Was this the best her father could do? Nothing but blame his daughter for being negative! Had he missed the point? Was he ignoring the point? Had he known? Had he been part of it all too? Had he carried out so many of Ma's crimes that she had him cornered? Lauren couldn't answer any of it, and would no longer try to tease it out. Her father was broken. Her father was damned. She'd known that for a long time. She also knew that he would remain impotent until the day he died. Her father would never go against Ma. Not even for her. It was clear that despite his flimsy promises, he would not do right. He would always choose to abandon his children.

Always.

This was Lauren's second revelation. It confused her almost as much as the first.

Once she comprehended that her father would not stand with her, she began to run every day on the treadmill. Fast. She turned the settings to the highest speed and the steepest incline. The intense workouts bathed her in salty sweat; it seeped out of her until her face was showered in perspiration and tears of anger and mourning, until her eyelashes meshed together and she could not see. She ran on, traveling the distance, picking up one foot and then another. The running was accompanied by music, cranked loud. Female voices belting out powerful tunes. The sopranos reached to grasp their highest notes and the altos strained to communicate their sorrow. They sang for justice, for freedom, for independence, for inspiration—a melodic calling for salvation, the healing of their broken hearts, and their will to endure. The low-pitched bass thumped along, underling each songstress and her harmonies. The music propelled Lauren forth—she was pushed ahead by the cumulative power of a great vocal sisterhood.

When she stopped running, Lauren knew this: she was not willing to lose. If she crumbled, lay down defeated and shattered like her father, Ma would win.

That would not happen.

Chapter 55

Nonna died in her sleep. Lauren suspected that the news killed her. Nonna behaved as if she hadn't understood, but perhaps she had. Perhaps she knew that her family was broken apart, splintered beyond repair, and there was nothing she could do to fix it. No motherly ministry could heal it. She could not help her granddaughter, and she certainly could not help her son. It was too late.

Auntie Rose called to tell Lauren about Nonna, and while Lauren knew that Rose and the other Aunties were aware that she had not spoken to her parents for over three years, she did not know if Nonna told Rose any more. She instinctively felt that Nonna had not, and Lauren let it be. Kept it to herself.

"Your Nonna loved you so much," Rose told Lauren, almost apologizing for Nonna's leave-taking. "She was old and not so well lately. She tried to put on a good face, but she missed your Nonno for so long. He was a good man."

Lauren agreed with Rose. Nonno was a good man. She remembered that much. Her father had once been a good man too.

❧

Michael worried for his wife. He needed to keep his abhorrence for Ma defused on a daily basis. He wanted to stamp Ma out, make her pay for what she had done to his family. It was evil. There were no excuses. Lauren read and reread book after book about narcissistic personality disorder, Munchausen syndrome by proxy, and criminal psychopathy. She found similarities for each diagnosis in Ma's behavior. She was searching for the why, longing for an explanation that would make sense. Michael was not interested. His explanation was simple: Ma committed heinous acts because she was evil. He would never give her a pass. Never offer a label that might be understood as an excuse, a reason to mitigate what she had done. Michael wanted to see Ma punished. He wanted to protect his family, but without current proof there was no legal recourse. And Ma was still out in the world. Michael was sure that if given the chance, she was ready to strike.

Lauren refused the doctor's ongoing suggestion for antidepressants. The last thing she wanted was to take a prescription drug. It was Father Gabriel who suggested that Lauren and Michael visit a spa, purify themselves, and find a solid path to renewal. Michael arranged for his parents to come and look after Little Michael, and they flew to Florida, to the Ritz Carlton in Naples.

It was in Naples, overlooking the Gulf of Mexico, that they tried to find grounding. They started with the business of detoxifying. There were steam rooms, saunas, and outdoor mineral pools. There were tranquility massages for two, where warm stones dotted their backs. Body wraps cocooned their bodies in green tea, and their skin was scrubbed clean with sand and salt. They bathed in seaweed and were lathered in lemongrass lotions and oils. They drank water infused with citrus and mint. At lunch, in pristine terrycloth robes, they ate poached salmon.

The couple lounged under umbrellas, in a private cabana under mangrove, cypress, and palm trees. They sipped cocktails from the Sand Bar. They exercised. They strolled the beach day and night, breathing in the ocean air, collecting seashells to bring back to Little Michael.

When they departed one week later, they felt cleansed and replenished—renewed with strength and determination. Lauren was determined to return to work with Carl Hill.

Carl only said one thing, but it was advice she would remember for the rest of her life. "You can't choose where you come from, but you can choose where you go."

At home, Lauren established a strict routine, something to steady her, keep her upright and advancing toward the future. She worked, tended to Little Michael and her husband, ran on her treadmill, took long baths, and kept up the spa ritual of drinking water infused with mint and lemon. She continued to write, filling journal after journal. The routine helped and her head stayed clear.

So when her cousin Jimmy O'Donnell phoned her, she did not welcome the call. She was afraid he would upset the fragile balance she so carefully built, and her impulse was to hang up the moment she realized whom he was.

It had been years since Lauren had thought about Jimmy—the cousin Ma invited to live in their home and tend to their recovering father, the cousin who subsequently went to jail and was happily forgotten. Lauren had never liked him and she did not want to engage with him now, even with a simple phone call. She didn't trust him. As Jimmy spoke, she heard an earnest timbre in his raspy voice, and it was the heartfelt tone that caught her curiosity. She held the receiver tighter than was necessary, but listened all the same.

Jimmy was out of jail, on probation. He tried to look up Tony, but Ma would not speak to him. Bill, Jimmy's father, told him that it would be difficult to reach Tony, as Tony, like all of the O'Donnell men, was on his way to prison for armed burglary and assault charges. He and Jimmy had crossed paths without knowing it: one cousin released from incarceration, one newly bound.

Lauren heard Jimmy's account of Tony and gasped.

"Come on, you can't be surprised? It's a fuckin' rite of passage for the O'Donnell men," Jimmy joked.

No, she was not surprised, but she didn't want to hear it and found no humor in his cavalier attitude. His tone had changed, and she recalled why she never liked him. So out of anger, or frustration, or desperation, or misjudgment, Lauren spewed the details of her discovery to her cousin.

"That sounds about right," Jimmy said. It was his way of offering something akin to sympathy. "Look," he counseled her, "beatings, drunks, heroin, assault, murder, rape, incest, prison, suicide, you name it, that's our family tree. I guess I'm an apple that didn't fall far, and neither did Tony. You're different. Well, you—you broke the cycle."

Lauren did not reply. But she was listening.

"It's funny," Jimmy said. "I thought your life was fuckin' perfect. I know your mother is as demented as they come. Just like my dad, just like the whole fuckin' family, but I always thought things were going okay for you. I thought you were the little favorite. Everybody treated you like a little fuckin' princess. Little Princess Lauren. And here you were getting shit too. Even you."

Lauren said good-bye to Jimmy, knowing that she would never talk with him again. For that, she was grateful. Any thoughts of contacting Tony now faded away as well. Tony had not shot himself in the head like his namesake, their Uncle Jack Anthony. Not yet, at least. Still, it was clear she could not help him.

Lauren tallied up Ma's wreckage. Louie was gone. Tony was gone. Her father might as well be gone. She was left the lone survivor. And that's what she intended. To survive. She knew the journey would be long and arduous. She would work as hard as she could to manage it.

Dear Journal,

I realize that the words I write have been a salve. I've always felt the need to have them close. The writing mitigates the pounding worry. It scrapes off the darkness, letting the gunk fall away, until my mind is clean and clear. And when the words line up on the page, lucid and transparent, they give me something concrete to examine. Mostly, I write about Ma. Once I have her on the page,

I can see her (I can see us) better. In my head, Ma still looms so large. On the page, Ma looks different. I can say what I want to her when she's trapped under my pen. I can move her around. I can investigate her as if she were a fictional character in someone else's life. She is less powerful then. In this place, she can't get away with her trickery. And I can always choose to close the book and put her away.

Lauren

Chapter 56

For years she read books. The stacks littered the floor of her bedroom. She moved on from the psychological analysis of personality disorders. She had plenty of those, and could produce a comprehensive list of symptoms that she might attribute to Ma. She read books on anger and forgiveness too. Those books were not particularly helpful, it was too early to forgive, but the anger made her feel worse, and so she wiggled into the cerebral space that recognized Ma as being incapable of loving herself and even her own children.

Whether it was mental illness or the devil, Ma was possessed. Ma knew what she was doing. She intentionally set out to harm people, family members included. This was a fact Lauren would never comprehend, and it was exactly what she must learn to accept. What made her father tick would also remain a lifelong mystery. She tried to convince herself that it wasn't necessary to understand. She didn't have to. She only had to release her parents for good and take her own place in the world. That seemed to be a monumental task.

One thing was clear: Lauren could make a different choice. She could be the exact opposite of Ma. So she yearned for stories about those who walked out, even crawled out, of their own rotten circumstances. She no longer was willing to identify with just the abused and downtrodden. Lauren wanted to put her energies into moving beyond, making her life have purpose.

She resolved to strip herself of her given name. She wanted to cast it out, along with a pile of objects that Ma had gifted her, presents with "Lauren" engraved like a deep scar. Whether it was a jewelry box, a bracelet, or her own being, she felt branded with Ma's insignia. And when she looked at the inscriptions or heard her name called it was all the same. *Lauren. Lauren. Lauren.* It was Ma. Ma in charge. Ma in control. Now she needed to be someone new, someone other than Lauren.

She submitted the paperwork with the County Circuit Court to make the legal change, to symbolize a final separation from her mother.

∽

On the Fourth of July, Lauren Napolitano turned thirty-three. Thirty-three—the same age that Christ was when He was crucified. Lauren thought something momentous should happen in this year of her life. She hadn't felt much like celebrating, but she and Michael had taken Little Michael and Christine to see the fireworks.

They arrived early on the National Mall to claim their spot on the lawn. There was a parade along Constitution Avenue, followed by the launch of fireworks from the Lincoln Memorial Reflecting Pool which illuminated the sky over the Washington Monument. Thousands of spectators cheered after each thunderous explosion. Lauren worried that the blasts might frighten her son. Secure in his father's lap, Little Michael joined the crowd, joyously offering his appreciation after each riotous display. As Lauren lay on the blanket, her mind drifted, mesmerized by the moment, and she closed her eyes in reflection, meditating on the origins of this great nation as well as her own life.

Far from this patriotic assembly—where sunburned tourists and patient locals crowded in tight to celebrate their country's independence—was a less artful display of pyrotechnics. This explosion, which received neither cheers nor applause, was only witnessed by one.

Two propane tanks in Westfield, New Jersey erupted into fire. First one and then the other. The booming blasts, sounding like fireworks, did not alarm the neighbors. The tanks, full of liquefied petroleum gas, had been oddly positioned in front of the home, which made it easy for the flames to tickle the front door, giving the inhabitants no warning. In minutes, the house resembled a wild, untamed bonfire. The inferno reduced the suburban home to ashes, leaving all of its contents, including one female resident, charred and destroyed. When the fire department arrived, it was over.

If Ma had survived the fire, she might have insisted that Lori Molinari had been the culprit for the conflagration, or she might have blamed Jimmy coming back to cross her, or even imagined that the ghost of Nonno was stirring up an apparition's revenge. It never would have occurred to Ma to consider the lone man who sat at the picnic table, silently watching the house glow, entranced by the unruly flames. She would be surprised to see her husband sitting where rats once scampered, ignoring the unbearable heat the house tossed off.

If Ma had emerged from the bonfire, red-hot flames circling her feet, to face him, Lou might have told his wife that he was tired. So very sleepy.

"You big clown, what have you done now?" Ma would say.

And Lou could tell her that he had finally taken care of the rodent problem, the problem that gnawed at him all these years. Perhaps he might have found it in himself to challenge her about his losses—two sons, one estranged and one ruined, his beloved dog Wylie, his father. And Lauren. He had lost his daughter.

But of course, Lou never had it in him to profess such things. So what could he do?

He could stay seated and watch the fire until the last flame popped. He could walk into the smoldering house and take his place next to the sassy, petite girl he married all those years ago. Or perhaps he should move away from the picnic table and walk out of the Belle Haven neighborhood and beyond. The choice was his, but Lou would stay still, befuddled. He couldn't imagine making any choice at all. For the first time, Ma wouldn't be there to call the shots. Finally able to make a decision without her overriding direction, Lou was stumped.

The truth was that it no longer mattered.

The thunderous display of the grand finale brought Lauren back from the reverie. She looked over to her son and husband as a tear fell from her cheek onto the blanket, forming a clear splotch with jagged edges like irregular flower petals as it soaked into the thick fabric.

Epilogue

Massachusetts Heights, Washington, D.C.

Lauren ceased trying to blot out her past. It was part of her, but the past would not define her future, nor the future of her son, a boy with O'Donnell blood. They were taking a new direction.

Her husband was a success and Lauren assisted him every step of the way. With that success came material rewards. They now lived in a 1920s Tudor in Massachusetts Heights, only a few blocks from the Greek Orthodox Cathedral. The home stood on the highest peak of the city, with a beautiful view of the Washington Monument. Lauren would have been happy to live anywhere with her husband and son, but she treasured the opportunity to care for this grand residence, with its steeply pitched gable roof and elaborate stone and brickwork. Inside, she felt protected by the sturdy structure, the surrounding walls her bulwark. Her favorite room was the kitchen, where she spent hours learning to cook, and where she gazed out the decorative windowpanes far into the distance—a world of beauty, freedom, and possibility.

There was possibility. Enveloped by Michael's family and their mutual friends who loved and admired her for her steadfast courage, Lauren was beginning to coax out a buried confidence, a trait that had lain dormant but had always been there. Confidence that helped her turn down Carl Hill's job promotion, offered a second time. This time, she didn't turn it down for lack of faith in her abilities, but instead due to an emerging recognition of her own passions. When she declined Carl's offer, he had sensed the change in her, a clear and strong shift, and said, "Good for you." And he'd also been the first to say it out loud. "You need to write your story. You have something important to say. You must write." His words lingered in the space between them before Lauren hugged him fiercely.

And a little over six months after the Fourth of July fireworks display, family and friends gathered to celebrate the legal change of her name. She chose her baptismal name, a saint appellation she selected when she joined the Greek Orthodox Church. Anna—after Saint Anna, mother of the Virgin Mary.

Michael's parents were in attendance, as well as Evangeline and her new beau. Christine came, of course, and Carl Hill and his wife. Amy attended as well. Auntie Rose came, as she was the only Auntie still able to travel.

Carl brought her a gift—a new journal, leather bound. On the first page Carl had written in gold ink:

Start by doing what's necessary; then do what's possible; and suddenly you are doing the impossible.

—Saint Francis of Assisi

She couldn't help but recall her first journal from Louie, the black speckled composition book he covered in shiny foil. Louie had given her a clear purpose with the title, *Lauren's Private and Secret Thoughts.*

"But what can I put in this book?" she had asked Louie, worried about making a mistake.

"You can write anything. Anything you want," he had told her.

For a moment, she believed that Louie might now walk through the door and tell her what she could put in the new journal from Carl. What she could write as Anna. But Louie wasn't coming back today or any other day. Still, she understood that what Louie told her remained true. She could write anything. And what she wanted to write now was neither secret nor private. She knew exactly how she would fill Carl's journal. With her story. She would mold, hammer, and polish the sentences and paragraphs, until the pages revealed her narrative. Over the last years, her purpose for words had evolved. They were no longer random scribbles filled with fear or shame and hidden away. Now, the tidings were for sharing, a communication to reach far beyond herself. She would craft her story into a novel. For her. And for Louie—and for all the others who struggled.

For Michael, it meant everything to see his wife delighted. Michael and Anna travelled a great distance together, and as she adopted her new identity, he beheld her. Dressed in a long white, summer gown, she greeted each and every guest. She'd gained a bit of weight over the last year, and her skin was lightly bronzed and clear. Anna looked healthy and radiant. In this moment, she reminded Michael of one of the beautiful illustrations he admired as a young boy—one of the female legends plucked from his picture book of Greek myths. She mingled in the crowd like Aphrodite or Athena or Artemis, a woman full of power, love, and purpose.

If you asked her, Anna would say that both her strength and her purpose was still a work in progress, for there wasn't a day that she didn't wish Ma and Lou had been different, had been capable of loving her. But she knew not to dwell there, and made the choice to stay focused on what she did have. Which was a lot—friends and family members who were there for her and meant more than she had previously realized.

Carl Hill supported her for years and she wasn't sure that she fully understood his fidelity. Had she even realized? She remembered the time that Carl telephoned her in May to wish Little Michael a happy birthday. "I'm honored to be a part of his life," he said. The memory made her shiver, as if she finally had the ability to translate the greater meaning, to grasp what should have been obvious all along—other people cared about her. "Only a mother will love you," Ma used to warn her. But that wasn't true. For it wasn't about the color of your skin, or your faith, or the blood that ran through your veins. It was possible that people outside of family could come together. It was possible to create kinship. Here they were today—her *de facto* family. A tribe of her own who were full of devotion. She only had to glance around the room, open her heart, and accept their gift.

Everyone danced that night. In the Greek tradition, they broke plates, smashing the white ceramic dishes to the floor. There was music, singing, and laughter. When she sat to catch her breath, Anna saw Michael and Little Michael link arms, rollicking across the floor. Dancing with joy. Together as harmonious counterparts, Anna and Michael would bequeath to their son a different legacy, one that they had created from honesty, loyalty, hard work, and mutual respect.

Yes, here was her healthy son and her husband—a husband who stood by her when others might have fled. She was so thankful that her life was joined with this man. The appreciation made her place her hand over her fertile belly, full of a new life that grew within her. She was Anna now, and she was blessed. Anna believed in miracles.

Adriana Sifakis

Adriana is cofounder of the Live Inspire Empower brand, which is focused on inspiring and empowering youth, women, and girls across the globe. She is a member of the PEN/Faulkner Foundation and the US Senate Toastmasters Club in Washington, D.C. Adriana is passionate about the development of a family social responsibility platform, which she advocates via blogging and freelance writing. She takes tremendous pride and joy in the creative writing process. Adriana is also cofounder of Axela LLC and Idea-gen.com, a cross-sector collaboration platform where the world's leading organizations convene to address some of the world's most vexing issues. Adriana is a graduate of Marian Court College and Endicott College. She believes in living a healthy, balanced lifestyle, and enjoys cooking and spending quality time with her family. Adriana resides in Washington, D.C. with her husband, George, and their three loving children.

George Sifakis

Since cofounding and leading Axela LLC over a decade ago and founding Idea-gen.com in early 2013, George has crafted countless cross-sector, collective impact partnerships among corporate, government, and non-profit organizations. Prior to entering the private sector, George served in all branches of the federal government, including as a presidential appointee and US Senate committee staffer. George is a frequent speaker on issues relating to collective impact and cross-sector collaboration. He is also cofounder of the Live Inspire Empower brand. George is an avid runner and is an alumnus of Suffolk University Graduate School, Rhode Island College, Northeastern University, and Harvard Kennedy School's Executive Education program in government.

The authors donate a portion of their proceeds to charities.